THE PAWNS OF NULL-A

Who and what was the Follower? That was the
question plaguing Gilbert Gosseyn
during his mighty efforts
to end the holocaust
that threatened to destroy whole solar systems and
wreck a universe.
Wherever he went, whatever he did, the shadow of
the Follower fell across his best-laid
plans,
thwarting even the amazing talents of Gosseyn's
Null-A trained double brain.
But when he finally pinned down that unseen
factor, he was face to face with a
mysterious force that
lay at the very origin of human intelligence.

D1419053

SOME OTHER DIGIT SCIENCE-FICTION TITLES

THE AMAZING MR. LUTTERWORTH Desmond Leslie 2/-

✦

JOURNEY TO THE CENTRE OF THE EARTH Jules Verne
2/6 (Royal)

✦

MISSION TO THE STARS E. A. Van Vogt 2/-

✦

SEARCH THE SKY C. M. Kornbluth and Frederik Pohl 2/-

✦

VOICES IN THE DARK Edmund Cooper 2/-

✦

THE SPACE MERCHANTS C. M. Kornbluth and Frederik Pohl
2/-

✦

THE HOUSE THAT STOOD STILL A. E. Van Vogt 2/-

✦

ASSIGNMENT IN ETERNITY Robert A. Heinlein 2/-

THE PAWNS OF
NULL-A

The unseen player in the gamble
of worlds

A. E. VAN VOGT

BROWN, WATSON LTD
London

THE PAWNS OF NULL-A

A DIGIT BOOK

First publication in the U.K.
U.S. edition by Ace Books, New York

By the same author
MISSION TO THE STARS (Digit Books series)
THE HOUSE THAT STOOD STILL (Digit Books series)

Digit Books are published by Brown, Watson Ltd
Digit House, Harlesden Road, London, N.W.10

Made and printed in Great Britain by
Hutchinson Printing Trust
at The Anchor Press, Ltd, Tiptree, Essex

I

Null-Abstracts

A normal human nervous system is potentially superior to that of any animal's. For the sake of sanity and balanced development, each individual must learn to orientate himself to the real world around him. There are methods of training by which this can be done.

SHADOWS. A movement on the hill where the Games Machine had once stood, where all was now desolation. Two figures, one curiously shapeless, walked by slowly among the trees. As they came out of the darkness, and into the light of a street lamp that stood like a lonely sentinel on this height from which they could overlook the city—one of the figures resolved into a normal two-legged man.

The other was a shadow, made of shadow stuff, made of blackness through which the street lamp was visible.

A man, and a shadow that moved like a man, but was not. A shadow man, who stopped as he reached the protective fence that ran along the lip of the hill. Who stopped and motioned with a shadow arm at the city below, and spoke suddenly in a voice that was not shadowy but very human.

'Repeat your instructions, Janasen.'

If the other man was awed by his strange companion, he did not show it. He yawned slightly.

'Kind of sleepy,' he said.

'Your instructions!'

The man gestured in irritation. 'Look, Mister Follower,' he said in an annoyed voice, 'don't talk like that to me. That get-up of yours doesn't scare me in the slightest. You know me. I'll do the job.'

'Your insolence,' said the Follower, 'will try my patience once too often. You know that there are time energies involved in my own movements. Your delays are calculated to offend, and I will say this: If I am ever forced into an unpleasant position because of that tendency on your part, I'll end our relationship.'

There was such a savage note in the Follower's voice that the man said no more. He found himself wondering why he taunted this immeasurably dangerous individual, and the only answer he could think of was that it burdened his spirit oppressively to realize that he was the paid agent of a being who was his master in every respect.

'Now, quick,' said the Follower, 'repeat your instructions.'

Reluctantly, the man began. The words were meaningless to the breeze that blew from behind them; they drifted on the night air like phantasms out of a dream, or shadows that dissipated in sunlight. There was something about taking advantage of the street fighting that would now shortly end. There would be a position open in the Institute of Emigration. 'The false papers I have will give me the job during the necessary time.' And the purpose of the scheming was to prevent a Gilbert Gosseyn from going to Venus until it was too late. The man had no idea who Gosseyn was, what it was Gosseyn was to be late for—but the means were clear enough. 'I'll use every authority of the Institute, and on Thursday, fourteen days from now, when the President Hardie leaves for Venus, I'll arrange for an accident to take place at a certain time—and you'll see to it that he's there for it to happen to him.'

'I don't see to anything of the kind,' said the Follower in a remote voice. 'I merely foresee that he will be there at the proper instant. Now, what is the moment of the accident?'

'9 : 28 a.m., zone 10 time.'

There was a pause. The Follower seemed to be in meditation. 'I must warn you,' he said at last, 'that Gosseyn is an unusual individual. Whether this will affect events or not, I do not know. There seems no reason why it should, but still there is the possibility. Take heed.'

The man shrugged. 'I can only do my best. I'm not worried.'

'You will be removed in due course in the usual fashion. You can wait here or on Venus.'

'Venus,' said the man.

'Very well.'

There was silence. The Follower moved slightly, as if to free himself from the restraint of the other's presence. The shadow shape of him seemed suddenly less substantial. The street lamp shone sharply through the black substance that was his body, but even as the misty thing grew duller, vaguer, less clearly marked, it held together, held its form. It vanished as a whole, and was gone as if it had never been.

Janasen waited. He was a practical man, and he was curious.

6

He had seen illusions before, and he was partially convinced that this was one. After three minutes, the ground glowed. Janasen retreated warily.

The fire raged furiously, but not so violently that he did not see the inner works of a machine with intricate parts as the white, hissing flames melted the structure into a shapeless mass. He did not wait for the end, but started to walk along the pathway that led down to a robocar station.

Ten minutes later he was deep in the city.

The transformation of time energy proceeded at its indeterminable pace to the hour of 8:43 a.m. on the first Thursday of March, 2561 A.D. The accident to Gilbert Gosseyn was scheduled for 9:28.

8:43 a.m. At the spaceport on the mountain above the city, the Venus-bound President Hardie floated into take-off position. It was due to leave at one o'clock in the afternoon.

Two weeks had passed since the Follower and his henchman looked down at the city from a world bathed in night. It was two weeks and a day since a bolt of electricity had spouted from an energy cup in the Institute of General Semantics, and bloodily sheared off the head of Thorson. As a result within three days the fighting in the city proper had ended.

Everywhere robotools whirred, buzzed, hissed and worked under the direction of their electronic brains. In eleven days a gigantic city came back to life, not without sweat, not without men having to bend their backs beside the machines. But the results were already colossal. Food supply was back to normal. Most of the scars of battle were gone. And, of overwhelming importance, the fear of the unknown forces that had struck at the solar system from the stars was fading more with each bit of news from Venus, and with each passing day.

8:30 a.m. On Venus, in the pit that had once been the secret galactic base of the Greatest Empire in the solar system, Patricia Hardie sat in her tree apartment studying an abridged stellar guidebook. She was dressed in a three-day casual which she would wear today only before destroying it. She was a slender young woman whose good looks were overshadowed by another more curious quality—an air of authority. The man who opened the door and came in at that moment paused to gaze at her, but if she had heard his entrance, she gave no sign.

Eldred Crang waited, faintly amused, but not offended. He respected and admired Patricia Hardie, but she was not yet fully trained in the Null-A philosophy, and therefore she still had set techniques of reaction, of which she was probably un-

7

aware. As he watched she must have gone through the unconsious process of accepting the intrusion, for she turned and looked at him.

'Well?' she asked.

The lean man walked forward. 'No go,' he said.

'How many messages is that?'

'Seventeen.' He shook his head. 'I'm afraid we've been slow. We took it for granted Gosseyn would find his way back here. Now our only hope is that he'll be on the ship that leaves Earth today for Venus.'

There was silence for a while. The woman made some marks with a needle-sharp instrument in the guidebook. Each time she touched the page, the material glowed with a faint bluish light. She shrugged finally.

'It can't be helped. Who'd have thought Enro would discover so quickly what you were doing? Fortunately, you were prompt, and so his soldiers in this area are scattered to dozens of bases, and are already being used for other purposes.'

She smiled admiringly. 'You were very clever, my dear, releasing those soldiers to the tender mercies of base commanders. They're all so eager to have more men in their sectors that when some responsible officer gives them a few million they actually try to hide them. Years ago, Enro had to evolve an elaborate system for locating armies lost in just that fashion.'

She broke off. 'Did you find out how much longer we can stay here?'

'Bad news on that point,' said Crang. 'They have orders on Gela 30 to cut Venus off the individual "matrix" circuit the moment you and I get to Gela. They're leaving the way open for ships to come this way, which is something, but I was told that the individual "Distorters" will be cut off in twenty-four hours, whether we get to Gela or not.'

He stood frowning. 'If only Gosseyn would hurry. I think I could hold them an extra day or so without revealing your identity. I think we should take the risk involved. As I see it, Gosseyn's more important than we are.'

'There's a tone in your voice,' Patricia Hardie said sharply. 'Something has happened. Is it war?'

Crang hesitated then: 'When I was sending the message just now, I tuned in on a confusion of calls from somewhere near the center of the galaxy. Some nine hundred thousand warships are attacking the central League powers in the Sixth Decant.'

The young woman was silent for a long time. When she finally spoke, there were tears in her eyes. 'So Enro has taken

8

the plunge.' She shook her head angrily and wiped her tears. 'That settles it. I'm through with him. You can do anything you please to him if you ever get the chance.'

Crang felt unmoved. 'It was inevitable. The quickness of it annoys me. We've been caught off base. Just imagine, waiting till yesterday to send Dr. Kair to Earth to look for Gosseyn.'

'When will he get there?' She waved her hand. 'Never mind. You've told me that before, haven't you? Day after tomorrow. Eldred, we can't wait.'

She stood up, and came over to him. Her eyes were narrowed with speculation as she studied his face. 'You're not going to make us take any desperate chances, I hope.'

'If we don't wait,' said Crang, 'Gosseyn'll be cut off here nine hundred seventy-one light-years from the nearest interstellar transport.

Patricia said quickly, 'At any moment Enro might have an atomic bomb "similarized" into the pit.'

'I don't think he'll destroy the base. It took too long to build up, and, besides, I have an idea he knows you're here.'

She looked at him sharply, 'Where would he obtain such information?'

Crang smiled. 'From me,' he said. 'After all, I had to tell Thorson who you were to save your life. I also told an intelligence agent of Enro.'

'Still,' said Patricia, 'all this is based on wishful thinking. If we get out safely, we can come back for Gosseyn.'

Crang stared at her thoughtfully. 'There's more to this than meets the eye. You forget that Gosseyn always assumed that beyond him, or behind him, was a being he called, for want of a better name, a cosmic chess player. That's, of course, a wild comparison, but if it had any application whatsoever, then we've got to assume a second player. Chess is not a game of solitaire. Another thing: Gosseyn regarded himself as approximately a seventh-row pawn. Well, I think he became a queen when he killed Thorson. I tell you, Reesha, it's dangerous, to leave a queen in a position where it can't move. He should be out in the open, out among the stars, where he'll have the greatest possible mobility. In my opinion, so long as the players are hidden and able to make their moves without being caught or observed, just so long is Gosseyn in deadly danger. I think a delay of even a few months might be fatal.'

Patricia was briefly silent, then: 'Just where are we going?'

'Well, we'll have to use the regular transmitters. But I plan on us stopping somewhere to get news. If it's what I think it will be, there's only one place for us to go.'

'Oh!' the woman said in a flat tone. 'Just how long do you intend to wait?'

Crang gazed at her somberly, and drew a deep breath. 'If Gosseyn's name,' he said, 'is on the passenger list of the President Hardie—and I'll get that list a few minutes after it takes off from Earth—we'll wait here till it arrives—three days and two nights from now.'

'And if his name is not on the list?'

'Then we leave here as soon as we've made sure of that.'

The name of Gilbert Gosseyn, as it turned out, was not on the passenger list of the President Hardie.

8:43 a.m. Gosseyn wakened with a start, and almost simultaneously became aware of three things: what the time was, that the sun was shining through the hotel room window, and that the videophone beside the bed was buzzing softly but insistently.

As he sat up, he came further out of sleep, and abruptly remembered that this was the day the President Hardie was scheduled to leave for Venus. The thought galvanized him. The fighting had reduced travel between the two planets to a once-a-week basis, and he still had the problem of obtaining permission to get aboard today. He bent down and clicked on the receiver but, because he was still in his pajamas, left the video plate blank.

'Gosseyn speaking,' he said.

'Mr. Gosseyn,' said a man's voice, 'this is the Institute of Emigration.'

Gosseyn stiffened. He'd known this was going to be the day of decision, and there was a tone to the voice on the phone that he didn't like.

'Who's talking?' he asked sharply.

'Janasen.'

'Oh!' Gosseyn scowled. This was the man who had put so many obstacles in his way, who had insisted upon his producing a birth certificate and other documents and had refused to recognize a favorable lie detector test. Janasen was a minor official, a rank which was surprising in view of his almost pathological refusal to do anything on his own initiative. He was no person to talk to on the day that a ship was due to leave for Venus.

Gosseyn reached down and clicked on the video plate. He waited till the image of the other's sharp face was clear, then: 'Look, Janasen, I want to talk to Yorke.'

'I have received my instructions from Mr. Yorke.' Janasen

was imperturbable. His face looked strangely sleek in spite of its thinness.

'Put me through to Yorke,' said Gosseyn.

Janasen ignored the interruption. 'It has been decided,' he said, 'that in view of the troubled situation on Venus. . . .'

'Get off the line!' Gosseyn said in a dangerous voice. 'I'll talk to Yorke, and to no one else.'

'. . . that in view of the unsettled situation on Venus, your application for entrance is refused,' said Janasen.

Gosseyn was furious. For fourteen days he had been held off by this individual, and now, on the morning of the departture of the ship, here was the decision.

'This refusal,' said the unfazable Janasen, 'will in no way debar you from making your application again when the situation on Venus has been clarified by directives from the Venusian Council for Immigration.'

Gosseyn said: 'Tell Yorke I'll be along to see him right after breakfast.'

His fingers flipped the switch, and broke the connection.

Gosseyn dressed swiftly, and then paused for a final survey of himself in the full length mirror of the hotel room. He was a tall, stern-faced young man of thirty-five or so. His vision was too sharp for him not to notice the unusual qualities of that image. At a casual glance, he looked quite normal, but to his own eyes his head was clearly too large for his body. Only the massiveness of his shoulder, arm and chest muscles made his head even tolerable in proportion. As it was he could think of it falling within the category of 'leonine'. He put on his hat, and now he looked like a big man with a strongly muscled face, which was satisfactory. As much as possible he wished to remain inconspicuous. The extra brain, which made his head nearly a sixth larger than that of an ordinary human being, had its limitations. In the two weeks that had passed since the death of the mighty Thorson, he'd been free for the first time to test its terrific powers—and the results had sharply modified his earlier feeling of invincibility.

A few minutes over twenty-six hours was the maximum time during which his 'memorized' version of a section of floor was valid. No change might be visible in the floor, but somehow it altered, and he could no longer retreat to it in the instantaneous 'similarity' fashion.

That meant he must, literally, rebuild his defenses every morning and evening in overlapping series, so that he'd never be caught without a few key points to which he could escape in an emergency. There were several puzzling aspects to the time limits involved. But that was something to investigate when he got to Venus.

As he stepped into the elevator a moment later, he glanced at his watch. 9:27.

One minute later, at 9:28, the time for which the accident was scheduled, the elevator crashed to destruction at the bottom of its shaft.

II

Null-Abstracts

General Semantics enables the individual to make the following adjustments to life: (1) He can logically anticipate the future. (2) He can achieve according to his capabilities. (3) His behaviour is suited to his environment.

GOSSEYN arrived at the mountain take-off point a few minutes before eleven o'clock. The air at this height was briskly cool, and the effect was of exhilaration. He stood for a while near the high fence beyond which the spaceship lay on its cradle. The first step, he thought, was to get through the fence.

That was basically easy. The area swarmed with people, and one more, once he got inside, would scarcely be noticed. The problem was to get in without anyone observing him materialize.

He felt no regrets, now that he had made up his mind. The slight delay caused by the accident—he'd escaped from the elevator by the simple process of similarizing himself back into his hotel room—had brought a keen awareness of how little time remained to him. He had a picture of himself trying to obtain a certificate of admission from the Institute of Emigration at this final day. The visualization was all he needed. The time for legality was past.

He selected a spot on the other side of the fence behind some packing cases, memorized it, stepped behind a truck —and a moment later walked out from behind the packing cases and headed towards the ship. Nobody tried to stop him. Nobody gave him more than a passing glance. The fact that

12

he was inside the fence was credential enough, apparently.

He walked aboard and spent his first ten minutes memorizing a dozen floor areas with his extra-brain—and that was that. During the take-off, he lay comfortably on the bed of one of the finest suites on the ship. About an hour later, a key rattled in the lock. Swiftly, Gosseyn attuned to a memorized area, and swiftly he was transported to it.

He'd chosen his materialization positions skillfully. The three men who saw him step out from behind a heavy girder obviously took it for granted that he had been there for several minutes, for they scarcely glanced at him. He walked easily to the rear of the ship, and stood before the great plexiglass port gazing down at Earth.

The planet was vast below him. It was an immense world that still showed color. As he watched, it slowly turned a grayish dark, and looked rounder every minute. It began to contract sharply, and for the first time he saw it as a great misty ball floating in black space.

Somehow it looked unreal.

He stayed that first night in one of the many unoccupied cabins. Sleep came slowly, for his thoughts were restless. Two weeks had passed since the death of the mighty Thorson, and he hadn't heard a word from Eldred Crang or Patricia Hardie. All his attempts to contact them through the Institute of Emigration had met with the unvarying reply, 'Our Venusian office reports your message undeliverable.' He'd thought once or twice that Janasen, the Institute official, took a personal satisfaction in giving him the bad news, but that seemed hardly possible.

There was no question, so it seemed to Gosseyn, that Crang had seized control of the galactic army on the very day Thorson died. The papers'd been full of the news of the withdrawal of the invaders from the cities of non-Aristotelian Venus. There was confusion as to the reason for the mass retreat, and the editors did not seem to be clear as to what was happening. Only to him who knew what had preceded the enormous defeat was the situation understandable. Crang was in control. Crang was shipping the galactic soldiers out of the solar system as fast as his two-mile-long similarity powered ships could carry them—before Enro the Red, military overlord of the Greatest Empire, discovered that his invasion was being sabotaged.

But that didn't explain why Crang had not delegated someone to get in touch with Gilbert Gosseyn who, by killing Thorson, had made all this possible.

Gosseyn slept uneasily on that thought. For though the

13

desperate danger of the invasion was temporarily averted, his own personal problem was unsolved—Gilbert Gosseyn, who possessed a trained extra brain, who had died, yet lived again in a highly similar body. His own purpose must be to find out about himself and his strange and tremendous method of immortality. Whatever the game that was being played around him, he seemed to be one of the important and powerful figures in it. He must have been tensed by the long strain he'd been under and by the hideous fight with Thorson's armored guard, or he would have realized sooner that, like it or not, for better or for worse, he was above the law. He should never have wasted his time with the Institute of Emigration.

Nobody questioned him. When officers came towards him, he stepped out of sight, and vanished to one of his memorized areas. Three days and two nights after the start, the ship eased down through the misty skies of Venus. He had glimpses of colossal trees, and then a city grew onto the horizon. Gosseyn came down the gangplank with the rest of the four hundred passengers. From his place in the fast moving line he watched the process of landing. Each person stepped up to a lie detector, spoke into it, was confirmed, and passed through a turnstile into the main part of Immigration Hall.

The picture clear in his mind, Gosseyn memorized a spot behind a pillar beyond the turnstile. Then, as if he had forgotten something, he returned aboard the ship and hid until dark. When the shadows lay deep and long in the land below, he materialized behind the pillar of the immigration building, and walked calmly toward the nearest door. A moment later he stepped down onto a paved sidewalk, and looked along a street that shone with a million lights.

He had an acute sense of being at the beginning and not the end of his adventure—Gilbert Gosseyn, who knew just enough about himself to be dissatisfied.

The pit was guarded by a division of Venusian Null-As, but there was no interference with the thin but steady stream of visitors. Gosseyn wandered disconsolately along the brightly lighted corridors of the underground city. The vastness of what had once been the secret base in the solar system of the Greatest Empire overshadowed his body. Silent distorter-type elevators carried him to the higher levels, through rooms that glittered with machines, some of which were still operating. At intervals he paused to watch Venusian engineers singly and in groups examining instruments and mechanical devices.

A communicator snatched Gosseyn's attention, and a sudden wonder made him stop and switch it on. There was a pause, then the voice of the roboperator said in a matter-of-

14

fact tone, 'What star are you calling?'

Gosseyn drew a deep breath. 'I'd like,' he said, 'to speak to either Eldred Crang or Patricia Hardie.'

He waited, with rising excitement. The idea had come like a flash, and he could hardly imagine its being successful. But even if no contact was established, that in itself would be information of a sort.

After several seconds, the robot said, 'Eldred Crang left the following message: "To anyone who may attempt to locate me, I regret that no communication is possible".' That was all. There was no explanation. 'Any other call, sir?'

Gosseyn hesitated. He was disappointed, but still the situation was not entirely adverse. Crang had left the solar system connected with the vast interstellar videophone organization. It was a tremendous opportunity for the Venusians, and it gave Gosseyn a personal thrill to imagine what they could do with it. Another question formed in his mind. The answer of the roboperator was prompt:

'It would take a ship about four hours to come here from Gela 30, which is the nearest base.'

It was a point Gosseyn was very much interested in. 'I thought Distorter transport was virtually instantaneous.'

'There is a margin of error in the transport of matter, although the traveler has no physical awareness of it. To him it appears to be an instantaneous process.'

Gosseyn nodded. He could understand that to some extent. Twenty decimal similarity was not perfect. He continued, 'Suppose I made a call to Gela. Would it take eight hours to get a message back?'

'Oh, no. The margin of error on the electronic level is infinitesimally small. The error to Gela would be about one-fifth of a second. Only matter is slow.'

'I see,' said Gosseyn. 'You can talk right across the galaxy with scarcely any delay.'

'That is right.'

'But suppose I wanted to talk to someone who didn't speak my language?'

'There is no problem. A robot translates sentence by sentence in as colloquial a manner as possible.'

Gosseyn wasn't sure about there being no problem in such a verbal transference. Part of the Null-A approach to reality had to do with the importance of word-word relationships. Words were subtle, and frequently had little connection with the facts they were supposed to represent. He could imagine innumerable mix-ups between galactic citizens who did not speak each other's languages. Since the galactic empires did

15

not teach Null-A, or practice it, they were apparently unaware of the dangers of misunderstanding implicit in the process of inter communication through robots.

The important thing was to be aware of the problem from moment to moment. Gosseyn said, 'That's all, thank you!' and broke the connection.

He arrived presently in the tree apartment which he had shared with Patricia Hardie while they were both prisoners of Thorson. He looked for a message that might have been left for him, a more complete and personal account than could be intrusted to the videophone exchange. He found several transcribed conversations between Patricia and Crang—and had what he wanted.

The references to Patricia's identity did not surprise him. He had always hesitated to accept her statements about her personal life, even though she had proved trustworthy in the fight against Thorson. The information that the great war in space had started shocked him. He shook his head to the suggestion that they would return for him in a 'few months'. Too long by far. But the gathering awareness that he was cut off in an isolated sun system made him sharply attentive to the rather complete account of the effort Crang had made to get in touch with him on Earth.

Janasen was responsible, of course. Gosseyn sighed with understanding. But what was the matter with the man, that he had taken it upon himself to frustrate one individual whom he did not know? Personal dislike? Could be. Stranger things had happened. But, on reflection, it seemed to Gosseyn that that was not the explanation.

More thoughtfully, he played over what Crang had said about possible hidden players and his danger from them. It was oddly convincing, and it directed his thought back to Janasen like a beacon.

The man was his starting point. Somebody had moved Janasen onto the 'board', perhaps only for a fleeting moment of universe time, perhaps only for a fleeting purpose, a mere pawn in this great game—but pawns, also, were looked after. Pawns came from somewhere and, when they were human, returned whence they came. There was probably no time to waste.

Yet, even as he accepted the logic of that, another purpose grew in Gosseyn's mind. He considered a few of the possibilities, then sat down at the apartment communicator, and made his call. When the roboperator asked him what star he wanted, he said, 'Give me the highest official available at the head offices of the Galactic League.'

'Who shall I say is calling?'

Gosseyn gave his name, and then settled down to wait. His plan was simple. Neither Crang nor Patricia Hardie would have been able to advise the League as to what had happened in the solar system. It was a chance that neither could have taken without grave risks. But the League, or at least a tiny division of it, had exerted its weak influence in an attempt to save Venus from Enro, and Patricia Hardie had stated that its permanent officials were interested in Null-A from an educational viewpoint. Gosseyn could see many advantages in making the contact. The roboperator's voice interrupted his thought:

'Madrisol, the secretary of the League, will speak to you.'

The words were scarcely uttered when a lean, intense face image grew onto the videoplate. The man seemed about forty-five years old, and many passions were written on his face. His blue eyes darted over Gosseyn's face. At last, apparently satisfied, Madrisol's lips moved in speech. There was a short delay, and then: 'Gilbert Gosseyn?'

The robot translator's tone had a query in it. If it was a reasonably exact representation of the original, then it was a remarkable job. Who, the tone suggested, was Gilbert Gosseyn?

That was one point that Gosseyn didn't discuss in any kind of detail. He kept his account to events in the solar system 'in which I have reason to believe the League has interested itself'. Yet even as he was speaking he had a sense of disappointment. He had expected a measure of Null-A appearance in the permanent secretary general of the League, but this man's face showed him to be a thalamic type individual. Emotions would rule him. Most of his actions and decisions would be reactions based upon emotional 'sets', and not upon Null-A cortical-thalamic processes.

He was describing the possibilities of using Venusians in the battle against Enro, when Madrisol interrupted both his train of thought and his narrative.

'You're suggesting,' he said pointedly, 'that the League States establish transport communication with the solar system, and permit trained Null-As to direct the League side of the war.'

Gosseyn bit his lip. He took it for granted that Venusians would achieve the highest positions in a short time, but thalamic individuals mustn't be allowed to suspect that. Once the process started, they'd be surprised at the swiftness with which men of Null-A, who had come originally from Earth, would

17

attain the highest positions which they felt it necessary to achieve.

Now, he mustered a bleak, humorless smile, and said, 'Naturally, Null-A men would be of assistance in a technical capacity.'

Madrisol frowned. 'It would be difficult,' he said. 'The solar system is hemmed in by star systems dominated by the Greatest Empire. If we attempted to break through, it might seem as if we attached some special importance to Venus, in which case Enro might destroy your planets. However, I will take the matter up with the proper officials, and you may be sure that what can be done will be. But now, if you please——'

It was dismissal. Gosseyn said quickly:

'Your excellency, surely some subtle arrangement can be made. Small ships could slip through, and take a few thousand of the most highly trained men out where they could be of assistance.'

'Possibly, possibly'—Madrisol looked impatient, and the mechanical translator made his voice sound the same way, —'but I'll take that up with——'

'Here on Venus,' Gosseyn urged, 'we have an intact distorter ship transmitter capable of handling spaceships ten thousand feet long. Perhaps your people could make use of that. Perhaps you could give me some idea as to how long such a transmitter remains similarized with transmitters on other stars.'

'I shall refer all these matters,' said Madrisol, 'to the proper experts, and decisions will be made. I presume there will be someone available and authorized to discuss the problem at your end.'

'I'll have the roboperator see to it that you talk to the, uh, properly constituted authorities here,' said Gosseyn, and suppressed a smile. There were no 'authorities' on Venus, but this was no time to go into the vast subject of Null-A voluntary democracy.

'Good-by and good luck.'

There was a click, and the intense face vanished from the plate. Gosseyn instructed the roboperator to switch all future calls from space to the Institute of Semantics in the nearest city, and broke the connection. He was reasonably satisfied. He had set another process in motion and, though he had no intention of waiting, at least he was doing what he could.

Next, Janasen—even if it meant going back to Earth.

III

Null-Abstracts

In order to be sane and adjusted as a human being, an individual must realize that he cannot know all there is to know. It is not enough to understand this limitation intellectually; the understanding must be an orderly and conditioned process, 'unconscious' as well as 'conscious'. Such a conditioning is essential to the balanced pursuit of knowledge of the nature of matter and life.

THE hour seemed late, and Janasen was not yet recovered from the surprise of having been snatched from the offices of the Institute of Emigration. He had not suspected the presence of a transport machine in his own office. The Follower must have other agents in this planetary system. He looked around him cautiously. He was in a dimly lighted park area. A waterfall cascaded from some invisible height beyond a clump of trees. The plume of spray glittered in the vague light.

The Follower stood partly silhouetted against the spray, but his formless body seemed to merge with the greater darkness on every side. The silence grew long, and Janasen fidgeted, but he knew better than to speak first. At last the Follower stirred, and drifted several feet nearer.

'I had difficulty adjusting myself,' he said. 'These intricate energy problems have always annoyed me, since I am not mechanically minded.'

Janasen held his silence. He had not expected an explanation, and he did not feel qualified to interpret the one he had received. He waited.

'We must take a chance,' said the Follower. 'I have followed my present course because I wish to isolate Gosseyn from those who could help him and, if necessary, destroy him. The plan that I have agreed to pursue in support of Enro the Red cannot be interfered with by a person of unknown potentialities.'

In the darkness, Janasen shrugged. For a moment, then, he wondered at his own indifference. For a moment there was a bright thought in his mind that there was something super-

19

normal about a man like himself. The thought passed. It didn't matter what chance he took, or what were the unknown potentialities of his opponents. He didn't care. 'I'm a tool,' he told himself with pride. 'I serve a shadow master.'

He laughed wildly. For he was intoxicated with his own ego, and the things that he did and felt and thought. Janasen he had called himself because it was as close as he could get to his real name. David Janasen.

The Follower spoke again. 'There are curious blurs,' he said, 'in the future of this man Gosseyn, but pictures do come through . . . though no Predictor can get them clearly. Yet I am sure that he will seek you out. Do not try to prevent him. He will find that your name was on the list of passengers of the President Hardie. He will wonder that he did not see you, but at least it will indicate to him that you are now on Venus. At this moment we are in a park in downtown New Chicago——'

'Huh!' Janasen glanced around in astonishment. But there were only the trees and shadow-like shrubs, and the hiss of the waterfall. Here and there in the darkness weak lights cast their pale glow, but there was no sign of a city.

'These Venusian cities,' said the Follower, 'have no parallel elsewhere in the galaxy. They are differently arranged, differently planned. Everything is free: food, transport, shelter—everything.'

'Well, that makes things simple.'

'Not quite. The Venusians have become aware of the existence of human beings on the planets of other stars. Having been invaded once they are likely to take precautions. However, you'll have a week or so, during which time Gosseyn should discover you.'

'And when he does?' Janasen was interested.

'Have him come to your apartment and give him this.'

The thing tumbled out of the darkness glittering, as it fell, like a white flickering flame. It lay on the grass shining like a mirror in sunlight.

'It won't seem so bright in daytime,' said the Follower. 'Remember, it must be given to him in your room. Now, any questions?'

Janasen reached down gingerly and picked up the glowing object. It seemed to be a plastic card of some kind. It felt smooth and glassy. There was printing on it, which was too small for him to read with the naked eye.

'What is he supposed to do with this?'

'Read the message.'

Janasen frowned. 'And what will happen?'

'It is not necessary for you to know that. Just carry out my instructions.'

Janasen pondered that, and then scowled. 'You said a little while ago that we must take a chance. It looks to me as if I'm the only one who is taking any chances.'

'My Friend,' said the Follower in a steely tone, 'I assure you, you are wrong. But let us have no arguments. Any more questions?'

Actually, he told himself, he had never worried the slightest bit. 'No,' said Janasen.

There was silence. Then the Follower began to fade. It was impossible for Janasen to decide just when that fade-out was complete. But presently he knew that he was alone.

Gosseyn looked down at the 'card', then up at Janasen. The calmness of the man interested him because it provided an insight into the other's character. Janasen was a solipsist who had struck a balance with his neurosis by developing a compensatory attitude value, since again and again it would depend on whether other stronger men would tolerate his insolence.

The setting of their face-to-face meeting was colorfully Venusian. They sat in a room that opened onto a patio, with young flowering shrubs just outside. It was a room with all conveniences including automatic delivery of food, automatic table cooking devices, which dispensed with the necessity of having a kitchen.

Gosseyn studied the hollow-cheeked man with hostile gaze. The task of finding Janasen had not been too involved. A few interplanetary messages—not obstructed this time, a quick canvassing of hotel roboregisters, and here was the end of the trail.

It was Janasen who spoke first. 'The system on this planet sort of interests me. I can't get used to the idea of free food.'

Gosseyn said curtly, 'You'd better start talking. What I do to you depends entirely on how much you tell me.'

The clear, blue, unafraid eyes stared at him thoughtfully. I'll tell you everything I know,' Janasen said at last with a shrug, 'but not because of your threats. I just don't bother keeping secrets either about myself or anyone else.'

Gosseyn was prepared to believe that. This agent of the Follower would be fortunate to survive another five years, but during that time he would maintain his self-respect. He made no comment, however, and presently Janasen began to talk. He described his relations with the Follower. He seemed to be quite candid. He had been in the secret service of the Greatest

Empire, and somehow he must have come to the attention of the shadow-shape. He proceeded to give a word for word account of his conversations with the Follower about Gosseyn. In the end he broke off, and returned to his earlier statement.

'The galaxy,' he said, 'swarms with anarchistic ideas, but I've never before heard of them working. I've been trying to figure out how this non-artist . . . to . . . to——'

'Call it Null-A,' said Gosseyn.

'——this Null-A stuff operates, but it seems to depend on people being sensible, and that I refuse to believe.'

Gosseyn said nothing more. For this was sanity itself that was being discussed, and that could not be explained with words alone. If Janasen was interested, let him go to the elementary schools. The other must have realized his mood, for he shrugged again.

'Read the card yet?' he asked.

Gosseyn did not answer immediately. It was chemically active but not harmfully so. He had the impression that it was an absorbing material. Still, it was a strange thing, obviously some development of galactic science, and he had no intention of being rash with it.

'This Follower,' he said finally, 'actually predicted that I would go into that elevator about 9:28 a.m.'

It was hard to credit. Because the Follower was not of Earth, not of the solar system. Somewhere out in the far reaches of the galaxy, this being had turned his attention to Gilbert Gosseyn. And pictured him doing a particular thing at a particular time. That was what Janasen's account implied.

The intricacy of prophecy involved was staggering. It made the 'card' valuable. From where he sat he could see that there was print on it, but the words were unreadable. He leaned closer. Still the print was too small.

Janasen shoved a magnifying glass towards him. 'I had to get this so I could read it myself,' he said.

Gosseyn hesitated, but presently he picked up the card and examined it. He tried to think of it as a switch that might activate a larger mechanism. But what?

He looked around the room. At the moment of entering he had memorized the nearest electric sockets and traced live wires. Some ran to the table at which he sat, and supplied power to the built-in compact electronic cooking machine. Gosseyn looked up finally.

'You and I are going to stick together for a while, Mr. Janasen,' he said. 'I have an idea that you're going to be removed from Venus either by a ship or a Distorter transporter. I intend to go with you.'

Janasen's gaze was curious. 'Don't you think that might be dangerous?'

'Yes,' said Gosseyn with a smile. 'Yes, it might be.'

There was silence.

Gosseyn attuned the card to one of his memorized areas, and simultaneously, he made the action cue a simple fear-doubt. If the emotion of fear and doubt should enter his mind, the card would instantly be similarized out of the room.

The precaution was not altogether adequate, but it seemed to him he had to take the chance.

He focused his glass on the card, and read:

Gosseyn:

A Distorter has a fascinating quality. It is electrically powered, but shows no unusual characteristics even when it is on. Such an instrument is built into the table at which you are sitting. If you have read this far, you are now caught in the most intricate trap ever devised for one individual.

If the emotion of fear came, he did not recall it then or afterwards.

For there was night.

IV

Null-Abstracts

A child's mind, lacking a developed cortex, is virtually incapable of discrimination. The child inevitably makes many false evaluations of the world. Many of these false-to-facts judgments are conditioned into the nervous system on the 'unconscious' level, and can be carried over to adulthood. Hence, we have a 'well educated' man or woman who reacts in an infantile fashion.

THE wheel glinted as it turned. Gosseyn watched it idly, as he lay in the cart. His gaze lifted finally from the gleaming metal wheel, and took in the near horizon, where a building spread itself. It was a wide structure which curved up from the ground like a huge ball, only a small part of which was exposed to view.

Gosseyn allowed the picture to seep into his consciousness, and at first did not feel either puzzled or concerned. He found himself making a comparison between the scene before him and the hotel room where he had been talking to Janasen. And then he thought: I am Ashargin.

The idea was nonverbal, an automatic awareness of self, a simple identification that squeezed up out of the organs and glands of his body and was taken for granted by his nervous system. Not quite for granted. Gilbert Gosseyn rejected the identification with amazement that yielded to a thrill of alarm and then a sense of confusion.

A summer breeze blew into his face. There were other buildings beside the great one, outbuildings scattered here and there inside a pattern of trees. The trees seemed to form a kind of fence. Beyond them, a backdrop of unsurpassed splendor, reared a majestic, snowcapped mountain.

'Ashargin!'

Gosseyn jumped as that baritone yell sounded no more than a foot from his ear. He jerked around, but in the middle of the action caught a glimpse of his fingers. That stopped him. He forgot the man, forgot even to look at the man. Thunderstruck, he examined his hands. They were slender, delicate, different from the stronger, firmer, larger hands of Gilbert Gosseyn. He looked down at himself. His body was slim, boyish.

He felt the difference, suddenly, inside, a sense of weakness, a dimmer life force, a mix-up-edness of other thoughts. No, not thoughts. Feelings. Expressions out of organs that had once been under the control of a different mind.

His own mind drew back in dismay, and once again on a nonverbal level came up against a fantastic piece of information: 'I am Ashargin.'

Not Gosseyn? His reason tottered, for he was remembering what the Follower had written on the 'card'. *You are now caught . . . in the most intricate trap . . . ever devised.* The feeling of disaster that came was like nothing else that he had ever experienced.

'Ashargin, you lazy good for nothing, get out and adjust the harness on the drull.'

He was out of the cart like a flash. With eager fingers he tightened the loosened cinch on the collar of the husky, oxlike beast. All this before he could think. The job done, he crawled back into the cart. The driver, a priest in work garb, applied the whip. The cart jogged on, and turned presently into the yard itself.

24

Gosseyn was fighting for understanding of the servile obedience that had sent him scurrying like an automaton. It was hard to think. There was so much confusion. But at last a measure of comprehension came.

Another mind had once controlled this body—the mind of Ashargin. It had been an unintegrated, insecure mind, dominated by fears and uncontrollable emotions that were imprinted on the nervous system and muscles of the body. The deadly part of that domination was that the living flesh of Ashargin would react to all that internal imbalance on the unconscious level. Even Gilbert Gosseyn, knowing what was wrong, would have scarcely any influence over those violent physical compulsions—until he could train the body of Ashargin to the cortical-thalamic sanity of Null-A.

Until he could train it . . . 'Is that it?' Gilbert Gosseyn asked himself. 'Is that why I am here? To train this body?'

Faster than his own questions, the flood of organic thought squeezed up into his brain—memories of that other mind. Ashargin. The Ashargin heir. The immense meaning of that came slowly, came dimly, came sketchily because there was so much that had happened. When he was fourteen, Enro's forces had come to the school he was attending. On that tense day he had expected death from the creatures of the usurper. But instead of killing him, they brought him back to Enro's home planet of Gorgzid, and placed him in the care of the priests of the Sleeping God.

There he labored in the fields, and hungered. They fed him in the morning, like an animal. Each night he slept with a shuddering uneasiness, longing for the morning that would bring the one meal a day that kept him alive. His identity as the Ashargin heir was not forgotten, but it was pointed out that old ruling families tended to thin away and become weak and decadent. In such periods the greatest empires had a habit of falling by default into the possession of masterful men like Enro the Red.

The cart rounded a clump of trees that ornamented a central portion of the grounds, and they came abruptly within sight of a skycar. Several men in black, priestly uniforms and one gorgeously arrayed individual stood in the grass beside the plane, and watched the approach of the cart.

The work priest leaned back in agitation, and nudged Ashargin with the blunt end of his whip, a hurriedly brutal gesture. He said hastily, 'Down on your face. It's Yeladji himself, Watcher of the Crypt of the Sleeping God.'

Gosseyn felt a violent jerk. He flipped over, and crashed to the bottom of the cart. He was lying there, dazed, as it slowly penetrated to him that the muscles of Ashargin had obeyed the command with automatic speed. The shock of that was still running its course when a strong, resonant voice said:

'Koorn, have the Prince Ashargin enter the plane, and consider yourself dismissed. The prince will not be returning to the work camp.'

Once more, the obedience of Ashargin was on an all-out basis. His sense blurred. His limbs moved convulsively. Gosseyn recalled collapsing into a seat. And then the skycar began to move.

It was all as fast as that.

Where was he being taken? It was the first thought that came when he could think again. Gradually, the process of sitting relaxed Ashargin's tensed muscles. Gosseyn made the Null-A cortical-thalamic pause, and felt 'his' body loosen even more. His eyes came into focus, and he saw that the plane was well off the ground, and climbing up over the snow-capped peak beyond the temple of the Sleeping God.

His mind poised at that point like a bird arrested in mid-flight. Sleeping God? He had a vague memory of other 'facts' Ashargin had heard. The Sleeping God apparently lay inside a translucent case in the inner chamber of the dome. Only the priests were ever allowed to look inside the case of the body itself, and then only during initiation, once in each individual's life-time.

Ashargin's memory reached that far. And Gosseyn had as much as he wanted. It was a typical variation of a pagan religion. Earth had had many such, and the details didn't matter. His mind leaped on to the vastly more important reality of his situation.

Obviously, this was a turning point in the career of Ashargin. Gosseyn looked around him with a gathering awareness of the possibilities of what was here. Three black uniformed priests, one at the control—and Yeladji. The Watcher of the Crypt, was a plumpish man. His clothes, which had seemed so dazzling, resolved on closer inspection into a black uniform over which was draped a gold and silver cloak.

The examination ended. Yeladji was number two priest in the Gorgzid hierarchy, second only to Secoh, religious overlord of the planet on which Enro had been born. But his rank and his role in all this meant nothing to Gilbert Gosseyn. He seemed a distinctly minor character in galactic affairs.

Gosseyn glanced out of the window; there were still mountains below. In the act of glancing down, he realized for the first time that the clothes he had on were not normal for Ashargin, the farm laborer. He was wearing an officer's dress uniform of the Greatest Empire—gold-braided trousers and pull-over coat with jeweled staff, the like of which Ashargin had not seen since he was fourteen, and that was eleven years before.

A general! The greatness of the rank startled Gosseyn. His thoughts grew clearer, sharper. There must be some very important reason why the Follower had put him here at this turning point in the career of the Ashargin heir—without his extra brain and helpless in a body that was controlled by an unintegrated nervous system.

If it was a temporary state, then it was an opportunity to observe a facet of galactic life such as might never have come his way normally. If, on the other hand, escape from this trap depended on his personal efforts, then his role was even clearer. Train Ashargin. Train him at top speed by Null-A methods. Only in that way could he ever hope to dominate his unique environment—in possession of a body not his own.

Gosseyn drew a deep breath. He felt amazingly better. He had made his decision; made it with determination and with a reasonably full knowledge of the limitations of his position. Time and events might add new facts to his purpose, but so long as he was imprisoned in Ashargin's nervous system, that training must be first in all his plans. It shouldn't be too hard.

The passive way that Ashargin accepted the flight fooled him. He leaned across the aisle toward Yeladji.

'Most noble Lord Watcher, where am I being taken?'

The assistant head priest turned in surprise. 'Why, to Enro. Where else?' he said.

Gosseyn had intended to watch the journey, but his ability to do so ended at that moment. Ashargin's body seemed to melt into a formless jelly. His vision blurred into the myopic blindness of terror.

The jar of the plane landing shocked him back to a semblance of normalcy. On trembling legs, he clambered out of the plane, and saw that they had landed on the roof of a building.

Eagerly, Gosseyn looked around. It seemed important that he get a picture of his surroundings. He realized he was out of luck. The nearest edge of the roof was too far away. Reluctantly, he let the three young priests direct him towards a staircase that led down. He caught a glimpse of a mountain far to his left—thirty, forty miles away. Was that the mountain beyond which lay the temple? It must be, for he could see no corresponding mountain range anywhere else.

He walked with his escort down three broad flights of stairs, and then along a bright corridor. They paused before an ornate door. The lesser priests stepped back. Yeladji came slowly forward, his blue eyes glittering.

'You will go in alone, Ashargin,' he said. 'Your duties are simple. Every morning, exactly at this hour—eight o'clock, Gorgzid city time—you will present yourself at this door, and enter without knocking.'

He hesitated, seemed to consider his next words, and then went on with a prim note in his voice:

'It shall never be any concern of yours what his excellency is doing when you come upon him, and this applies even if there is a lady in the room. To such incidents you literally pay no attention. Once inside, you will place yourself completely at his disposal. This does not mean that you will necessarily be required to do menial work, but if the honor of performing some personal service for his excellency is requested of you, you will do it instantly.'

The positivity of command went out of his manner. He grimaced as if in pain, and then smiled graciously. It was a lordly gesture of condescension intermixed with a slight anxiety, as if all this that had happened was unexpected. And there was even the suggestion that the Watcher of the Crypt regretted certain actions which he had taken against Ashargin as a matter of discipline. He said:

'As I understand it, we now part company, you and I, Ashargin. You have been brought up with a strict regard for your rank, and the great role which is now thrust upon you. It is part of our creed that the first duty of man to the Sleeping God is that he learn humility. At times you may have wondered if perhaps your burden was not too great, but now you can see for yourself that it was all for the best. As a parting admonition, I want you to remember one thing: From time immemorial it has been the custom of new princes such as Enro to exterminate rival royal houses root, stock and branch. But you are still alive. That alone should make you grateful to the great man who governs the largest empire in all time and space.'

Once more, a pause. Gosseyn had time to wonder why Enro had left Ashargin alive; time to realize that this cynical priest was actually trying to make him feel grateful, and then:

'That is all,' said Yeladji. 'Now, enter!'

It was a command, and Ashargin obeyed it in the all-out fashion that Gosseyn could not resist. His hand snatched forward. He grasped the knob with his fingers, turned it, and pushed the door open. He stepped across the threshold.

The door closed behind him.

.   .   .   .   .

28

On the planet of a far sun, a shadow thickened in the center of a gray room. It floated finally above the floor. There were two other conscious people in that narrow chamber, separated from each other and from the Follower by thin, metal grilles —but the shadow shape paid them no attention. He glided instead over to a cot on which lay the inert body of Gilbert Gosseyn.

He bent close, and seemed to listen. He straightened finally. 'He's alive,' he said aloud.

He sounded baffled, as if something had happened which was not within the purview of his own plans. He half-turned to face the woman through the bars that separated them—if a faceless thing could confront anyone.

'He arrived at the time I predicted?'

The woman shrugged, then nodded sullenly.

'And he's been like this ever since?' His resonant voice was insistent.

This time the woman did not answer directly. 'So the great Follower has run up against someone who doesn't conform.'

The shadowy substance trembled, almost as if he were shaking off her words. His reply was a long time in coming. 'It is a strange universe out there,' said the Follower finally. 'And here and there, on the myriad planets, are individuals who, like myself, have a unique faculty that lifts them above the norm. There is Enro—and now here is Gosseyn.'

He stopped, then said softly as if he was thinking out loud, 'I could kill him this instant by hitting him over the head or by knifing him or by any one of a dozen methods. And yet——'

'Why don't you?' The woman's tone taunted him.

He hesitated. 'Because . . . I don't know enough.' His voice grew cold and decisive. 'And besides I don't kill people I might be able to control. I shall be back.'

He began to fade, and presently he was gone from the squalid, concrete room where a woman and two men were imprisoned in cells that were separated from each other by a thin, fantastic network of metal.

Gosseyn-Ashargin found that he had entered a large room. At first sight, it seemed to be filled with machinery. To Ashargin, whose education had ended when he was fourteen, the picture was all confusion. Gosseyn recognized mechanical maps and videoplates on the walls, and almost everywhere he looked were Distorter instrument boards. There were several devices which he had never seen before, but he had so sharp a scientific comprehension that the very way in which they were

29

fitted with the other machines gave him an inkling of their purpose.

This was a military control room. From here Enro directed, as much as one man could, the inconceivably large forces of the Greatest Empire. The videoplates were his eyes. The lights that twinkled on the maps could theoretically provide him with an over-all picture of any battle situation. And the very quantity of the Distorter equipment suggested that he tried to maintain a tight control over his far-flung empire. Perhaps he even had a linked system of Distorter transport whereby he could go instantly to almost any part of his empire.

Except for the fixtures, the great room was empty and unguarded.

There was a large window in one corner, and Gosseyn raced for it. A moment later, he was standing looking from a height down at the city Gorgzid.

The capital of the Greatest Empire glittered below him in the rays of its bright blue sun. Gosseyn remembered with Ashargin's memory that the old capital of Nirene had been leveled by atomic bombs, and that the entire area that had once been a city of thirty million was a radioactive desert.

The recollection startled Gosseyn. Ashargin, who had not witnessed the scenes of destruction on that nightmarish day, was indifferent to it with the thoughtless indifference of people who cannot imagine an unobserved disaster. But Gosseyn stiffened before the details of one more major crime that Enro had committed. The deadly thing was that this one individual had now plunged the galactic civilization into a war that was already vast beyond all imagination. If Enro could be assassinated. . . .

His heart pattered. His knees started to buckle. Swallowing, Gosseyn made the Null-A pause, and halted Ashargin's frightened reaction to the hard purpose that formed like a flash in Gosseyn's mind.

But the purpose stayed. It stayed. The opportunity that was here was too tremendous for anything or anyone to stand in its way. This faint-heart must be persuaded, must be cajoled, built up, propagandized into making one supreme effort. It could be done. The human nervous system could be whipped up into ecstatic effort and unlimited sacrifice.

But he'd have to watch out. At the moment the assassination was consummated, there would be danger of death, and there might even be the problem of a return to his own brain.

He stood there, eyes narrowed, lips compressed with determination. He felt the difference within the body of Ashargin, the gathering strength as that utterly different type of thought

30

changed the very metabolic processes of the glands and organs. He had no doubt about what was happening. A new, stronger mind was in possession of this frail body. It was not enough, of course. Not by itself. Null-A training of muscle and nerve co-ordination was still necessary. But the first step was taken.

Kill Enro. . . .

He gazed out on the city of Gorgzid with a genuine interest; it looked like a government city. Even its skyscrapers were covered with lichens and climbing 'ivy'—it seemed to be ivy—and the roots were built with old-fashioned towers and odd slopes that appeared to crisscross each other. Of the city's fourteen million inhabitants, four-fifths of the working population occupied key positions in government buildings that had direct liaison with work offices on other planets. About five hundred thousand inhabitants—Ashargin had never learned the exact figure—were hostages who lived sulkily in the remote green suburbs. Sulkily, because they considered Gorgzid a provincial city and felt themselves insulted. Gosseyn could see some of the houses in which they lived, magnificent homes hidden among trees and evergreen shrubbery, homes that straddled entire hilltops and crept down into the valleys, and were lost in the mists of distance.

Gosseyn turned slowly away from the vista that spread there. For more than a minute, odd sounds had blurred from beyond a door on the opposite wall. Gosseyn walked towards it, conscious that he had already delayed longer than was good for a first morning. The door was shut, but he opened it firmly, and stepped across the threshold.

Instantly, the sound filled his ears.

V

Null-Abstracts

Because children—and childlike grownups—are incapable of refined discrimination, many experiences shock their nervous systems so violently that psychiatrists have evolved a special word for the result: trauma. Carried over into later years, these traumas can so tangle an individual that unsanity

—that is, neurosis—or even insanity (psychosis) can result. Almost everyone has had several traumatic experiences. It is possible to alleviate the effect of many shocks with psychotherapy.

I T took a moment, then, to accept the picture. He was in a large bathroom. Through a door to his right, partly open, he could see half of an enormous bed in an alcove at the far corner of a tremendous bedroom. There were other doors leading from the bathroom, but they were closed. And, besides, after one glance, Gosseyn brought his mind and his gaze out of the bedroom, and back to the scene that spread before him.

The bathroom was built of mirrors—literally. Walls, ceiling, floor, fixtures—all mirrors, so perfectly made that wherever he looked he saw images of himself getting smaller and smaller but always sharp and clear. A bathtub projected out from one wall. It, too, was made of mirrors. It curved rakishly up from the floor to a height of about three feet. Water poured into it from three great spouts, and swirled noisily around a huge, naked, red-haired man who was being bathed by four young women. He saw Gosseyn, and waved the women out of the way.

They were alert, those young women. One of them turned off the water. The others stepped aside. As silence settled over the bathroom, the bather sat back with pursed lips and narrowed eyes, studied the slim Gosseyn-Ashargin. The strain of that examination on Ashargin's nervous system was terrific. A dozen times, by an effort of will, Gosseyn made the Null-A cortical-thalamic pause. He had to do it, not merely to retain control, but for the simple, basic purpose of keeping Ashargin's body from losing consciousness. The situation was as desperate as that.

'What I'd like to know,' said Enro the Red slowly, 'is what made you pause in Control Center and look out of the window? Why the window?' He seemed intent and puzzled. His eyes were without hostility, but they were bright with the question he had asked. 'After all, you've seen the city before.'

Gosseyn couldn't answer. The direct interrogation was threatening to dissolve Ashargin into a flabby jelly. Grimly, Gosseyn fought for control, as Enro's face took on an expression of sardonic satisfaction. The dictator stood up and climbed out of the tub onto the mirrored tile of the floor. Smiling faintly, a remarkable muscular figure of a man, he waited while the women wrapped a gigantic towel around his dripping body. That towel was removed, and then he was dried by small towels vigorously wielded. Finally, a robe the color

32

of his flaming hair was held for him. He slipped into it, and spoke again, still smiling:

'I like women to bathe me. There is a gentleness about them that soothes my spirit.'

Gosseyn said nothing. Enro's remark was intended to be humorous, but like so many people who did not understand themselves he merely gave himself away. The whole bathing scene here was alive with implications of a man whose development to adulthood was not complete. Babies, too, loved the feel of a woman's soft hands. But most babies didn't grow up to gain control of the largest empire in time and space. And the way Enro had sat in his bath, aware of what Gosseyn-Ashargin was doing in the adjoining room, showed that no matter how immature he was on the one hand, a part of his constitution had attained comparatively superior state. How valuable that quality would be in an emergency remained to be seen.

For a moment, standing there, he had forgotten Ashargin. It was a dangerous lapse. The direct remark by Enro about the women had been too much for his unstable nervous system. His heart quickened, his knees shook and his muscles quivered. He staggered and would have fallen if the dictator had not signaled to the women. Gosseyn saw the movement out of the corner of his eyes. The next second, firm hands caught him.

When Gosseyn could stand again, and see clearly again, Enro was striding through one of two doors in the left wall into a room that was bright with sunlight. And three of the women were in the act of leaving the bathroom by the partly open bedroom door. Only the fourth young woman continued to brace his quivering body. The muscles of Ashargin started to shrink away from her eyes, but just in time Gosseyn made the pause. It was he who realized that her gaze was not contemptuous but pitying.

'So this is what's been done to you,' she said softly. She had gray eyes and classically beautiful features. She frowned, then shrugged. 'My name is Nirene—and you'd better get in there, my friend.'

She started to shove him toward the open door through which Enro had disappeared, but Gosseyn was in control again. He held back. He had already been struck by her name.

'Is there any connection,' he said, 'between Nirene the girl and Nirene the old capital?'

Her frown grew puzzled. 'One moment you faint,' she said. 'The next you ask intelligent questions. Your character is more complicated than your appearance suggests. But now, quick! You must——'

'What does my appearance suggest?' asked Gosseyn.

Cool, gray eyes studied him. 'You asked for it,' she said. 'Defeated, weak, effeminate, childlike, incapable.' She broke off impatiently, 'I said, hurry. I meant it. I'm not staying another minute.'

She whirled around. Without looking back, she walked swiftly through the bedroom door, and shut it behind her.

Gosseyn made no attempt at speed. He was not enjoying himself. And he felt tense whenever he thought of his own body. But he was beginning to get a picture of what he must do if he—and Ashargin—were to survive the day without being utterly disgraced.

Hold back. Delay reactions in the Null-A fashion. It would be learning in action, with its many disadvantages. He had a conviction that for many hours, still, he'd be under the watchful, measuring eyes of Enro, who would be startled by any sign of self-control in the man he had tried to destroy. That couldn't be helped. There'd be unpleasant incidents as it was, enough, perhaps, to persuade even the dictator that all was as it should be.

And the moment he got into whatever room he was given, he'd make an all-out attempt to 'cure' Ashargin by Null-A methods.

Walking forward slowly, Gosseyn passed through the door beyond which Enro had disappeared. He found himself in a very large room where under an enormous window a table was laid for three. He had to take a second look before he estimated the size of the window at a hundred feet high. Waiters hovered around, and there were several distinguished-looking men with important documents held limply in their fingers. Enro was bending over the table. As Gosseyn paused, the dictator lifted, one after the other, the gleaming covers from several dishes, and sniffed at the steaming food underneath. He straightened finally.

'Ah,' he said, 'fried mantoll. Delicious.' He turned with a smile to Ashargin-Gosseyn. 'You sit over there.' He indicated one of the three chairs.

The knowledge that he was to have breakfast with Enro did not surprise Gosseyn. It fitted with his analysis of Enro's intentions toward Ashargin. Just in time, however, he realized that the young man was beginning to react in his terrible, self-conscious manner. He made the cortical-thalamic pause. And saw that Enro was staring at him, thoughtfully.

'So Nirene is taking an interest in you,' he said slowly. 'That's a possibility I hadn't considered. Still, it has its aspects. Ah, here is Secoh.'

The new arrival passed within a foot of Gosseyn, and so his

34

first look at the man was from the side and the rear. He was dark-haired, about forty years old and very good-looking in a sharp-faced manner. He wore a single-piece, form-fitting blue suit with a scarlet cloak neatly draped over his shoulder. As he bowed to Enro, Gosseyn already had the impression of a fox-like man, quick, alert, and cunning. Enro was speaking:

'I can't get over Nirene talking to him.'

Secoh walked to one of the chairs, and took up a position behind it. His keen black eyes glanced at Enro questioningly. The latter explained succinctly what had passed between Ashargin and the young woman.

Gosseyn found himself listening in amazement. Here it was again, the dictator's uncanny ability to know what was going on where he could neither see nor hear in a normal fashion.

The phenomenon changed the direction of his thoughts. Some of the strain on Ashargin lifted. For a moment, then, he had a picture of this vast environment of galactic civilization, and of the men who dominated it.

Each individual had some special qualification. Enro could see into adjoining rooms. It was a unique skill, and yet it scarcely justified the height of power it had helped him to attain. At first sight it seemed to prove that men didn't need much of an edge over their fellows to gain ascendancy over them.

Secoh's special position seemed to derive from the fact that he was religious overlord of Gorgzid, Enro's home planet. Madrisol of the League was still an unknown quality.

Finally, there was the Follower, whose science included accurate prediction of the future, a gadget for making himself insubstantial and which gave him such control of other people's minds that he had imposed Gilbert Gosseyn's upon Ashargin's. Of the three men, the Follower seemed the most dangerous. But that also had yet to be shown. Enro was speaking again.

'I have half a mind to make her his mistress,' he said. He stood scowling, then his face lighted. 'By heaven, I will.' He seemed suddenly in good humor, for he began to laugh. 'That ought to be something to see,' he said. Grinning, he told an off-color joke about the sexual problems of certain neurotics, and finished on a more savage note. 'I'll cure that female of any plans she has.'

Secoh shrugged, and then said in a resonant voice, 'I think you're overestimating the possibilities. But it won't hurt to do as you suggested.' He waved imperiously at one of the attendants. 'Make a note of his excellency's request,' he ordered in a tone of assured command.

The man bowed abjectly. 'Already noted, your excellency.'

Enro motioned to Gosseyn. 'Come along,' he said. 'I'm hungry.' His voice grew bitingly polite. 'Or would you like to be assisted to your chair?'

Gosseyn had been fighting the Ashargin body's reactions to the import of Secoh's 'request'. Fighting successfully, it seemed to him. He walked toward the chair, and he was taking up his position behind it when the sharpness of Enro's tone must have penetrated to Ashargin. Or perhaps it was a combination of overpowering events. Whatever the cause, what happened was too swift for defense. As Enro seated himself, Ashargin-Gosseyn fainted.

When he returned to the conscious state, Gosseyn found himself sitting at the breakfast table, his body being held upright by two waiters. Instantly, the body of Ashargin cringed, expecting censure. Startled, Gosseyn headed off the potential collapse.

He glanced at Enro, but the dictator was busily eating. Nor did the priest as much as glance at him. The waiters let go of his arms and began to serve him. The food was all strange to Gosseyn, but as each dish cover in turn was lifted, he felt a favorable or unfavorable reaction inside him. For once the unconscious compulsions of the Ashargin body had their uses. Within a minute or so he was eating food that was familiar and satisfying to the taste buds of Ashargin.

He began to feel shocked at what had happened. It was hard to participate in such a humiliating experience without feeling intimately a part of the disaster. And the worst part was that he could do nothing immediately. He was caught in this body, his mind and memory superimposed on the brain and body of another individual, presumably by some variation of Distorter similarity. And what was happening meantime to the body of Gilbert Gosseyn?

Such possession of another body could not be permanent —and, besides, he must never forget that the system of immortality which had enabled him to survive one death would protect him again. Therefore, this was a tremendously important incident. He must savor it, try to understand it, be aware of everything that went on.

'Why,' he thought in wonder, 'I'm here at the headquarters of Enro the Red, the reigning overlord of the Greatest Empire. Actually eating breakfast with him.'

He stopped eating, and stared at the big man in abrupt fascination. Enro, of whom he had heard vaguely through Thorson and Crang and Patricia Hardie. Enro, who had ordered the destruction of Null-A because it would be the simplest method of starting a galactic war; Enro, dictator, leader, caesar, usurper, absolute tyrant, who must gain some of his ascendancy by his ability to hear and see what was going on in nearby rooms. Rather a good-looking man in his way. His face was strong, but it was slightly freckled, which gave him a boyish appearance. His eyes were clear and bold, and blue in color. His eyes and mouth looked familiar, but that must be an illusion. Enro the Red, whom Gilbert Gosseyn had already helped to defeat in the solar system, and who was now waging the vaster galactic campaign. Failing an opportunity to assassinate the man, it would be a fantastic achievement to discover here in the heart and brain of the Greatest Empire, a method of defeating him.

Enro pushed his chair away from the table. It was like a signal. Secoh immediately ceased eating, though there was still food on his plate. Gosseyn put down his own fork and knife, and guessed that breakfast was over. The waiters began to clear the table.

Enro climbed to his feet, and said briskly, 'Any news from Venus?'

Secoh and Gosseyn stood up, Gosseyn stiffly. The shock of hearing the familiar word at this remote distance from the solar system was personal, and therefore controlled. The jittery nervous system of Ashargin did not react to the name Venus.

The priest's thin face was calm. 'We have a few more details. Nothing that matters.'

Enro was intent. 'We'll have to take some action about that planet,' he said slowly. 'If I could be sure Reesha was not there——'

'That was only a report, your excellency.'

Enro whirled, his expression grim. 'The mere possibility,' he said, 'is enough to hold my hand.'

The priest was equally bleak. 'It would be unfortunate,' he said coldly, 'if the League powers discovered your weakness, and spread the report that Reesha was on any one of thousands of League planets.'

The dictator stiffened, hesitated for a moment. Then he laughed. He walked over and put his arm around the smaller man's shoulder.

'Good old Secoh,' he said sarcastically.

The Temple lord squirmed at the touch, but bore it for a moment with a distasteful expression on his face. The big man guffawed. 'What's the matter?'

Secoh withdrew from the heavy grasp, gently but firmly. 'Have you any instructions to give me?'

The dictator laughed once more, then swiftly he grew

thoughtful. 'What happens to that system is unimportant. But I feel irritated every time that I remember Thorson was killed there. And I would like to know how we were defeated. Something went wrong.'

'A Board of Inquiry has been appointed,' said Secoh.

'Good. Now, what about the battle?'

'Costly but progressively decisive. Would you care to see the figures of losses?'

'Yes.'

One of the attending secretaries handed a paper to Secoh, who passed it silently over to Enro. Gosseyn watched the dictator's face. The potentialities of this situation were becoming vaster every moment. This must be the engagement which Crang and Patricia had referred to ; nine hundred thousand warships—fighting the titanic battle of the Sixth Decant.

Decant? He thought in a haze of excitement: *The galaxy is shaped like a gigantic wheel——*' Obviously, they had divided it into 'decants.' There'd be other methods of locating the latitude and longitude of planets and stars of course, but——

Enro was handing the paper back to his adviser. There was a pettish expression on his face, and his eyes were sulky.

'I feel indecisive,' he said slowly. 'It's a personal feeling, a sense of my own life force not having been fulfilled.'

'You have more than a score of children,' Secoh pointed out.

Enro ignored that. 'Priest,' he said, 'it is now four sidereal years since my sister, destined by the ancient custom of the Gorgzid to be my only legal wife, departed for—— where?'

'There is no trace.' The lean man's voice had a remote quality.

Enro gazed at him somberly, and said softly, 'My friend, you always were taken with her. If I thought you were withholding information——' He stopped, and there must have been a look in the other's eyes, for he said hastily, with a faint laugh, 'All right, all right, don't be angry. I'm mistaken. It would be impossible for a man of your cloth to do such a thing. Your oaths, for one thing.' He seemed to be arguing with himself.

He looked up bleakly, and said, 'I shall have to see to it that of the children of my sister and myself—yet to be born—the girls are not educated in schools and on planets where the dynastic principle of brother-sister marriages is derided.'

No reply. Enro hesitated, staring hard at Secoh. He seemed unaware for the moment that others were witnessing the interchange. Abruptly, he changed the subject.

'I can still stop the war,' he said. 'The members of the

38

Galactic League are nerving themselves now, but they'll almost fall over themselves to give me my way if I showed any willingness to stop the battle of the Sixth Decant.'

The priest was quiet, calm, steady. 'The principle of universal order,' he said, 'and of a universal State transcends the emotions of the individual. You can shirk none of the cruel necessities.' His voice was rocklike. 'None,' he said.

Enro did not meet those pale eyes. 'I am undecided,' he repeated. 'I feel unfulfilled, incomplete. If my sister were here, doing her duty . . .'

Gosseyn scarcely heard. He was thinking gloomily. So that's what they're telling themselves; a Universal State, centrally controlled, and held together by military force.

It was an old dream of man, and many times destiny had decreed a temporary illusion of success. There had been a number of empires on Earth that had achieved virtual control of all the civilized areas of their day. For a few generations then, the vast domains maintained their unnatural bonds—unnatural because the verdict of history always seemed to narrow down to a few meaningful sentences: 'The new ruler lacked the wisdom of his father——' 'Uprisings of the masses——' 'The conquered states, long held down, rose in successful rebellion against the weakened empire——' There were even reasons given as to why a particular state had grown weak.

The details didn't matter. There was nothing basically wrong with the idea of a universal state, but men who thought thalamically would never create anything but the outward appearance of such a state. On Earth Null-A had won when approximately five percent of the population was trained in its tenets. In the galaxy three percent should be sufficient. At that point, but not till then, the universal state would be a feasible idea.

Accordingly, this war was a fraud. It had no meaning. If successful, the resultant universal state would last possibly a generation, possibly two. And then, the emotional drives of other unsane men would impel them to plotting and to rebellion. Meanwhile, billions would die so that a neurotic could have the pleasure of forcing a few more high-born ladies to bathe him every morning.

The man was only unsane, but the war he had started was maniacal. It must be prevented from development. . . . There was a stir at one of the doors, and Gosseyn's thought ended. A woman's angry voice sounded:

'Of course I can go in. Do you dare to stop me from seeing my own brother?'

The voice, in spite of its fury, had a familiar ring in it. Gosseyn whirled, and saw that Enro was racing for the door at the far end, opposite the great window.

'Reesha!' he shouted, and there was jubilance in his voice.

Through the watering eyes of Ashargin, Gosseyn watched the reunion. There was a slim man with the girl, and as they came forward, Enro carrying the girl in his arms and hugging her fast against his dressing gown, it was that slim man who drew Gosseyn's fascinated gaze.

For it was Eldred Crang. Crang? Then the girl must be—— must be—— He turned and stared, as Patricia Hardie said peevishly, 'Enro, put me down. I want you to meet my husband.'

The dictator's body grew rigid. Slowly then, he set the girl down, and slowly turned to look at Crang. His baleful gaze met the yellowy eyes of the Null-A detective. Crang smiled, as if unaware of the other's immense hostility. Something of his tremendous personality was in that smile and in his manner. Enro's expression changed ever so slightly. For a moment he looked puzzled, even startled, then he parted his lips and he seemed on the point of speaking when out of the corner of his eyes, he must have caught a glimpse of Ashargin.

'Oh,' he said. His manner altered radically. His self-possession returned. He beckoned Gosseyn with a brusque gesture. 'Come along, my friend. I want you to act as my liaison officer with Grand Admiral Paleol. Tell the admiral——' He began to walk toward a nearby door. Gosseyn trailed him, and found himself presently in what he had previously identified as Enro's military control room. Enro paused before one of the Distorter cages. He faced Gosseyn.

'Tell the admiral,' he repeated, 'that you are my representative. Here is your authority.' He held out a thin, glittering plaque. 'Now,' he said, 'in here.' He motioned to the cage.

An attendant was opening the door of what Gosseyn had already recognized as a transport Distorter. Gosseyn walked forward, nonplussed. He had no desire to leave Enro's court just now. He hadn't yet learned enough. It seemed important that he remain and learn more. He paused at the cage door.

'What shall I tell the admiral?'

The other's faint smile had broadened. 'Just who you are,' Enro said suavely. 'Introduce yourself. Get acquainted with the staff officers.'

'I see,' said Gosseyn.

He did see. The Ashargin heir was being exhibited to the military men. Enro must expect opposition from high-ranking officers, and so they were to have a look at Prince Ashargin —and realize how hopeless it would be for them ever to build up resistance around the only person who would have any legal or popular position. He hesitated once more.

'This transport will take me straight to the admiral?'

'It has only one control direction either way. It will go there, and it will come back here. Good luck.'

Gosseyn stepped into the cage without another word. The door clanged behind him. He sat down in the control chair, hesitated for a moment—after all, Ashargin wouldn't be expected to act swiftly—and then pulled the lever.

Instantly, he realized that he was free.

VI

Null-Abstracts

Children, immature adults and animals 'identify'. Whenever a person reacts to a new or changing situation as if it were an old and unchanging one, he or she is said to be identifying. Such an approach to life is aristotelian.

FREE. That was the tremendous fact. Free of Ashargin. Himself again. Odd how he knew that. It seemed to grow out of the very elements of his being. His own transport experience with his extra brain made the transition feel familiar. Almost, he was aware of the movement. Even the blackness seemed incomplete, as if his brain did not quite stop working.

Even as he came out of the darkness, he sensed the presence of a powerful electric dynamo and of an atomic pile. And simultaneously, with intense disappointment, he realized that they were not near enough for him to make use of them, or control them, in any way.

Quickly, then, he came to consciousness. As vision returned, he saw that he was neither in the Venusian apartments of Janasen, nor in any place to which Enro would have sent Ashargin.

He was lying on his back on a hard bed staring up at a high, concrete ceiling. His eyes and his mind absorbed the scene in one continuous glance that followed through. The room he was in was small. A needle-studded grille came down from the ceiling. Beyond it, sitting on a bunk watching him, was a dis-tinguished-looking young woman. Gosseyn's eyes would have paused, would have stared, but there was another metal grille on the other side of her cell. In it, sprawled on a bunk, seemingly asleep, was a very large man who was naked except for a pair of discolored sport shorts. Beyond the giant was concrete wall.

As he sat up, more intent now, Gosseyn saw that that was the scene. Three cells in a concrete room, three windows, one in each cell, at least fifteen feet above the floor, no doors. His summing up stopped short. No doors? Like a flash, he ran his gaze along the walls searching for cracks in the cement. There were none.

Quickly, he went over to the bars that separated his cell from the woman's. Quickly, he memorized a portion of the floor of his own cell, then of hers, and then of the cell of the sleeping colossus. Finally, he tried to similarize himself back to one of his safety points on Venus.

Nothing happened. Gosseyn accepted the implications. Between distant points there was a time lag, and in this case the twenty-six hour period during which a memorized area remained similarizable had been used up. Venus must be immensely far away.

He was about to make a more detailed survey of his prison when once more he grew aware of the woman. This time his attention held. His first fleeting impression had been of someone whose appearance was very distinctive. Now, with measured glance, he saw that his picture was correct.

The woman was not tall, but she held herself with an air of unconscious superiority. Unconscious; that was the telling reality. What the conscious mind of an individual thought was important only insofar as it reflected or helped to anchor the set of the nervous system. The only comparison Gosseyn could think of was Patricia Hardie, who so surprisingly had turned out to be the sister of the mighty Enro. She also had that pride in her eyes, that automatic, innate conviction of superiority—different from the Null-A trained Venusians, whose dominant characteristic of complete adequateness seemed part of their body and their faces.

Like Patricia, the stranger was a *grande dame*. Her pride was of position and rank, of manners and—something else. Gosseyn stared at her with narrowed eyes. Her face showed that she acted and thought thalamically, but then, so did Enro and Secoh, and so had virtually every individual in history before the development of Null-A.

Emotional people could build up their talents along one or two channels, and achieve as greatly as any Null-A Venusian in a particular field. Null-A was the system of integrating the human nervous system. Its greatest values were social and personal.

The important thing about assessing this woman was that, as he studied her, the extra component of the neural vibrations that flowed from her seemed to take on greater proportions with each passing moment.

She was dark-haired, with a head that seemed a shade too large for her body, and she returned his gaze with a faint, puzzled, anxious yet supercilious smile.

'I can see,' she said uneasily, 'why the Follower has taken an interest in you.' She hesitated. 'Perhaps you and I could escape together.'

'Escape?' echoed Gosseyn, and looked at her with steady eyes. He was astonished that she spoke English, but the explanation of that could wait while he gained more vital information.

The woman sighed, then shrugged. 'The Follower is afraid of you. Therefore this cell cannot be quite as much of a prison to you as it is to me. Or am I wrong?'

Gosseyn didn't answer that, but he felt grim. Her analysis was wrong. He was as completely a prisoner as she was. Without an outside point to which he could similarize himself, without a power socket before his eyes to memorize, he had no resources.

He studied the woman with a faint frown. As a fellow prisoner, she was, theoretically, an ally. As a lady of quality, and, possibly, an inhabitant of this planet, she might be very valuable to him. The trouble was that she was very likely an agent of the Follower. And yet, he had a conviction that a fast decision was needed here.

The woman said, 'The Follower has been in here three times wondering why you didn't wake up when you first arrived more than two days ago. Have you any idea?'

Gosseyn smiled. The idea that he would be giving out information struck him as naive. He was not going to tell anyone that he had been in the body of Ashargin, although surely the Follower, who had put him there——

He stopped. He felt himself grow taut. He thought, almost blankly, *But that would mean——*

He shook his head in wonder, and then stood in blank amazement. If the Follower had lost control of him, that would indicate the existence of still another being of enormous power. Not that that was out of the question. He must never forget his theory. Somewhere out here were the players of this mighty game, and even a queen, such as he had estimated himself to be, could be moved or forced, checked and endangered, or even taken and removed from the board.

He parted his lips to speak, but restrained himself. His slightest word would be noted and analyzed by one of the sharp and dangerous minds of the Galaxy. He pondered for a moment, and came back to his own first question.

Aloud, he said, 'Escape?'

The woman was sighing. 'It seems incredible,' she said. 'A man whose movements cannot be predicted. Up to a point, I have a clear picture of what you're going to do, then, because one of those actions is without logic, I get only blur.'

Gosseyn said, 'You can read the future—like the Follower?' He was intent. He walked to the bars, separating their two cells, and stared down at her in fascination. 'How is it done? Who is this Follower who has the appearance of a shadow?'

The woman laughed. It was a slightly tolerant laugh, but it had a musical note in it that was pleasing to the ear. The laughter ended.

'You're in the Follower's Retreat, of course,' she said, and frowned. 'I don't understand you,' she complained. 'And your questions. Are you trying to mislead me? Who is the Follower? Why, everyone knows that the Follower is an ordinary Predictor who discovered how to put himself out of phase.'

There was an interruption. The giant in the third cell stirred on his cot, and sat up. He stared at Gosseyn.

'Get over to your bunk,' he said in a bass voice. 'And don't let me catch you talking to Leej again. Now, get!'

Gosseyn did not move, simply watched the other with curious eyes.

The stranger climbed to his feet, and came over to the bars of his cell. On the cot he had looked like a giant. Now, for the first time, Gosseyn realized how big the man really was. He towered. He spread. He was seven and a half feet tall, and as broad as a gorilla. Gosseyn estimated his chest at eighty inches.

He was taken aback. He had never seen such an enormous man before. The giant exuded abnormal physical power. For the first time in his life, Gosseyn felt himself in the presence of an untrained individual whose sheer muscular strength visibly exceeded the possibilities of a normal Null-A.

'Better back down fast,' the monster said in a menacing voice. 'The Follower told me she's mine, and I don't intend to have any competition.'

Gosseyn glanced questioningly toward the woman, but she had lain down with her face to the wall. He faced the giant again.

'What planet is this?' he asked conversationally.

His tone must have been right, because the giant lost some of his belligerence.

'Planet?' he said. 'What do you mean?'

That was startling. Gosseyn, whose mind had leaped ahead, devising other questions, teetered and came back. Was it possible that he was in another isolated planetary system similar to that of Sol? The probability shook him.

'The name of your sun?' he urged. 'Surely, you have a name for it. It must have been assigned a recognition symbol in the galactic nomenclature.'

The other's mood chilled visibly. His blue eyes misted with suspicion. 'What are you trying to pull off?' he asked roughly.

Gosseyn said grimly, 'Don't try to pretend that you don't know the planets of other suns are inhabited by human beings.'

The huge man looked disgusted. 'Got yourself a little addled in the brain, haven't you?' he said significantly. 'Look,' he went on, 'my name is Jurig. I live on Crest, and I'm a Yalertan citizen. I killed a man by hitting him too hard, and so here I am, subject to execution—but I don't want to talk to you any more. You bother me with that foolishness.'

Gosseyn hesitated. Jurig's protests were convincing, but he wasn't prepared to let the matter drop. There was one point that needed clearing up.

'If you're so innocent,' he said accusingly, 'how is it that you can speak the English language so perfectly?'

He realized the answer to that as he spoke the word 'English'. Jurig completed the thought with finality.

'What language?' he said. He began to laugh. 'You are crazy.' He seemed to realize the implications of what he was saying. He groaned. 'Is it possible the Follower has put me in here with a crazy man?'

He caught hold of himself. 'Man,' he said, 'whoever you are —the language we're speaking, you as well as I, is Yalertan. And I can tell you right now, you speak it like a native.'

For a few minutes, then, Gosseyn abandoned the conversation. He walked to his bunk and sat down. The flow of neural sensations that streamed from the giant were not friendly. There was cunning in them, and a kind of smug, murderous self-satisfaction.

The question was, why did the man dissemble? In point of muscular strength, the Yalertan was in a class by himself. If they ever came to grips, then Gilbert Gosseyn would have to use his extra brain to similarize himself to various parts of the prison. He must keep clear of those gorilla-like arms and fight like a boxer, not a wrestler.

But any use of his extra brain would reveal the nature of his

45

special ability. Gosseyn climbed to his feet, and walked slowly over to the grille that divided his cell from that of Leej. He recognized that his position was bad. The cell had no power sockets. He was caught in it as completely as if he was the most ordinary of human beings.

The bars of the grille were thin, and about four inches apart. They looked as if a strong man might be able to bend them.

No strong man in his right mind would ever try. The metal was encrusted with needles. Thousands of them. He drew back, defeated, then bent down and examined the connection of the grille with the floor.

There was a crossbar that was free of needles, but the needles from the horizontal bars reached down over it, guarding it from probing fingers. Gosseyn straightened, and turned to his one remaining hope, the cot. If he could move it against the wall, end up, he'd be able to reach the window.

The cot was a metal affair, its legs cemented into the concrete floor. After several minutes of straining at it vainly, Gosseyn stood back. A doorless cell, he thought, and silence. His mind paused. The silence was not complete. There were sounds, movements, rustlings, a faint throb of voices. This prison must be part of a larger building—what was it the woman had called it—the Follower's Retreat. He was trying to visualize that when Jurig said from behind him:

'Funny clothes you got on.'

Gosseyn turned and stared at the man. Jurig's tone indicated that he had made no connection between the clothing and what Gosseyn had said about other planets.

He glanced down at his 'funny' suit. It was a light, plastic coverall with hidden zipper and, also hidden, a thermostat controlled heating and refrigeration network that was mazed evenly through the artificial textile material. It was very neat and expensive looking and very handy to have on, particularly for a man who might find himself in an unaccustomed climate. In cold or hot weather, the suit would maintain a uniform temperature next to his skin.

The shock of realizing that he had been using a foreign language so naturally, so easily, that he hadn't even been aware of it, had come at the moment that he tried to fit the word 'English' into the Yalertan tongue. It had sounded wrong. He'd gathered from Thorson and Crang that the galactic civilization had developed language machines by which soldiers, diplomats and space travelers could be taught the tongues of the peoples of far planets. But he hadn't pictured anything like this.

The card must have done it. Gosseyn sank down on his cot, and closed his eyes. He had really been trapped in Janasen's

46

room. Imagine actually sitting on a Distorter. In one instant, he thought, I was transported from Venus. My body headed unerringly for this cell, and arrived at a predetermined instant. In midflight, another player in this vast game, similarized my brain into the brain case of Ashargin on a far planet. The moment that connection was broken, I woke up here, already educated in the local language. And, if the Follower really expected me to awaken the moment my body arrived, then I must have been taught the language during or immediately after the time that I looked at the card.

He glanced again at the woman, but her back was still turned. He looked at Jurig appraisingly; here must be his immediate source of information.

The big man answered his questions without hesitation. The planet was made up of thousands of large islands. Only the skytrailer people, the Predictors, could move freely over the entire surface. The rest of the population was confined, each individual group to its own island. There was trade among them, and some migration, but always on a limited scale as between nations. There were numerous trade and immigration barriers but . . .

Gosseyn listened with the attention of a man who was swiftly grasping at a new idea. He was trying to imagine the Null-A Venusians against these Yalertans. He tried to think of a comprehensive word that would describe the Predictors, but nothing seemed to fit. Neither side yet realized that two utterly different systems for dealing with reality existed in the galaxy. Neither side had as yet become aware of the other. Both were systems that had developed in isolation from the main stream of galactic civilization. Both were now about to be drawn into the maelstrom of a war being fought on so vast a scale that entire planetary systems might be wiped out.

He commented finally, 'You seem to dislike these Predictors. Why?'

The giant had wandered away from the bars of his cell, and was leaning against the wall under the window. 'Are you kidding?' he said. His eyes narrowed with annoyance, and he came back to the bars. 'You've pulled enough of that stuff for one day.'

'I'm not kidding. I really don't know.'

'They're stuck-up,' said Jurig abruptly. 'They can tell the future, and they're ruthless.'

'That last point sounds bad,' Gosseyn admitted.

'They're all bad!' Jurig exploded. He stopped and swallowed hard. 'They enslave other people. They steal the ideas of the island folk. And because they can tell the future, they

47

win every battle and repress every rebellion.'

'Listen!' Jurig leaned closer to the bars in front of him. His tone was earnest. 'I noticed you didn't like my saying that Leej belonged to me. Not that it matters what you like, you understand. But don't ever feel sorry for one of them. I've seen these women flay alive some lesser being'—his voice grew sarcastic, then angry—'and get a kick out of it. Now, this one has run up against the Follower for a private reason, and so, for the first time in centuries—I never heard of any other—one of us lesser folk has a chance at last to get back a little at these murderous scum. Am I going to take advantage of that? You bet I am.'

For the first time since she had turned her back, the young woman stirred. She swung around, sat up, and looked at Gosseyn.

'Jurig's neglected to mention one thing,' she said.

The giant let out a bellow. His lips drew back in a snarl. 'You tell him,' he raged, 'and I'll smash in your teeth the moment we get together.'

The woman flinched visibly, and there was no question of her fear. Her voice when she spoke, trembled, but there was defiance in it, too.

'He's suposed to kill you the moment the bars are removed,' she said.

Jurig's face was a study. 'All right for you, my fine lady. That finishes you.'

The woman was white. 'I think,' she said shakily, 'the Follower wants to see how well you can defend yourself.' She stared at him appealingly. 'What do you think? Can you do anything?'

It was a question that Gosseyn was urgently asking himself.

Gosseyn had an impulse to reassure the young woman, but he suppressed it. He had no intention of standing by while Jurig's blood-thirsty threats were carried out, but he must never forget that somewhere beyond these drab walls was an alert observer—and that his every movement, word and action would be carefully weighed and analyzed.

'Can you do anything?' she asked, 'or is the Follower worried about you without reason?'

'What I'd like to know,' countered Gosseyn, 'is what action do you forsee me taking?'

Her answer proved, if it was necessary to prove it, that this was no academic argument. Without warning, she burst into tears.

'Oh, please,' she sobbed, 'don't keep me in suspense. That man's threats are driving me insane.' She shook her head tear-

48

fully. 'I don't know what's the matter. When I look into your future, everything blurs. The only time that ever happens is with the Follower, and with him it's natural. He's simply out of phase.'

She broke off, wiped her tears with the back of her hand, and said earnestly, 'I know you're in danger, too. But if you can do anything against the Follower, you'll have to be able to do it in the open.'

Gosseyn shook his head. He felt sorry for the woman, but her logic was wrong. 'In the history of the planet that I come from, surprise has been a major factor in determining what countries and groups shall dominate civilization.'

All the tears were gone now from her eyes, and her gaze was steady again. 'If the Follower can defeat you in the open, he can baffle any surprise system you may have.'

Gosseyn scarcely heard. 'Listen,' he said earnestly, 'I'm going to try to help you, but whether I can or not depends on how you answer my questions.'

'Yes?' She sounded breathless, her eyes wide, her lips parted.

'Have you any pictures at all of my future actions?'

'What I see you doing,' said Leej, 'doesn't make sense. It just doesn't make sense.'

'But what is it?' He felt exasperated. 'I've got to know.'

'If I told you,' she said, 'it would introduce a new factor and change the future.'

'But maybe it should be changed.'

'No.' She shook her head. 'After you do it everything blurs. That gives me hope.'

Gosseyn controlled himself with an effort. Anyway it was something. The implication was that his extra brain was going to be used. Apparently, whenever that happened this system of prediction failed to function.

Their faculty remained remarkable, and he'd have to try to find out how neurotics like this woman could automatically foretell the future. But that was for later.

'Look,' said Gosseyn, 'when does all this happen?'

'In about ten minutes,' said Leej.

Gosseyn was shocked into temporary silence. Finally, he said, 'Is there any kind of transport between Yalerta and the planets of other stars?'

'Yes,' said Leej. 'Without warning, without previous knowledge on our part, the Follower informed all the skytrailer people that they must accept commissions on military spaceships of some being who calls himself Enro. And immediately he had a ship here with some method for transporting us.'

Gosseyn took the shock of that without change of expression, but he flinched inwardly. He had a sudden picture of seers on every warship foretelling the future actions of enemy warships. How could any normal human being fight such a superhuman crew? He had known from what Janasen had said that the Follower was working with Enro, but that was one individual. Here were reinforcements by the—He asked the question in a piercing tone, 'How many . . . how many of you are there?'

'About five million,' said Leej.

He had guessed more than that, but the lesser figure brought him no sense of relief. Five million was enough to dominate the galaxy.

'Still,' said Gosseyn, hoping aloud, 'they won't all go.'

'I refused,' said Leej in a flat tone. 'I'm not the only one, I understand, but I've talked against the Follower for five years, and so I'm to be made an example of.' She sounded weary. 'Most of the others are going.'

Gosseyn estimated that four of the ten minutes were gone. He wiped his damp forehead, and pressed on.

'What about the accusations Jurig made against the Predictors?'

Leej shrugged listlessly. 'I suppose they're true. I remember a silly girl in my service talked back to me, and I had her whipped.' She looked at him, her eyes wide and innocent. 'What else can you do with people who don't know their place?'

Gosseyn had almost forgotten the man, but now he was forcibly reminded. There was a roar of outrage from the cell beyond the woman.

'You see,' yelled the giant. 'See what I mean?' He paced the floor. 'Just wait till these grilles go up, and I'll show you what you can do with people who don't know their place.' He raised his voice in a frenzied shout. 'Follower, if you hear me, let's get some action. Pull up these grilles. Pull 'em up.'

If the Follower heard, he showed no sign. The grilles did not go up. Jurig subsided and retired to his cot. He sat there muttering the words, 'Just wait! Just wait!'

For Gosseyn, the waiting was past. Jurig, in his outburst, had given him the clue to the action he must take. He realized he was shaking, but he didn't care. He had his answer. He knew what he was going to do. The Follower himself would supply the opportunity at the moment of crisis.

No wonder Leej had disbelieved her advance picture of his future action. Apparently, it would be a meaningless move.

Crash! The interrupting sound came as he was settling back onto the cot. A metallic sound.

The grilles were lifting.

VII

Null-Abstracts

In making a statement about an object or an event, an individual 'abstracts' only a few of its characteristics. If he says, 'That chair is brown!' he should mean that brownness is one of its qualities, and he should be aware, as he speaks, that it has many other qualities. 'Consciousness of abstracting' constitutes one of the main differences between a person who is semantically trained and one who is not.

With the speed of a hunting cat, Gosseyn was off his cot. His fingers gripped the crossbar of the grille at the bottom. He felt himself irresistibly lifted up.

The effort to hold on cost him every ounce of strength in his arms and fingers. The area to which he had to cling was less than an inch in thickness, and it curved the wrong way. But he had taken his grip just under the needles, under that fantastic pattern of needles, and he either hung on or suffered ultimate defeat.

He hung on. As he came up above the level of the window, he was able to see out. He had a glimpse of a courtyard in the immediate foreground, of a high fence in the near distance made of sharply pointed metal spears, and of a land of trees beyond. Gosseyn barely glanced at the vista. One look at the scene as a whole, and then he turned his attention to the courtyard.

There was an agonizingly slow moment while he memorized the surface structure of a part of a cobblestone. And then, his purpose accomplished, he dropped nearly twenty feet to the concrete floor of the cell.

He landed on all fours, physically relaxed, but with his mind as taut as a metal bar. He had an outside area to which he could escape by using the special powers of his extra brain, but he still had to make up his mind what his immediate course of action should be.

His problem with regard to the Follower was not radically altered. Deadly and imminent danger remained but at least he could now get out into the open.

Warily, like a fighter parrying a dangerous opponent, Gosseyn watched the gorilla-like Jurig who was supposed to kill him.

'Leej,' he said, without looking at the Predictor woman, 'come over here behind me.'

She came without a word, her feet almost noiseless on the floor. He had a glimpse of her face as she slipped past him. Her cheeks were colorless, her eyes blurred, but she held her head high.

From the far side of what was now one room, Jurig snarled, 'That won't do you any good, hiding behind him.'

It was a purely thalamic threat, serving no useful purpose even to Jurig. But Gosseyn did not let it go by. He had been waiting for an opening. A man who could not make up his mind about a larger issue had to appear to concentrate on a smaller one. So long as he gave the impression of being concerned with Jurig, as if that were the danger, just so long would the Follower await events. He said in a steely voice:

'Jurig, I'm tired of that kind of talk. It's time you made up your mind whose side you're on. And I'm telling you right now that it had better be mine.'

The Yalertan, who had been bracing himself and edging forward, stopped. The muscles of his face worked spasmodically, quivering between doubt and rage. He glared at Gosseyn with the baffled eyes of a bully whose smaller opponent was not afraid.

'I'm going to smash your head against the cement,' he said from between clenched teeth. But he spoke the words as if he were testing their effect.

'Leej,' said Gosseyn.

'Yes?'

'Can you see what I'm going to do?'

'There's nothing. Nothing.'

It was Gosseyn's turn to be baffled. True, if she couldn't foresee his actions, then neither could the Follower. But he had hoped to obtain a vague picture which would help him make up his mind. What should he do when he got outside? Run? Or enter the Retreat and seek out the Follower?

His role in this affair was on a vaster level than that of either Jurig or Leej. Like the Follower, he was a major piece in the galactic game of chess. At least, he must consider himself one until events proved otherwise. It imposed restraints upon him. Escape alone would not solve his problems. He must also, if it could possibly be done, plant the seeds of future victory.

'Jurig,' he temporized aloud, 'you've got a big decision to make. It involves more courage than you've yet shown, but I'm sure you have it in you. From now on, regardless of conse-

52

quences, you're against the Follower. I tell you, you have no choice. The next time we meet, if you're not working unconditionally against him, I shall kill you.'

Jurig stared at him uncertainly. It seemed hard for him to realize that a fellow prisoner was actually giving him an order. He laughed uneasily. And then the immensity of the insult must have penetrated. He became enormously angry, the anger of a man who feels himself outraged.

'I'll show you what choice I have!' he shouted.

His approach was swift but heavy. He held his arms out, obviously intending to hug and squeeze, and the surprise for him was when Gosseyn stepped right into the circle of those bearlike limbs, and sent a powerful right to his jaw. The blow failed to land squarely but it stopped Jurig short. He grappled with Gosseyn with a sick look on his face. His expression grew sicker as he fought to gain a stranglehold on a man who, now that so telling a blow had been struck, was not only faster but stronger than himself.

The Yalertan yielded suddenly, like a door that has been smashed open with a battering ram. Gosseyn felt it coming, and with a final burst of strength sent the other staggering back across the floor, routed, defeated in mind and body.

The shock would be lasting, and Gosseyn regretted it. But there was no doubt that it had been necessary. On such identifications, people like Jurig built their egos. All through his life, like the goats in the famous experiment, Jurig had butted his way to dominance. It was his way, not Gosseyn's, of expressing his superiority.

Consciously, he would resent the defeat, find a dozen excuses for himself. But on the unconscious level he would accept it. So far as Gilbert Gosseyn was concerned, his confidence in his physical prowess was gone. Only Null-A training would ever enable him to reorientate himself to the new situation, and that was not available.

Satisfied, Gosseyn similarized himself out onto the courtyard. Swiftly, then, the greater purpose of escape took full possession of his nervous system.

He was vaguely aware of people in the courtyard turning to look at him as he ran. He had a glimpse, in turning his head, of an enormous pile of buildings, spires and steeples, masses of stone and marble, colored glass windows. That picture of the Follower's Retreat remained in his mind even as he kept 'watch' on every energy source in the castle. He was ready to similarize himself back and forth to escape blasters and power-driven weapons. But there was no change in the flow from the dynamo or the atomic pile.

Automatically, he similarized Leej to the memorized area behind him, but he did not look to see if she was following him.

He reached the tall fence, and saw that the spears which looked formidable enough in themselves were encrusted with the same kind of needles as had been the grilles in the prison cell he'd just left. Nine feet of unscalable metal—but he could see between the spears.

It required the usual long—it seemed long—moment to memorize an area beyond the fence. Actually, it was not a memory. When he concentrated in a definite fashion on a spot, his extra brain automatically took a 'photograph' of the entire atomic structure of the matter involved to a depth of several molecules. The similarization process that could then follow resulted from the flow of nervous energy along channels in the extra brain—channels which had been created only after prolonged training. The activating cue would send a wash of that energy out, first along the nerves of his body, and then beyond his skin. For an instant then, every affected atom was forced into a blurred resemblance to the photographer pattern. When the approximation of similarity was made accurate to twenty decimal places, the two objects became contiguous, and the greater bridged the gap to the lesser as if there were no gap.

Gosseyn similarized himself through the fence and started to run toward the woods. As he ran he felt the presence of magnetic energy and saw a plane glide toward him over the trees. He kept on running, watching it from the corner of his eyes, striving to analyze its power source. It had no propeller, but there were long metal struts jutting down from its stubby wings. Similar type plates ran along its fuselage, and that gave him confirmation. Here was the source of the magnetic power.

Its weapons would be bullets or a magnetic beam blaster.

The machine had been off to one side. Now, its nose twisted toward him. Gosseyn similarized himself back to the fence.

A plume of colored fire puffed along the ground where he had been. The grass smoked. There were flashes of yellow flame from the brush, but that only mingled with the red-green-blue-orange of the blaster's own chromatic display.

As the plane hissed past him, Gosseyn took a photograph of its tail assembly. And once more, at top speed, he started to run toward the trees more than a hundred yards away.

He kept a watch on the plane, and saw it turn and dive down at him again. This time Gosseyn took no chances. He was a hundred feet from the fence, which was dangerously close. But he similarized the tail assembly of the plane to the memorized area beside the fence.

There was a crash that rocked the ground. The metallic shriek of the plane, its speed undiminished by the process of similarization, was ear splitting as it screeched along parallel to the fence, tearing the fence with fantastic ripping sounds. It came to a rest an eighth of a mile away, a tattered fragment.

Gosseyn ran on. He reached the woods safely, but he was no longer satisfied with merely escaping. If one attacking device existed, then so might others. Swiftly, he memorized an area beside a tree, stepped aside and brought Leej up to it. Next, he transported himself back to the area just outside the cell window, and headed at a run for the nearest door leading into the Retreat. He wanted weapons that would match anything the Follower had mustered to prevent his escape, and he intended to get them.

He found himself in a broad corridor, and the first thing he saw was a long line of magnetic lights. He memorized the nearest one, and immediately felt a lot better. He had a small but potent weapon that would operate anywhere on Yalerta.

He continued along the corridor but no longer at top speed. The dynamo and the pile were near, but just where he had no way of knowing. He sensed the presence of human beings around, but the neural flow was neither tense nor menacing. He came to a basement stairway, and without hesitation headed down the long flight of steps. Two men were standing at the bottom, talking to each other earnestly but without anxiety.

They looked up at him in surprise. And Gosseyn, who had already made his plan, said breathlessly, 'Which way to the power plant? It's urgent.'

One of the men looked excited. 'Why . . . why—that way. That way. What's the matter?'

Gosseyn was already racing in the direction indicated. The other called after him, 'The fifth door to your right.'

When he came to the fifth door, he stopped just inside the threshold. Just what he had expected he didn't know, but not an atomic pile feeding power to an electric dynamo. The huge dynamo was turning softly. Its great wheel glinted as it moved slowly. To either side were walls lined with instrument boards. A half dozen men were moving around, and at first they didn't see him. Gosseyn walked boldly towards the power outlet of the dynamo, and memorized it. He estimated it at forty thousand kilowatts.

Then, still without hesitation, he strode to the pile itself. There were the usual devices for looking into the interior, and an attendant was bending over a gauge making minute adjustments on a marked dial. Gosseyn stepped up beside him, and

55

peered through one of the viewing devices into the pile itself.

He was aware of the man straightening. But the long moment the other required to grasp the nature of the intrusion was all that Gosseyn needed. As the attendant tugged at his shoulder, too surprised for speech or anger, Gosseyn stepped back and, without a word, walked to the door and out into the corridor.

The moment he was out of sight, he transported himself into the woods. Leej stood a dozen feet away, almost facing him.

She jumped as he appeared, and babbled something he didn't catch. He waited for the expression on her face to indicate that she was recovering. He didn't have long to wait.

Her body trembled, but it was a quaver of excitement. Her eyes were slightly glazed, but they became bright with eagerness. She grabbed his arm with quivering fingers.

'Quick,' she said, 'this way. My trailer will be over here.'

'Your what?' said Gosseyn.

But she had started off through the brush, and she seemed not to hear.

Gosseyn ran after her, his eyes narrowed, and he was thinking: *Has she been fooling me? Has she known all this time that she was going to escape now? But then why wouldn't the Follower know, and be waiting?*

He couldn't help remembering that he was caught in 'the most intricate trap ever devised for one man.' It was something to think about even if he apparently succeeded in getting away.

Ahead of him, the woman plunged through a screen of tall shrubs, and then he didn't hear her any more. Following her, Gosseyn found himself on the edge of a limitless sea. He had time to remember that this was a planet of vast oceans broken at intervals by islands, and then an airship came floating over the trees to his left. It was about a hundred and fifty feet long, snub-nosed, and about thirty feet high at its thickest. It plunged lightly into the water in front of them. A long, sleek gangplank came sliding down toward them. It touched the sand at the woman's feet.

In a flash, she was up and along it. She called over her shoulder, 'Hurry!'

Gosseyn pressed across the threshold behind her. The moment he was inside, the door flowed shut, and the machine began to glide forward and up. The swiftness with which everything happened reminded him of a similar experience he'd had at the Temple of the Sleeping God on Gorgzid while in the body of Prince Ashargin.

There was one difference, vital and urgent. As Ashargin, he had not felt immediately threatened. Now, he did.

VIII

Null-Abstracts

Aristotle's formulations of the science of his time were probably the most accurate available during his lifetime. His followers for two thousand years subscribed to the identification that they were true for all time. In more recent years, new systems of measurement disproved many of these 'truths', but they continue to be the basis of the opinions and beliefs of most people. The two-valued logic on which such folk-thought is founded has accordingly been given the designation aristotelian—abbreviation: A—and the many-valued logic of modern science has been given the name non-aristotelian—abbreviation: Null-A.

GOSSEYN found himself in a corridor at the bottom of a flight of steps. The corridor extended both right and left, curving gradually out of sight. At the moment he had no impulse for exploration. He followed Leej up the stairway toward a bright room, and he was already noticing the radical design of the ceiling lights. It confirmed his first 'feel' of the ship's power source. Magnetic power.

The fact was interesting because of the picture it gave him of Yalertan scientific development, comparable to twenty-second century Earth. But it also gave him a shock. For him now the magnetic engine had a flaw. It was too complete. It performed so many functions that people who used it had a tendency to discard all other forms of power.

The Predictors had made the old mistake. There was no atomic power aboard. No electricity. Not even a battery. That meant no really potent weapons, and no radar. These Predictors obviously expected to be able to foresee the approach of anything inimical to them, but this was not so any more. He had a vision in his mind of galactic engineers sending electrically guided aerial torpedoes with proximity fuses and atomic warheads, or any of a dozen devices that, once attuned to a target, would follow it till they destroyed it or were themselves destroyed.

The worst part of it was that he could do nothing but find out as swiftly as possible just how much Leej could foresee.

And of course, he could hope.

The bright room into which Leej led him was longer, broader and higher than it had seemed from the entrance below. It was a drawing room, complete with couches, chairs, tables, a massive green rug and, directly across from where he had paused, a sloping window that bulged out like a streamlined balcony from the side of the ship.

The woman flung herself with an audible sigh onto a couch near the window, and said, 'It's wonderful to be safe again.' She shook her dark hair with a tiny shudder. 'What a nightmare.'

She added in a savage tone, 'That will never happen again.'

Gosseyn, heading for the window, was stopped short by her words. He half turned to ask her on what she based her confidence. He didn't speak the question. She had already admitted that she couldn't foretell the actions of the Follower, and that was all he needed to know. Deprived of her gift, she was a good-looking, emotional young woman about thirty years old without any particular astuteness to protect her from danger. He could find out all she knew after he had done what he could to ward off possible attacks.

As he started forward again, he felt the nerve sensation that indicated the approach of a human being. A moment later, a man emerged from a door that led to the forward part of the vessel. The fellow was slim, with an edge of gray in his hair. He ran over to Leej, and knelt beside her.

'My dear,' he said, 'you're back.'

He kissed her with a quick movement.

At the window now, Gosseyn ignored the lovers. He was looking down and back at a fascinating scene. An island. A green island, set like an emerald in a sapphire sea. There was a gem within the green gem, a pile of buildings that shone gray-white in the sun, and already it was hard to make out the details. They seemed unreal, and actually did not resemble buildings at this distance. His knowledge that they were enabled his mind to fill in the gaps.

The ship was climbing a long, shallow slope of air. Its speed was evidently greater than he had thought from the smoothness of the acceleration, because, as he watched, the island shrank visibly in size. And he could see now that there was no apparent movement either on the ground or in the air above it.

That braced him, though there had been in his mind through all the dangerous moments the knowledge that, even if he were killed, the continuity of his memories and thoughts would immediately be carried on by another Gosseyn body, which would wake up automatically in a remote hiding place.

58

Unfortunately, as he had learned from an earlier version of his body, now dead, the next group of Gosseyns were eighteen years old. He couldn't escape the conviction that no eighteen year old could handle the crisis that had been created by Enro. People had confidence in mature men and not in children. That confidence might make a difference between victory and defeat in a critical moment.

It was important that he remain alive in this body.

His eyes narrowed thoughtfully as he considered the immediate possibilities. He had work to do. He must stop further transportation of Predictors to Enro's fleet, seize the warships that had landed, and, as soon as possible, attack the shadow-thing on his island.

There were preliminaries to be accomplished, but those were the things he must work toward—and swiftly. Swiftly. The great and decisive battle of the Sixth Decant was hourly growing in fury. If he knew anything of human nature, then the League was already shaken to its tenuous foundations. Certainly, Enro expected it to collapse, and, childish though the dictator might be when it came to women, on the political and military level he was a genius.

He was about to turn from the window when it struck him that Jurig, under sentence of death as he was, might be bearing the brunt of the Follower's wrath. Hastily, he similarized Jurig to the woods outside the fence. If the man was at all afraid, he would hide there and so be available for transportation to the ship later on.

The action taken, he twisted back into the room in time to hear the woman say calmly, 'I'm sorry, Yanar, but he will want a woman, and naturally I must be the one. Good-by.'

The man was on his feet, his face dark. He looked up and his eyes met Gosseyn's. The hatred that sparkled in their dark depths was matched by the sensation that jumped from his nervous system to Gosseyn's extra brain. He said with a sneer, 'I don't give my mistress up to anyone without a fight, even someone whose future is a blur.'

His hand disappeared into a pocket, and came out with a small, fanlike instrument. He brought it up, and pressed the charger.

Gosseyn walked forward, and took the weapon from Yanar's fingers. The other did not resist. There was a strained look on his face, and the nervous rhythm that exuded from him had altered to a fear pattern. He was obviously stunned at the way his fragile appearing but powerful gun had failed to 'fire.' Gosseyn moved off several paces and examined the instrument curiously. The radial flanges that made up the antenna was typical, and verified, if verification was needed, the nature of the energy involved. Magnetic weapons operated on outside power, in this case the field set up by the magnetic engines in the hull. The field extended with dimming strength for a distance of nearly five miles beyond the hull.

Gosseyn slipped the instrument into his pocket, and tried to imagine the effect on Yanar of what had happened. He had photographed the entire weapon, and allowed one of the discharge points to flow to a similarized area into the prison cell of the Follower's Retreat. The distance in space prevented the current from coming back to the ship, and so the weapon, its energy diverted, had failed to function. The psychological effect must be slightly terrific.

The man's face remained a bleached white, but he brought his teeth together with a snap.

'You'll have to kill me,' he said, bitterly.

He was a middle-aged nonentity, set in his ways, thalamically bound up in A—as distinct from Null-A—habits, and because he could shoot for purely emotional reasons, he would be dangerous so long as they were both aboard the ship. He must be killed, or exiled, or—Gosseyn smiled grimly—guarded. He knew just the man who could do it. Jurig. But that was for later. Now, he half-turned to Leej, and questioned her pointedly about the marriage customs of the Predictors.

There was no marriage. 'That,' said Leej with disdain, 'is for the lesser breeds.'

She did not say so in so many words, but Gosseyn gathered that Yanar was one of a long line of lovers, and that, being older, he had had even more mistresses. These people wearied of each other, and because of their gift were usually able to name the exact hour when they would separate. The unexpected appearance of Gosseyn had terminated this affair sooner than anticipated.

Gosseyn was neither repelled nor attracted by the moves involved. His first thought had been to reassure Yanar that he needn't worry about losing his mistress. He didn't say it. He wanted a Predictor beside him from now on, and Leej might be insulted if she discovered that he did not make love to women who did not have some Null-A training.

He asked Leej one more question. 'What does Yanar do besides eat and sleep?'

'He runs the ship.'

Gosseyn motioned at Yanar. 'Lead the way,' he said curtly.

Further conversation with Leej could wait. He was a man who must depend on what he knew, and the sense of urgency was strong upon him again.

As he examined the ship, Gosseyn's mind jumped back to what Leej had said when they were running through the underbrush on the Follower's island. Trailer, she had called her machine.

A skytrailer. He could imagine the easy life these Predictors had lived for so many years on their world of islands and water. Floating lazily through the sky, landing when the mood touched them, and where they desired; seizing control of any 'lesser' human being whom it pleased them to enslave, and snatching any object they wanted to possess—there was a part of man's nature that longed for such a carefree existence. The fact that in this case it included a ruthless subjugation of people who did not have the precious gift of prophecy was easy to understand also. Overlordship could always be justified by minds that were not too critical. And, besides, recent generations had grown up from babyhood in an environment where slavery was not questioned by the Predictor hierarchy. The attitude was part of the set of their nervous systems.

Though they did not seem to realize it, the appearance of the Follower on their idyllic scene had forever broken the casual pattern of their existence. And now, the arrival of the galactic warship and the presence of Gilbert Gosseyn were further indicators of their changing conditions. They must either adjust or be swept aside.

The control room was in the nose of the vessel. It didn't take long to examine it. The controls were of the simple discharger type common to energy derived from the planet's own magnetic currents.

The dome of the control room was limpidly transparent. Gosseyn stood for a long moment gazing down at the sea that was rushing by below. As far as he could see ahead there was only a mass of heaving waters, and not a sign of land.

He turned away to continue his exploration. There was a steel stairway in one corner. It led up at a steep slant to a closed hatch in the ceiling. Gosseyn started up immediately.

The loft turned out to be a storeroom. Gosseyn examined the labels on boxes and containers, not quite sure what he was looking for, but ready to follow up on any idea that suggested itself. Suddenly, as he examined a drum filled with degravitated air, the idea came.

As he continued his conducted tour, his plan grew more plausible. He glanced in at each of four bedrooms, a dining room, and a rear control room on the main floor, and then went down to the lower deck, but by now he was searching for something. He had previously sensed the presence of other human beings below deck. He finally counted six men and six women. They were submissive in manner, and judging from the neural flow from their bodies, obviously accepted their lot. He dismissed them from his calculations and, after peering in at spacious kitchens and more storerooms, he came to a work-room.

It was what he had been looking for. He sent Yanar about his business, and locked the door.

Gosseyn emerged three hours later with two tubes set up on a plate that would take power from the magnetic field of the ship's engines. Straight up to the loft he climbed, and spent more than fifteen minutes piping degravitated air into the air-tight container inside which he had set up his tubes.

At first the oscillation was faint. It grew stronger. The rhythmic pulse beat in his extra brain steadily and evenly. On earth, the graviton tube was known as a member of a group that was said to possess 'radiation hunger.' Lacking the gravitonic particle, it craved stability. Up to that point its reactions were normal, for all things in nature fought constantly to achieve a balance. It was the tube's methods that were fantastic.

It sent out radiations of its own to search for normal matter. Every time it touched an object, a message was dispatched back to the tube. Result: excitement. A change in the rhythm so long as the object remained in the vicinity. On Earth, technicians said of such moments, 'There's old Ehrenhaft wagging his tail again.'

Not that it did any good. And the tube never seemed to learn from experience. The process went on and on, without its hunger ever being satisfied. Surprisingly, as with many other things, such 'stupidity' was useful to those who cared to exploit it.

Gosseyn manoeuvred the ship to a height of five miles, and then down almost to the surface of the water. He was able in this way to accustom himself to the normal rhythm variation of movement above a sea. Finally, he set the cue. If there was any variation in the rhythm, then his extra brain would be warned, whereupon he would similarize himself into either front or rear control room and decide on further measures.

It was a personal detector system on a very limited level, useless against weapons traveling miles a second, and certainly useless if a galactic Distorter ever got a 'fix' on his ship. But it was something.

Gosseyn hesitated, then found himself an end of wire and memorized it. Quickly he memorized two floor areas in the control room. And then, as the sun disappeared behind the shimmering horizon of water, and the twilight quickened toward night, he headed for the living room, conscious that he was ready for more positive action.

When Gosseyn entered the living room, Yanar was sitting in a chair near the window, reading a book. The room glowed with soft, magnetic lights ; cold lights, yet they always looked so warm and intimate, because of the way their colors changed ever so little from moment to moment.

Gosseyn stopped just inside the doorway, and watched the other narrowly. This was the test. He similarized the wire end back in the control room to the first memorized area, and waited.

The older man looked up with a start from his book. He stared at Gosseyn grimly, then climbed to his feet, walked to a chair at the far end of the room, and sat down. A steady stream of unfriendly neural sensations, tinged with spasmodic discharges indicating doubt, flowed from the Predictor's nervous system.

Gosseyn studied the man, convinced that he had got as much of a response as he could hope for. It could be an attempt to fool him. His every move could have been foreseen and allowed for. But he thought not.

Accordingly, his major problem with these Predictors was solved. Each time he 'moved' the wire with his extra brain, he would confuse their ability to predict his actions. There would, in short, be a blur. He could carry on an interview, and be fairly sure that his questions were not being anticipated. There was one more problem: Should he or should he not be conciliatory with Yanar?

That was more important than it might seem. It took time to make friends, but it only required a shock moment to impress another person with the fear that he was in the presence of a superior. The power of Gilbert Gosseyn on Yalerta was going to depend on his ability to put over the idea that he was invincible. In no other way could he hope to operate at the top speed necessary to his plans and to the basic war situation in the galaxy.

The question was, at what speed would it be right for him to operate?

Gosseyn walked over to the window. It was almost pitch dark now, but the glint of the sea was visible in the half light. If there was a moon circling the planet, it was not yet above the horizon, or else it was too small to reflect a noticeable amount of sunlight.

He gazed at the light-flecked waters, and wondered how far he was from Earth. It seemed strange, even unsettling, to realize how great the distance must be. It brought a sense of smallness, an awareness of how much remained to be done.

He could only hope he would be able to develop to the height of power that would be necessary in the critical days ahead. He was not a man who need ever think of himself as belonging to any one planet, but, still, he did have a strong feeling for the solar system.

A sound drew his attention. He turned away from the window, and saw that the slaves from the lower deck were busy in the dining room. He watched them thoughtfully, noting that the youngest and prettiest girl was the target for little, spiteful acts of domination by the other two women. She was about nineteen, Gosseyn estimated. She kept her eyes down, which was a significant sign. If he knew anything about thalamic people—and he did—then she was biding her time and awaiting an opportunity to repay her tormentors. Gosseyn guessed from the nature of the neural sensations that flowed from her that she would be able to do her greatest damage by playing the coquette with the men servants.

He studied Yanar again, and made up his mind. Definitely, irrevocably, no friendliness.

He walked slowly toward the man, making no effort to be stealthy. The Predictor glanced up, and saw him coming. He stirred uneasily in his chair, but remained where he was. He looked unhappy.

Gosseyn considered that a good sign. Except for those who had been in contact with the Follower, none of these Predictors had ever been subjected to the pressure of not knowing from instant to instant what the future might hold. It should be interesting to observe the effect on Yanar. And besides, he himself needed information badly.

Gosseyn began by asking the simple questions. And before each one—not only in the beginning, but during the entire interview—he shifted the wire in the control room back and forth between the floor areas 'one' and 'two.'

With occasional exceptions, Yanar answered freely. His full name was Yanar Wilvry Blove, he was forty-four years old, and had no occupation—that was where the first hesitation came.

Gosseyn noted the point mentally, but made no comment. Blockage in connection with occupation, distinct interruption in neural flow.

'Is there any significance to your names?' he asked.

Yanar seemed relieved. He shrugged. 'I'm Yanar of the Wilvry birth center on the island of Blove.'

So that was how it worked. He shifted the wire again, and said affably, 'You people have quite a gift of foreseeing. I've never run into anything like it before.'

64

'No good against you,' said Yanar darkly.

That was worth knowing for sure, though, of course, the statement that it was not usable did not make the words true. Fortunately, he had other verification.

Not that he had any alternative but to proceed as if Yanar didn't foresee his questions.

The interview continued. Gosseyn wasn't sure what he was searching for. A clue perhaps. His belief that he was still in the Followers' trap was becoming greater and not less. If that was so, then he was fighting against time, in a very real sense.

But what was the nature of the trap?

He learned the Predictors were born in a normal fashion, usually aboard skytrailers. A few days after being born they were taken to the nearest birth center that had space available.

'What does the birth center do to the child?' Gosseyn asked.

Yanar shook his head. And there was blockage again in the neural flow from him. 'We don't give information like that to strangers,' he said stubbornly, 'not even to——' He stopped, shrugged, then finished curtly, 'To no one.'

Gosseyn did not press the matter. He was beginning to feel distracted. The facts he was unearthing were valuable but not vital. They did not fit his needs of the moment.

Yet there was nothing to do but go on.

'How long have there been Predictors?' he asked.

'Several hundred years.'

'Then it's the result of an invention?'

'There's a legend——' Yanar began. He stopped, and stiffened. Blockage. 'I refuse to answer that,' he said.

Gosseyn said, 'At what stage does the prophetic ability appear?'

'Above twelve. Sometimes a little sooner.'

Gosseyn nodded, half to himself. There was a theory forming in the back of his mind, and this fitted. The faculty developed slowly, like the human cortex and like his own extra brain. He hesitated over his next question, because there was an assumption in it that he didn't want Yanar to notice until it was too late. As before, he shifted the wire first, then:

'What happens to children of Predictors for whom there's no room in the birth center?'

Yanar shrugged. 'They grow up and run the islands.'

He sat smug. He seemed unaware that he had revealed by implication that only those children who went to the birth centers became Predictors.

His impassivity started another train of thought in Gosseyn's mind. He had been intent, but now it struck him sharply that Yanar was not reacting like a man being subjected for the first time to such an interview as this. He knew what it felt like not to have advance awareness of questions. Knew it so well that it didn't upset him.

Like lightning Gosseyn saw the possibilities. He stepped back in his chagrin. It seemed incredible that it had taken him so long to realize the truth. He stared down at the Predictor, and said finally in a level but steely voice:

'And now, you will please describe exactly how you have been communicating with the Follower.'

If ever a man was caught by surprise, then Yanar was that man. He seemed unprepared in the extreme thalamic fashion. His face turned livid. The neural flow from his nervous system blocked and then burst, and then blocked and burst again.

'What do you mean?' He whispered the words finally.

Since the question was rhetorical, Gosseyn did not repeat his statement. He glowered down at the Predictor. 'Quick!' he said. 'Before I kill you.'

Yanar sagged limply back into his chair, and once more he changed color. He flushed. 'I didn't,' he stammered. 'Why should I endanger myself by calling the Follower and telling him where you were? I wouldn't do a thing like that.'

He shook himself, 'You can't prove it,' he said.

Gosseyn didn't need proof. He had been dangerously remiss in not keeping a watch on Yanar. And so the message had been sent and the damage done, Gosseyn had no doubt of that. The Predictor's reactions were too violent and too realistic. Yanar had never had to control his emotions, and so now he didn't know how. Guilt poured from every reflex in his body.

Gosseyn felt chilled. But he had done what he could to protect himself, and so there was nothing to do but obtain more information. He said curtly, 'You'd better talk fast, my friend, and truthfully. Did you contact the Follower himself?'

Yanar was sullen. He shrugged, and once more that was a signal for a block to break. 'Of course,' he said.

'You mean, he expected a call from you?' Gosseyn wanted that clear. 'You're his agent?'

The man shook his head. 'I'm a Predictor,' he said.

There was pride in his tone, but it was a bedraggled variety. A lock of his iron-gray hair had sagged over one temple. He looked like anything but a nobleman of Yalerta.

Gosseyn did not comment on the boast. He had his man on the run, and that was what counted.

'What did you tell him?'

'I said you were aboard.'

'And what did he say?'

'He said he knew that.'

66

'Oh!' said Gosseyn. He paused, but only for a moment.

His mind jumped ahead to other aspects of the situation. In quick succession he rapped out a dozen vital questions. The moment he had his facts he similarized the both of them into the control room, and stood over the trembling Yanar while he produced maps, and showed the wide circular course the ship had been following round and round the Follower's island, at a radius of a hundred miles.

Gosseyn reset the course for the island of Crest, only a few hundred miles north by northwest. Then he turned to confront the Predictors.

'And now,' he said in a threatening tone, 'we come to the problem of what to do with a traitor.'

The older man was pale, but some of his fear had departed. He said boldly, 'I owe you nothing. You can kill me, but you can't expect loyalty from me, and you won't get it.'

It wasn't loyalty that Gosseyn wanted. It was fear. He must make certain that these Predictors learned to think twice before they acted against him. But what to do?

It seemed impractical to make a definite decision. He turned on his heel and headed back into the drawing room. As he entered, Leej appeared from the direction of the bedrooms. He walked toward her, a faint frown on his face. *A few questions, madam,* he thought bleakly. *How was it that Yanar could warn the Follower without his action being predictable? Please explain that.*

The woman stopped, and waited for him, smiling. Her smile changed abruptly. Her gaze plunged past him and slightly to one side. Gosseyn spun around, and stared.

He felt nothing, heard nothing, and there was no sense of a presence even now that he could see. But a shape was taking form a dozen feet to his right. It grew black, and yet he could see the wall beyond it. It thickened, but it was not substance.

He felt himself become tense. The moment of his meeting with the Follower had come.

IX

Null-Abstracts

Semantics has to do with the meaning of meaning, or the meaning of words. General Semantics has to do with the relationship of the human nervous system to the world around it, and therefore it includes semantics. It provides an integrating system for all human thought and experience.

THERE was silence. The Follower seemed to be regarding him, for the shadowy mass was holding steady now. Gosseyn's brief, intense anxiety began to fade. He stared at his enemy alertly, and, swiftly, his attitude changed.

Actually, what could the Follower do against him?

Cautiously, Gosseyn shifted his gaze for a flickering moment to take in the rest of the scene before him. If there was going to be a battle, he wanted to be in the best possible position for it.

Leej was standing where she had paused. Her body was rigid, her eyes still unusually wide open. During the fleeting instant that his attention lingered upon her, he noted that the neural sensations that flowed from her showed an unvarying anxiety. It could be an alarm for her own safety exclusively, but Gosseyn thought not. Her fate was too closely bound up with his. He dismissed all thought of danger from her.

His eyes shifted toward the door of the corridor that led to the control room. For the barest moment, then, he lost sight of the Follower. He twisted back immediately, but he had his fact. The door was too far to the right. He had to turn his head too sharply in order to see it.

Gosseyn began to back toward the wall behind him. He moved slowly. There were several thoughts in his mind, several possibilities of danger. Yanar. The Predictor, he discovered with a swift probe of his extra brain, was still in the control room. Unfriendly vibrations flowed from him.

Gosseyn smiled grimly. He could just imagine how the older man might do him great damage in a critical moment. From memory, he visualized the wall behind him, and it had the air-conditioning slits that he wanted for his purpose. He twisted slightly to one side, until the soft breeze was blowing directly

68

It was clear that he was now expected to make an answer. Well, what ought he to say?

From the corner of his eyes, Gosseyn saw that Leej was edging cautiously toward a chair. She made it, and sighed audibly as she sank into it. That brought a bleak amusement to Gosseyn, which passed as the Follower said in his steeliest tone, 'Well?'

There was the beginning of purpose in Gosseyn now, a half determination to test the strength of the other. Test it now. But first, as much information as he could get.

'What's the war situation?' he temporized.

'I predict unqualified victory for Enro in three months,' was the reply.

Gosseyn hid his shock. 'You actually see the moment of victory?'

The pause, then, was so slight that Gosseyn wondered afterwards if it had occurred, or if he imagined it.

'I do,' was the firm reply.

He couldn't accept that, since it failed to take his extra brain into account. The strong possibility that he was being lied to made him sardonic again.

'No blurs?' he said.

'None.'

There was an interruption, a movement from Leej. She sat up.

'That,' she said in a clear voice, 'is a lie. I can foresee everything that anyone else can. And it is difficult to prophesy in detail for more than three weeks. Even that is always within certain limits.'

'Woman, hold your tongue!'

Leej's color was high. 'Follower,' she said, 'if you can't win with the power you really have, then you are as good as lost. And don't think for an instant that I feel myself bound to obey your orders. I do not desire, and never have desired, your victory.'

'Good girl,' said Gosseyn.

But he frowned, and noted a point for future reference. There was in her words a veiled implication of previous collaboration with the Follower.

'Leej,' he said without looking at her, 'are there any blurs in the next few weeks?'

'There is no picture at all,' was the answer. 'It's as if everything is cut off. The future is a blank.'

'Perhaps,' said the Follower softly but resonantly, 'that is because Gosseyn is about to die.'

He added quickly, 'My friend, you have five seconds to make up your mind.'

The five seconds passed in silence.

Gosseyn had expected, if an attack came, it would be one of three types. First, the Follower might try to utilize the magnetic power of Leej's ship against him. He'd quickly discover that that wouldn't work.

Second, and most likely, he'd use a source of power in the Retreat, since that was his base of operations. He'd quickly discover that that wouldn't work either. Third, he would use an outside source of power. If it was the latter, Gosseyn's hope was that it operated across space and not by mechanical similarity.

If it came by space, the tubes he had set up would detect it and his extra brain could then similarize electric energy onto the carrier beam of the tubes.

It turned out to be a combination. A Distorter and an electric power source in the Retreat. Gosseyn felt the abrupt re-direction of the current from the forty thousand kilowatt dynamo. It was what he had been waiting for, was ready for. There were 'switches' in his extra brain which, once set to cues, operated faster than any electric switch.

The problem, with his special method of controlling matter and energy, was that in a comparative sense it took a long time to 'set' the initial pattern.

The cue was automatic.

All the power of the dynamo flowed, not as the Follower directed, into a blaster, but according to the extra brain pattern. At first Gosseyn let it churn harmlessly into the ground at one of his memorized areas on the island. He wanted the Follower to realize that the attack was not proceeding according to plan.

'One, two, three,' he counted deliberately, and then without further pause similarized it into the air directly in front of the shadow shape.

There was a flash of flame, brighter than the sun.

The shadowy stuff absorbed it, and held. It took every volt and watt, wavering as it did so, but it held.

Presently the Follower said, 'We seem to be at an impasse.'

It was a reality that had already struck home to Gosseyn. He was all too keenly aware of his own shortcomings. It was not apparent, but Gilbert Gosseyn was ridiculously vulnerable. A surprise blast from a source of power over which he had not previously established control, and he would be dead.

The fact that his memory would go on in the body of an eighteen year old, and that there would be an apparent life

72

continuity did not alter the meaning of the defeat. No youth of eighteen would ever save a galaxy. And if such an individual, or even several such individuals interfered too much, they also could be removed from the scene by older and more powerful individuals like the Follower.

The perspiration stood out on his face. Just for a moment, there was a plan in his mind, to attempt something he had never tried before. But he rejected it almost instantly. Atomic energy was simply one more power that he could control with his extra mind. But to know that he could do it and actually to do it, were entirely different aspects of the problem.

In this confined space, atomic radiation could be as deadly to the user as to the person it was used against.

'I think,' the Follower's voice cut across his thoughts, 'we'd better come to an agreement. I warn you I have not used all my resources.'

Gosseyn could well believe that. The Follower need merely turn to an outside source of power, and instantly he would be the victor in this tense and deadly battle. At best, Gilbert Gosseyn could retreat to the Follower's island. The possibility of an ignominious recapture was as close as that.

And still he dared not use the atomic energy from the pile in the Retreat.

He made the famous thalamo-cortical pause, and consciously said to himself, *'There is more to this situation than is apparent. No individual can take the output of a forty thousand kilowatt dynamo. Therefore, I am making an identification. There must be an explanation for the shadow shape which is beyond my own understanding of physics.'*

But whose physics? The Follower had confessed that he knew little of such things. Whose vast knowledge was he using?

The mystery seemed as great as that posed by the existence of such a being as the Follower.

The shadow shape broke the silence. 'I admit,' he said, 'that you've caught me by surprise. Next time I'll operate on a different basis.' He broke off. 'Gosseyn, will you consider any kind of partnership?'

'Yes, but on my conditions.'

'What are they?' After a brief hesitation.

'First, that you turn the Predictors against Enro.'

'Impossible.' The Follower's voice was curt. 'The League must go down, civilization briefly lose its cohesion. I have a very special reason for requiring the makings of a universal state.'

Gosseyn remembered wryly where he had heard that before.

He stiffened. 'At a cost of a hundred billion dead,' he said. 'No, thank you.'

'I suppose you're a Null-A.' Grimly.

There was no point in denying that. The Follower knew that Venus existed, knew where it was, and could presumably order its destruction at any time. 'I'm a Null-A,' Gosseyn admitted.

The Follower said: 'Suppose I told you I was prepared to have a Null-A universal state.'

'I'd hesitate to accept that as a fact.'

'And yet, I might consider it. I haven't had time to examine this non-aristotelian philosophy in detail, but as I see it, it's a method of scientific thinking. Is that correct?'

'It's a way of thinking,' said Gosseyn cautiously.

The Follower's voice had a musing tone when he spoke again. 'I've never yet,' he said, 'had reason to fear science in any of its branches. I don't think I need to begin now. Let me put it like this: Let us both give this matter further consideration. But next time we meet you must have made up your mind. Meanwhile, I shall try to prevent you from making any more use of power on this planet.'

Gosseyn said nothing, and this time the silence continued. Slowly, the shadow shape began to withdraw.

Even in that bright light it was difficult to decide when the last wisp of it faded out of sight.

There was a pause. And then the dynamo in the Follower's Retreat began to give off less power. In thirty seconds the power was off.

Another pause. And then the pile went dead. Almost at the same instant, the magnetic power in the Retreat faded off into nothingness.

The Follower had made a shrewd guess as to what had happened. Even if he didn't suspect the full truth, he had now taken action that had all the effect of a complete and accurate analysis.

Only the magnetic power of a small ship remained in the control of Gilbert Gosseyn.

X

Null-Abstracts

For the sake of sanity, DATE: Do not say, 'Scientists believe. . . .' Say, 'Scientists believed in 1956 . . .' 'John Smith (1956) is an isolationist . . .' All things, including John Smith's political opinions, are subject to change and can therefore only be referred to in terms of the moment.

SLOWLY, Gosseyn let himself become aware again of his surroundings. He turned his head and glanced toward the dining room, where the servants had been so busy a short time before. They were not in sight. He could see the edge of the table, and all the dishes seemed to be on it, though no food was visible.

His gaze leaped to Leej, paused long enough for him to notice that she was climbing to her feet, and then flashed on to the door that led to the control room. From where he stood, the full length of the corridor and even a part of the dome window were visible, but there was no sign of Yanar.

The ship remained steady on its course.

Leej broke the silence between them. 'You've done it,' she whispered.

Gosseyn walked forward from the wall. He shook off her words, but he did not tell her that the Follower had just nullified whatever victory he had gained.

Leej came toward him now, her eyes glowing. 'Don't you realise,' she said, 'you've beaten the Follower?'

She touched his arm with a quick, tremulous caress of her fingers.

Gosseyn said, 'Come along.'

He headed toward the control room. When he entered, Yanar was bending expectantly over the magnetic radio receiver. For Gosseyn it was apparent at a glance what the man was doing—still waiting for instructions. Without a word he walked forward, reached past Yanar's shoulder and shut off the instrument.

The other started violently, then straightenend, and turned with a sneer on his lips. Gosseyn said, 'Pack your bags if you have any. You're getting off at the first stop.'

The Predictor shrugged. Without a word he stalked from the room.

Gosseyn stared after him thoughtfully. The man's presence annoyed him. He was an irritation, a minor nuisance whose only importance in the galactic scheme of things was that he was a Predictor. That, in spite of his obstinate and petty character, made him interesting.

Unfortunately, he was but one man out of more than two million, neither typical nor atypical of his kind. It was possible to make certain cautious hypotheses about the Predictors from his observation of Yanar and Leej. But such conclusions must be subject to change without notice.

He dismissed Yanar from his mind, and turned to Leej. 'How long will it take us to get to Crest, where the warship is?'

The young woman walked over to a plate on the wall, which Gosseyn hadn't noticed before. She pressed a button. Instantly, a map sprang into sharp relief. It showed water and islands, and a tiny point of light.

She indicated the brightness. 'That's us,' she said. She pointed at a land mass higher up. 'There's Crest.' Carefully, she counted finely ruled lines that crisscrossed the map. 'About three hours and twenty minutes,' she said. 'We'll have plenty of time to eat dinner.'

'Eat!' Gosseyn echoed. And then he smiled, and shook his head in a half apology to himself. He was tremendously hungry, but he had almost forgotten that such normal instincts existed.

It was going to be pleasant to relax.

Dinner.

Gosseyn watched as the young girl served him a cocktail glass that contained segments of what seemed to be fish. He waited alertly while Yanar was served by one of the older women, and then transposed the two glasses by similarization.

He tested his own cocktail. It was fish, sharply flavored. But, after the initial shock to his taste buds, delicious. He ate it all, then put down his fork, sat back and looked at Leej.

'What goes on in your mind when you foresee?'

The young woman was serious. 'It's automatic.'

'You mean, there's no pattern you follow?'

'Well——'

'Do you pause? Do you think of an object? Do you have to see it?'

Leej smiled, and even Yanar seemed more relaxed, even slightly, if tolerantly, amused. The woman said, 'We just have it, that's all. It's not something that has to be thought about.'

So those were the kind of answers they gave themselves.

76

They were different. They were special. Simple answers for simple people. Actually, the complication was of an unparalleled order. The Predictor processes occurred on a nonverbal level. The whole system of Null-A was an organized attempt to co-ordinate nonverbal realities with verbal projections. Even on Null-A Venus the gap between interpretation and event had never been more than partially bridged.

He waited while the empty glasses were removed, and they were each served a plate containing a brownish red meat, three vegetables and a thin sauce of greenish color. He exchanged his for Yanar's, tasted each of the vegetables in turn, and then cut off a piece of meat. Finally, he sat back.

'Try to explain,' he said.

Leej closed her eyes. 'I've always thought of it as floating in the time stream. It's a spreading out. Memories are coming into my mind, but they aren't really memories. Very clear, very sharp. Visual pictures. What is it you want to know? Ask about something not connected with yourself. You blur everything.'

Gosseyn had laid down his fork. He would have liked a prediction about Venus, but that would require projection of his future. He said, 'The girl who's serving me.'

'Vorn?' Leej shook her head and smiled at the girl, who was standing rigid and colorless. 'It's too hard on their nervous systems. I'll tell you her future privately later on, if you wish.' The girl sighed.

'The galactic warship,' said Gosseyn, 'on Crest?'

'You must be connected with that because it's blurred.'

'Blurred now?' He was surprised. 'Before we actually get there?'

'Yes.' She shook her head. 'This is not answering your questions, is it?'

'Could we get through to another star system if somebody was going there?'

'It depends on the distance. There is a limitation.'

'How far?'

'I don't know. I haven't had enough experience.'

'Then how do you know about it?'

'The galactic recruiting ship gives out bulletins.'

'Bulletins?'

She smiled. 'They're not depending entirely on the Follower's orders. They're trying to make it seem exciting.'

Gosseyn could imagine how that would work. The project was being made to sound fascinating for the benefit of minds that had many childlike qualities. And the publicists were smart enough to indicate that there were obstacles.

'These mental pictures,' he said. 'Can you follow the future-lines of some person you know who volunteered for warship service?'

She sighed and shook her head. 'It's too far. The bulletin once mentioned about eighteen thousand light-years.'

Gosseyn remembered that Crang had indicated in his conversation with Patricia Hardie, or rather Reesha, sister of Enro, that the Distorter transport bases of galactic civilization could not be more than about a thousand light-years apart.

Theoretically, similarity transport was instantaneous, and theoretically spatial distance made no difference. In practice there seemed to be a margin of error. The instruments were not perfect. Twenty decimal similarity, the critical point where interaction occurred, was no total similarity.

Apparently, the Predictor gift was also imperfect, even when not impeded by the presence of Gilbert Gosseyn. Still, whatever the distance over which they could predict, it would be adequate for the purposes of a battle in space.

Gosseyn hesitated, then: 'About how many ships' movements could they take into account at the same time?'

Leej looked surprised. 'It really doesn't matter. All of them, of course, that had any connection with the event. It's very limited in that way.'

'Limited!' said Gosseyn.

He stood up, and without a word headed for the control room.

He had been undecided about the Predictors. Prepared to let the galactic ship go on recruiting them until he made up his mind just when he would try to seize it. Now, it seemed to him that it might be a long way off. One man didn't capture a battleship without planning.

A preliminary move was necessary.

At the end of the living room, Gosseyn stopped and turned. 'Leej,' he called, 'I'll be needing you.'

She was already on her feet, and she joined him a minute later in the dome. 'That was a short dinner,' she said anxiously.

'We'll finish it later,' said Gosseyn. He was intent. 'Is there any band on this radio that can be used for sending a general message?'

'Why, yes. We have what we call an emergency band that——' She stopped. 'It's used to co-ordinate our plans when we are threatened.'

Gosseyn said, 'Set it.'

She gave him a startled look, but there must have been something in his expression that decided her to say no more. A moment later, Gosseyn was on the air. As before—it was now quite automatic—he shifted the wire immediately before each sentence he spoke. He said in a ringing voice:

'Calling all Predictors! From this moment every Predictor who is discovered or captured aboard a warship of the Greatest Empire will be executed. Friends are advised to communicate this warning to people who are already aboard such ships.

'You may all judge the effectiveness of this threat by the fact that you did not foresee the call that I am now making. I repeat: Every Predictor found aboard an Enro warship will be executed. There are no exceptions.'

He returned to the dining room, finished his dinner, and then went back to the control room. From its vantage point two and a half hours later he saw the lights of a city in the distance. At Yanar's request, the ship was brought down at what Leej called a Predictor air station. As soon as they were up in the air again, Gosseyn set the accelerator to *Full*, and then slipped to the window, and looked down at the city below. So many people. He saw the lights entwined with innumerable curling fingers of water. In some cases the ocean twisted right through the center of the city.

As he watched, all the lights went out. Gosseyn stared, but there was blackness. Beside him Leej uttered an exclamation.

'I wonder why they did that.'

Gosseyn could have answered the question, but he didn't. The Follower was taking no chances. He evidently had a theory about the nature of Gilbert Gosseyn's control over energy, and he intended to see that no energy was available.

Leej said, 'Where are we going now?'

When he told her, some of the color went out of her face. 'It's a warship,' she said. 'There are hundreds of soldiers aboard, and weapons that could kill you from many different directions at once.'

That was true enough. The danger of trying to use his special powers to seize a ship was that it would be virtually impossible to nullify or control many scores of hand weapons. It was under such circumstances that fatal accidents could occur all too easily.

But what had happened put a pressure on him to act more swiftly than he had planned. The reality was that he had already used his strongest weapons against the Follower. Therefore, the sooner he got away from Yalerta the better. Somewhere out in the galaxy there might be scientific understanding of what made the Follower invulnerable, and, actually, until he found a rational approach, he'd better stay away from the man.

Besides, the galactic warship was the only method he knew of to get off this isolated planet.

The greatest risks were in order.

In half an hour there was light ahead. At first, the galactic ship was little more than a bright blur in the midnight darkness, but presently, so brilliant were the lights around it, it was clearly visible. Gosseyn set Leej's airship into a wide orbit around the bigger ship, and studied the approaches through a magnetic powered telescope.

The stranger was about six hundred feet long. A small ship indeed by galactic standards. But then, it had only one purpose on Yalerta. Aboard was a Distorter transport instrument of the type that produced mechanical similarity. As an invention it had probably no equal in the history of science. With it, man could move across the vast distances of space as if there were no space. A Predictor on Yalerta need merely step into the Distorter aboard the warship, and he would be transported a hundred or a thousand light-years away almost instantly. The margin of error, as he had discovered with the organic distorter in his head, was as small as to be almost not noticeable.

The ship lay on a level plain. During the forty minutes that Gosseyn watched it, two skytrailers came out of the darkness. They came at different times, and floated down to a landing near a blaze point that must be an air lock. Gosseyn presumed that these were volunteers, and what interested him was that, on each occasion, the trailer departed before the volunteer was allowed aboard the galactic ship.

It was just such details that he had been waiting to find out.

They approached boldly. At five miles he was able to sense the energy aboard—and received his great disappointment. Electricity only, and in unimportant quantities. The drive pile had been damped.

Mentally, Gosseyn drew back from the venture. In his anxiety, he began to whistle under his breath. He was aware of Leej watching him.

'Why, you're nervous,' she said wonderingly.

Nervous, he thought grimly, uncertain, undecided. Very true. As things stood now, he could wait in the hope of improving his position with regard to the ship—or he could make an attempt to capture it immediately.

'This power of yours,' said Leej, 'the way you do things——how does it work?'

She was wondering about that at last, was she? Gosseyn smiled, and shook his head.

'It's a little involved,' he said, 'and without wishing to be offensive, I think it's beyond your scientific training. It goes something like this: The extensional area we call space-time is probably an illusion of the senses. That is, any reality they have

80

bears little relation to what you see, feel or touch. Just as you seem to be better orientated as a Predictor to the real space-time continuum, with emphasis on the time element—that is, better orientated than the average individual—so I am better orientated, but in my case the emphasis seems to be on space.'

She seemed not to have heard. 'You're not actually all-powerful, are you? Just what are your limitations?'

'Do you mind,' said Gosseyn, 'if I tell you later? I've just made up my mind about something.'

A pale Leej guided the airship through the night, and grew paler as she listened to his instructions. 'I don't think you have any right,' she said shakily, 'to ask me to do such a thing.'

Gosseyn said, 'I'd like to ask you one question.'

'Yes?'

'When you were in the cell with Jurig, what would have happened if he had killed me? Would the Follower have rescued you?'

'No, I was merely a device to incite you to your greatest effort. If I failed—it was my failure, also.'

'Well?' said Gosseyn softly.

The woman was silent, her lips pursed. The neural flow from her had changed from an anxious unevenness to a tense but steady pattern. She looked up at last.

'All right,' she said, 'I'll do it.'

Gosseyn patted her arm in silent approval. He did not fully trust Leej. There was a possibility that this also was a trap. But the shadow thing had already discovered that imprisoning Gilbert Gosseyn was easier said than done.

Gosseyn's eyes narrowed with determination. He was a man who had to keep moving. He felt immensely confident of his ability to do so, as long as he did not become too cautious in the face of necessity.

His reverie broke, as the beam of a searchlight penetrated the dome. There was a click as the magnetic receiver went on, and a man's voice said, 'Please land in the lighted area a hundred yards from our entrance.'

Leej took the ship down without a word. When they had come to rest, the voice spoke again from the receiver. 'How many are coming?'

Gosseyn held up a finger to Leej, and motioned for her to answer. 'One,' she said.

'Sex?'

'Female.'

'Very well. One female person will emerge from your ship and approach the admission office at the foot of the gangplank.

The trailer will leave immediately and go to a distance of five miles. As soon as it has retreated the required distance, the volunteer will be allowed aboard our ship.'

So it was five miles that the trailers were supposed to go. It seemed to Gosseyn that the two volunteers he had observed earlier had been admitted before anything like that distance had been covered by the ships that had brought them.

It was the same way with Leej. Gosseyn, who had similarized himself to the rear control room, watched her pause at the small structure beside the lower end of the gangplank. After little more than a second she started up the gangplank.

He glanced at the speedometer. The trailer had gone one and one-eighth Yalertan miles.

It could mean one of two things. First, this was a trap, and he was being lured. Or second, the space veterans had become bored, and were no longer adhering to the rules.

Of course, it could be a combination. A trap by the Follower, of which the ship's crew knew nothing. Or perhaps they had even been warned, and didn't take the threat seriously.

One by one Gosseyn ticked off the possibilities in his mind, and each time came back to the same reality. It made no difference. He had to make the attempt.

As he watched, Leej disappeared through the lock. He waited patiently. He had set himself four minutes after she got inside. In a way it was a long time to leave her alone.

He waited, and he felt strangely without regrets. For a moment, when she had protested her inclusion, he had wondered if he was not pushing her too hard. That wonder was past. It had seemed to him then, and still did, that the ship's crew would have been warned against a man, not a woman. Therefore, hers must be the risk of making the initial entry.

If she got inside, then so would he. There were other methods, but that was the fastest. He had plans for Leej, but first of all she must acquire the feeling that her fate was bound up with his.

He glanced at the clock, and experienced a thrill. The four minutes were up.

He hesitated a moment longer, and then similarized himself to the open porthole beside the air lock. It was touch and go for a second as he clawed for a hold. And then his arm was straddling the metal seat of the porthole.

It had seemed like a good place to enter, and so he had photographed it through the telescope while the trailer was still on the ground.

He drew himself into the tunnel-like porthole.

XI

Null-Abstracts

For the sake of sanity, INDEX: Do not say, 'Two little girls . . .' unless you mean, 'Mary and Jane, two little girls, different from each other, and from all the other people in the world . . .'

FROM where he lay straddling the porthole, Gosseyn could hear the murmur of conversation. It was subdued, so that no word came through. But the talking was between a woman and a man.

Cautiously, Gosseyn peered around the inner rim of the porthole. He looked down into a broad corridor. About thirty feet to his left was the open air lock through which Leej had come. To his right he could see Leej herself standing in a doorway and beyond her, with only his shoulder and arm visible, was a man in the uniform of an officer of the Greatest Empire.

Except for the three of them, the corridor was deserted.

Gosseyn lowered himself to the floor, and keeping to the far wall, approached the couple.

As Gosseyn came up, Leej was saying: '. . . I think I'm entitled to the details. What arrangements have been made for women?'

Her tone was calm, with just the right note of demand in it. The officer's voice, when he answered, held a resigned patience.

'Madam, I assure you, a six-room apartment, servants, every convenience, and authority second only to that of the captain and his first officers. You are——'

He stopped, as Gosseyn stepped into the doorway beside Leej. His surprise lasted only a few seconds.

'I beg your pardon,' he said. 'I didn't see you come aboard. The admission officer outside must have forgotten to——'

He stopped again. He seemed to realize the improbability of the admission officer having forgotten anything of the kind. His eyes widened. His jaw sagged slightly. His plump hand moved perkily toward the blaster at his side.

Gosseyn hit him once on the jaw. And caught him as he fell.

He carried the unconscious body to a couch. He searched the man quickly, but found only the blaster in the holster. He straightened, and looked around. He had already noticed that

83

in addition to the ordinary furnishings, the room contained a number of Distorter type elevators. Now, he counted them. One dozen, and not elevators, really. He'd called them that ever since he had mistaken them for elevators when he was in Enro's secret Venusian base.

One dozen. The sight of them in a row against the wall farthest from the door clarified his mental picture. This was the room from which Yalerta's Predictors were sent to their assigned posts. The process was even simpler than he had thought. There seemed to be no preliminaries. The admission officer allowed a volunteer into the gangplank. And then this plump man led them into this room, and shipped them to their destination.

The rest of the ship was apparently unaffected. The officers and men lived their routine existence, apart from the purposes for which their ship had come to Yalerta. And since it was after midnight, they might possibly be asleep.

Gosseyn felt stimulated at the mere idea.

He stepped back to the door. As before, the corridor was deserted.

Behind him, Leej said, 'He's awakening.'

Gosseyn returned to the couch, and stood waiting.

The man stirred, and sat up, nursing his jaw. He glanced swiftly from Leej to Gosseyn and back again. Finally, he said in a querulous tone, 'Are you two crazy?'

Gosseyn said: 'How many men are there aboard this ship?'

The other stared at him, then he started to laugh. 'Why you fool,' he said. For a moment he seemed to be overcome with renewed amusement. 'How many men,' he mimicked. His voice rose. 'There are five hundred. Just think that over, and get out of this ship as fast as you can.'

The crew complement was about what Gosseyn had expected. Spaceships were never crowded in the same fashion as ground vehicles. It was a matter of air and food supply. Still, five hundred men.

'Do the men live in dormitories?' he asked.

'There are eight dormitories,' replied the officer. 'Sixty men in each one.' He rubbed his hands together. 'Sixty,' he repeated, and his voice relished the figure. 'Would you like me to take you down and introduce you?'

Gosseyn allowed the humor to pass him by. 'Yes,' he said, 'yes, I would.'

Leej's fingers plucked at his arm nervously. 'There's a continuous blur,' she said.

Gosseyn nodded. 'I've got to do it,' he said. 'Otherwise he would know what I'm doing.'

She nodded doubtfully. 'So many men. Doesn't that make it complicated?'

Her words were like a spur to the officer. He climbed to his feet. 'Let's go,' he said jovially.

Gosseyn said, 'What's your name?'

'Oreldon.'

Silently, Gosseyn motioned him toward the corridor. When they came to the open outer lock, Gosseyn stopped.

'Can you close these doors?' he asked.

The man's plumpish face glowed with conscious good humor. 'You're right,' he said. 'We wouldn't want any visitors while I was off duty.' He stepped briskly forward, and he was about to press the button when Gosseyn stopped him.

'A moment, please,' he said. 'I'd like to check those connections. Wouldn't want you setting off an alarm, you know.'

He unfastened the plate and swung it open. By count, there were four wires too many. 'Where do they go?' he asked Oreldon.

'To the control room. Two for opening, two for shutting.'

Gosseyn nodded, and closed the panel. It was a chance he had to take. There would always be a connection with the control board.

Firmly, he pressed the button. Metal stirred, thick slabs of it glided across the opening and clanked shut with a steely sound.

'Mind if I talk to my partner outside?' Oreldon asked.

Gosseyn had been wondering about the man outside. 'What do you want to say to him?' he asked.

'Oh, just that I've closed the door, and that he can relax for a while.'

'Naturally,' said Gosseyn, 'you will be careful how you word it.'

'Of course.'

Gosseyn checked the wiring, then waited while Oreldon switched on a wall phone. He recognized that the other was in a state of thalamic stimulation. Accordingly, he would be swept along by the intoxicating flood of his own humor until the shock of imminent disaster sobered him. That would be the moment to watch for.

Apparently, the doors were not always open, for the admission officer did not seem surprised that they were closed. 'You're sure, Orry,' he said, 'that you're not going off with that female who just came in?'

'Regretfully, no,' said Oreldon, and broke the connection. 'Can't have these conversations going on too long,' he said heartily to Gosseyn. 'People might get suspicious.'

85

They came to a stairway. Oreldon was about to start down it when Gosseyn restrained him. 'Where does this lead?' he asked.

'Why, down to the men's quarters.'

'And where's the control room?'

'Oh, you wouldn't want the control room. You have to climb for that. It's up front.'

Gosseyn said gravely that he was happy to hear that. 'And how many openings are there into the lower deck?' he asked.

'Four.'

'I hope,' said Gosseyn pleasantly, 'that you're telling me the truth. If I should discover that there are five, for instance, this blaster might go off suddenly.'

'There's only four, I swear it,' said Oreldon. His voice was hoarse suddenly.

'You see,' said Gosseyn, 'I notice there's a heavy door that can slide over this stairway.'

'Wouldn't you say that was normal?' Oreldon was back in the groove again. 'After all, a spaceship has to be built so that whole sections can be sealed off in case of accident.'

'Let's slide it shut, shall we?' said Gosseyn.

'Huh!' His tone showed that he hadn't even thought of such a thing. His pasty face showed that this was the moment of shocked realization. His eyes rolled as he glared helplessly along the corridor. 'You don't think for one second,' he snarled, 'that you're going to get away with this.'

'The door,' said Gosseyn in an inexorable tone.

The officer hesitated, his body rigid. Then slowly he walked to the wall. He opened a sliding panel, waited tensely until Gosseyn had checked the wiring and then jerked the lever. The door panels were only two inches thick. They closed with a faint thud.

'I sincerely hope,' said Gosseyn, 'that they are now locked, and that they can't be opened from beneath, because if I should discover differently I would always have time to fire this blaster at least once.'

'They lock,' said Oreldon sullenly.

'Fine,' said Gosseyn. 'But now let's hurry. I'm eager to have those other stairways cut off also.'

Oreldon kept glancing anxiously along side corridors as they walked, but if he hoped that they would see a member of the crew, he was disappointed. There was silence except for the faint sound of their own movements. No one stirred.

'I think everyone must have gone to bed,' said Gosseyn.

The man did not respond. They completed the task of shutting off the lower floor before another word was spoken, then

Gosseyn said, 'That should leave twenty officers including you and your friend outside. Is that right?'

Oreldon nodded, but he said nothing. His eyes looked glazed.

'And if I remember my ancient history of Earth correctly,' said Gosseyn, 'there used to be an old custom—due to the intransigent character of some people—of confining officers to their quarters under certain circumstances. That always meant a system of outside locks. It would be interesting if Enro's warships also had problems, and solutions, like that.'

He had to take only one glance at his prisoner's face to realize that Enro's ships had.

Ten minutes after that, without a shot having been fired, he was in complete control of the galactic warship.

It had been too easy. That was the feeling that grew on Gosseyn as he peered into the deserted control room. Herding Oreldon ahead of him, and with Leej bringing up the rear, he entered the room. Critically, he looked around.

There was slackness here, not a single man on duty, except the two officers who looked after the Predictors.

Too easy. Considering the precautions that the Follower had already taken against him, it seemed unbelievable that the ship was his in reality.

And yet, it seemed to be.

Once more he gave his attention to the room. The instrument board curved massively beneath the transparent dome. It was divided into three sections: electric, Distorter and atomic. First, the electric.

He manipulated the switches that started an atomic powered dynamo somewhere in the depths of the ship. He felt better. As soon as he had memorized enough sockets, he would be in a position to release intolerable energy into each room and along every corridor. It was tremendously convincing. If this was a trap, then the crew members were not in on it.

But still he was dissatisfied. He studied the board. There were levers and dials on each section, the purposes of which he could only partially guess. He did not worry about the electric or the atomic; the latter could not be used within the confines of the ship, and the former he would shortly control without qualification.

That left the Distorter. Gosseyn frowned. There was no doubt of it. Here was the danger. Despite his possession of an organic Distorter in what he called his extra brain, his knowledge of the mechanical Distorter system of the galactic civilization was vague. In that vagueness his weakness must lie, and the trap, if there was a trap.

In his preoccupation, he had moved back from the board. He was standing there, teetering between several possibilities, when Leej said, 'We'll have to sleep.'

'Not while we're on Yalerta,' said Gosseyn.

His main plan was fairly clear. There was a margin of error between perfect similarity and the twenty decimal similarity of the mechanical Distorter. Measured by spatial distance, it came to about a thousand light-years every ten hours. But that also, Gosseyn had already surmised, was an illusion.

He explained to Leej: 'It's not really a question of speed. Relatively, one of the earliest and most encompassing of Null-A formulations, shows that factors of space and time cannot be considered separately. But I'm coming around to another variation of the same idea. Events occur at different moments, and separateness in space is merely part of the image that forms in our nervous systems when we try to interpret the time gap.'

He saw that once more he had left the woman far behind. He went on, half to himself: 'It's possible that two given events are so closely related that in fact they are not different events at all, no matter how far apart they seem to be, or how carefully defined. In terms of probability——'

Gosseyn stood frowning over the problem, feeling himself on the edge of a much greater solution than that required by the immediate situation. Leej's voice distracted his attention.

'But what are you going to do?'

Gosseyn stepped once more to the board. 'Right now,' he said, 'we're taking off on normal drive.'

The control instruments were similar to those on the ships that plied the space between Earth and Venus. The first upward thrust tensed every plate. The movement grew continuous. In ten minutes they were clear of the atmosphere, and gathering speed. After twenty-five minutes more, they emerged from the umbral cone of the planet, and sunlight splashed brilliantly into the control room.

In the rearview plate, the image of the spinning world of Yalerta showed as a saucer of light holding a vast, dark, misty ball. Gosseyn turned abruptly from the scene, and faced Oreldon. The officer turned pale when Gosseyn told him his plan.

'Don't let him guess I'm responsible,' he begged.

Gosseyn promised without hesitation. But it seemed to him that if a military board of the Greatest Empire should ever investigate the seizure of the Y-381907 the truth would be quickly discovered.

It was Oreldon who knocked on the captain's door, and presently emerged accompanied by a stocky, angry man. Gosseyn cut his violent language short.

'Captain Free, if it should ever be discovered that this ship was captured without the firing of a shot, you will probably pay with your life. You'd better listen to me.'

He explained that he wanted the use of the ship temporarily only, and Captain Free calmed enough to start discussing details. It appeared that Gosseyn's picture of how interstellar ships could operate was correct. Ships were set to go to a distant point, but the pattern could be broken before they got there.

'It's the only way we can stop at planets like Yalerta,' the captain explained. 'We similarize to a base more than a thousand light-years farther on, then make the break.'

Gosseyn nodded. 'I want to go to Gorgzid, and I want the pattern to break about a day's normal flight away.'

He was not surprised that the destination startled the other. 'Gorgzid!' the captain exclaimed. His eyes narrowed, and then he smiled grimly. 'They should be able to take care of you,' he said. 'Well, do you want to go now? It will take seven jumps.'

Gosseyn did not answer immediately. He was intent on the neural flow from the man. It was not quite normal, which actually was natural enough. There were uneven spurts, indicating emotional disturbances, but there was no purposeful pattern. It was convincing. The captain had no plans, no private schemes, no treachery in mind.

Once more he considered his position. He was attuned to the electric dynamo, and the atomic pile of the ship. He was in a position to kill every man aboard in a flash. His position was virtually impregnable.

His hesitation ended. Gosseyn drew a deep breath, and then:

'Now!' he said.

XII

Null-Abstracts

*For the sake of sanity, use ET CETERA: When you say,
'Mary is a good girl!' be aware that Mary is much more than
'good.' Mary is 'good,' nice, kind, et cetera, meaning she also
has other characteristics. It is worth remembering, also, that
modern psychology—1956—does not consider the placidly
'good' individual a healthy personality.*

HE had held himself tense, half expecting that an attempt
would be made to use the momentary blackout against
him. Now, he turned, and said, 'That was certainly fast
enough. We——'

His voice faltered—because he was no longer in the control
room of the destroyer.

Five hundred feet away was a control board on a vaster
plane than the one which he had left only an instant before.
The transparent dome that curved up from it was of such
noble proportions that for a moment his brain refused to
grasp the size.

With a sickening comprehension, he stared down at his
hands and body; his hands were thin, bony; his body slim,
and dressed in the uniform of a staff officer of the Greatest
Empire.

Ashargin!

The recognition was so sharp that Gosseyn felt the body
that he again occupied, tremble and start to cringe. With an
effort he fought off the weakness, but there was despair in him
as he thought of his own body far away in the control room
of the Y-381907.

It must be lying unconscious on the floor. At this very
minute, Oreldon and Captain Free would be overpowering
Leej, preparatory to capturing the two interlopers. Or rather
—Gosseyn made the distinction bleakly—approximately eighteen thousand light-years away, several days before so far as
the destroyer was concerned, Leej and Gilbert Gosseyn's body
had been seized.

He must never forget that a time difference resulted from
similarity transport.

He grew abruptly aware that his thoughts were too violent

for the fragile Ashargin in whose body he was once more trapped. With blurred eyes he looked around him, and slowly he began to adjust. Slowly, because this was not his own highly trained nervous system which he was trying to control.

Nevertheless, presently, his brain cleared, and he stopped trembling. After a minute, though the waves of weakness made a rhythm inside him, he was able to realize what Ashargin had been doing at the moment that he was possessed.

He had been walking along with a group of fleet admirals, He saw them now ahead of him. Two had stopped, and were looking back at him where he stood. One of these said, 'Your excellency, you look ill.'

Before Gosseyn-Ashargin could reply, the other man, a tall, gaunt, old admiral, whose uniform sparkled with the jeweled medals and insignia that he wore, said sardonically, 'The prince has not been well since he arrived. We must commend him for his devotion to duty at such a time.'

As the second man finished speaking, Gosseyn recognized him as Grand Admiral Paleol. The identification brought him even further back to normalcy. For it was something only Ashargin would know.

Clearly, the two minds, his and Ashargin's, were starting to integrate on the unconscious level.

The realization stiffened him. Here he was. Once more he had been picked up by an unseen player, and the essence that was his mind similarized into a brain not his own. The quicker he adjusted, the better off he would be.

This time he had to try to dominate his situation. Not a trace of weakness must show. Ashargin would have to be driven to the limit of his physical capacity.

As he hurried forward, to join the other officers, all of whom had stopped now, the memory of Ashargin's last week was beginning to well up. Week? The realization that seven days had passed for Ashargin, while he had had less than a full day and night of conscious existence, briefly startled Gosseyn. But the pause it gave him was only momentary.

The picture of the previous week was surprisingly good. Ashargin had not fainted once. He had successfully bridged the initial introductions. He had even tried to put over the idea that he would be an observer until further notice. For a man who had collapsed twice in the presence of Enro, it was an achievement of the first order.

It was one more evidence that even so unintegrated a personality as Ashargin responded quickly, and that only a few hours of control by a Null-A trained mind could cause definite improvement.

'Ah,' said a staff officer just ahead of Gosseyn-Ashargin, 'here we are.'

Gosseyn looked up. They had come to the entrance of a small council room. It was evident—and Ashargin's memory backed him up—that a meeting of high officers was about to take place.

Here he would be able to make his new, determined personality of Ashargin felt.

There were officers already in the room. Others were bearing down from various points. As he watched, still others emerged from Distorter cages a hundred feet farther along the wall. Introductions came thick and fast.

Several of the officers looked at him sharply when his name was given. But Gosseyn was uniformly polite to the newcomers. His moment would come later.

Actually, his attention had been distracted.

He had suddenly realized that the great room behind him was the control room of a super-battleship. And more. It was the control room of a ship that was at this very moment engaged in the fantastic battle of the Sixth Decant.

The excitement of the thought was like a flame in his mind. During a lull in the introductions, he felt compelled to turn and look, this time with comprehending eyes. The dome towered a good five hundred feet above his head. It curved up and over him, limpidly transparent, and beyond were the jewel-bright stars of the central mass of the galaxy.

The Milky Way, close-up. Millions of the hottest and most dazzling suns of the galaxy. Here, amid beauty that could never be surpassed, Enro had launched his great fleets. He must believe that it was the area of final decision.

Faster, now, came Ashargin's memories of the week he had watched the great battle. Pictures took form of thousands of ships simultaneously similarized to the base of an enemy planetary stronghold. Each time, the similarization was cut off just before the ships reached their objective.

Out of the shadowless darkness, then, they darted toward the doomed planet. More ships attacking than all the surrounding sun systems could muster. Distances that would have taken many months, even years, by ordinary flight were bridged almost instantly. And always the attacking fleet gave the victim the same alternative. Surrender, or be destroyed.

If the leaders of any planet, or group of planets, refused to credit the danger, the ruthless rain of bombs that poured from the sky literally consumed their civilization. So violent and so concentrated were the explosions that chain reactions were set up in the planet's crust.

The majority of systems were more reasonable. The segment of fleet which had paused to capture or destroy merely left an occupying force, and then flashed on to the next League base.

There was no real defense. It was impossible to concentrate sizable fleets to oppose the attackers, since it was impossible to know which planetary system was next in line. With uncanny ability, the invading forces fought those fleets that were brought against them. The attacking forces seemed always to know the nature of the defense, and wherever the defense was fiercest there appeared a dozen Enro ships for every one that was available to the League power.

To Ashargin that was almost magical, but not to Gosseyn. The Predictors of Yalerta were fighting with the fleets of the Greatest Empire, and the defenders literally had no chance.

The flood of memory ended as the Grand Admiral's voice said ironically from behind him: 'Prince, the meeting is about to begin.'

It was a relief to be able to sit down at the long council table.

He saw that his chair was next to and at the right of the admiral. Swiftly, his eyes took in the rest of the room.

It was larger than he had first thought. He realized what had given him the impression of smallness. Three walls were veritable maps of space. Each was sprinkled with uncountable lights, and on each wall about ten feet up from the floor there were series of squares on which numbers flickered and whirled. One square had red numbers on it, and the figure shown was 91308. It changed as Gosseyn watched and jumped to 91749. That was the largest change he observed as he glanced around.

He waited for some explanation of the numbers to well up from Ashargin's memory. Nothing came except the information that Ashargin had not before been in this room.

There were squares with numbers in blue, and squares with yellow, green, orange and gray numbers, pink numbers, purple and violet numbers. And then there were squares in which alternate figures were different colors. It was obviously a method of distinguishing facts at a glance, but the facts themselves were unstable.

They changed from moment to moment. The figures went through violent gyrations. They seemed to dance as they shifted and altered. And there was no question but that they told a story. It seemed to Gosseyn that in square after square of cryptic numbers the ever changing pattern of the battle of the Sixth Decant was revealed.

It cost him a tremendous effort to withdraw his fascinated

93

gaze from the squares, and to realize that Admiral Paleol had been speaking for several moments.

'. . . Our problems,' the gaunt and grim old man was saying, 'will scarcely be more difficult in the future than they have already been. But I called you here today to warn you that incidents have already occurred which will probably become more numerous as time goes on. For instance, on seventeen different occasions now, we have been unable to similarize our ships to bases, the Distorter patterns of which were secured for our great leader by the most highly organized spy system ever conceived.

'It is clear that some of the planetary governors have become suspicious and in their panic have altered the patterns. In every case so far brought to my attention, the planets involved were approached by our ships similarizing to a base beyond them, and then breaking. In every case, the offending planet was given no opportunity to surrender, but was mercilessly destroyed.

'These eventualities, you will be happy to know, were foreseen by our great leader, Enro the Red. History has no previous record of one man gifted with such foresight, sagacity and with so great a will to peace.'

The final remark was an aside. Gosseyn looked quickly at some of the other men, but their faces were intent. If they saw anything odd in the description of Enro as a man of peace they held their counsel.

He had several thoughts of his own. So an involved spy system had procured for Enro the Distorter patterns of thousands of league bases. It seemed to Gosseyn that there was a fateful combination of forces now working in Enro's favor. In the period of a few short years he had risen from the hereditary rulership of a small planetary group to the height of galactic power. And as if to prove that destiny itself was on his side, during that same period a planet of Predictors had been discovered, and those gifted minds were now working for him.

True, the Follower who supplied them had plans of his own. But that would not stop the war.

'. . . Of course,' Grand Admiral Paleol was saying, 'the main league centers in this area are not rubbing out their Distorter patterns. It takes time to build up similarity connections, and their own ships would be cut off from any bases in which the patterns were altered. However, in the future we must reckon with the possibility that more and more groups will try to break away into isolation. And some of them will succeed.

'You see'—his long face creased into a cold smile—'there

94

are systems which cannot be approached by similarizing to bases beyond them. In planning our campaign we made a point of launching all our initial attacks against planets that could so be approached. Now, gradually, our position will become more flexible. We must improvise. Fleets will find themselves in a position to attack objectives that were not formerly considered to be within our reach. To know when such opportunities exist will require the highest degree of alertness on the part of officers and crew members of all ranks.'

Unsmiling now, the old man looked around the table. 'Gentlemen, that about concludes my report. I must tell you that our casualties are heavy. We are losing ships at the average rate of two battleships, eleven cruisers, seventy-four destroyers and sixty-two miscellaneous craft every hour of operations. Of course, these are actuarial figures, and vary greatly from day to day. But, nevertheless, they are very real, as you can see by glancing at the wall estimators in this room.

'But basically our position is excellent. Our great obstacle is the vastness of space and the fact that it takes the time of a portion of our fleet to handle each separate conquest. However, it is now possible to estimate mathematically the length of the campaign. So many more planets to conquer, so much time for each—altogether ninety-four sidereal days. Any questions?'

There was silence. Then at the far end of the table, an admiral climbed to his feet.

'Sir,' he said, 'I wonder if we could have the views of the Prince Ashargin.'

The grand admiral arose slowly. The smile was back on his long, usually dour face. 'The prince,' he said dryly, 'is with us as a personal emissary of Enro. He has asked me to say that he has no comments to make at this time.'

Gosseyn climbed to his feet. His purpose was to have Ashargin sent back to Gorgzid, to Enro's headquarters, and it seemed to him the best way to do that was to start talking out of turn.

'That,' he said, 'is what I said to the grand admiral yesterday.'

He paused to wince at the high tenor of Ashargin's voice, and to relax the tenseness that swept Ashargin's body. In doing so he glanced at the old man beside him. The grand admiral was gazing up at the ceiling, but with such an expression that Gosseyn had an insight into the truth. He said quickly:

'I am momentarily expecting a call from Enro to return to make my report, but if I have time I should like to discuss some of the philosophical implications of the war we are waging.'

He got no further. The ceiling grew bright, and the face that took form on it was the face of Enro. Every man in the room sprang to his feet, and stood at attention.

The red-haired dictator stared down at them, a faint, ironic smile on his face. 'Gentlemen,' he said at last, 'because of previous business, I have just now tuned into this council meeting. I am sorry to have interrupted it, particularly sorry because I see that I came on the scene just as the Prince Ashargin was about to speak to you. The prince and I are in accord on all major aspects of the conduct of the war, but right now I desire him to return to Gorgzid. Gentlemen, you have my respects.'

'Your excellency,' said Grand Admiral Paleol, 'we salute you.'

He turned to Gosseyn-Ashargin. 'Prince,' he said, 'I shall be happy to accompany you to the transport section.'

Gosseyn said, 'Before I leave I wish to send a message to Y-381907.'

Gosseyn planned his message in the belief that he would shortly be back in his own body. He wrote:

SHOW EVERY COURTESY TO THE TWO PRISONERS YOU HAVE ABOARD YOUR SHIP. THEY ARE NOT TO BE TIED OR HANDCUFFED OR CONFINED. BRING THE PREDICTOR WOMAN AND THE MAN, WHETHER HE IS UNCONSCIOUS OR CONSCIOUS, TO GORGZID.

He slipped the message sheet into the slot of the roboperator. 'Send that immediately to Captain Free on Y-381907. I'll wait here for an acknowledgment.'

He turned and saw that Grand Admiral Paleol was watching him curiously. The old man smiled, and said with a tolerant sneer, 'Prince, you're something of an enigma. Am I right in believing you think Enro and myself will some day be called to account for what we are doing?'

Gosseyn-Ashargin shook his head. 'It could happen,' he said. 'You might overreach yourself. But actually it wouldn't be a bringing to account. It would be a vengeance, and immediately there would be a new power group as venal, though perhaps more cautious for a while, as the old. The childish individuals who think in terms of overthrowing a power group have failed to analyze the character that binds such a group. One of the first steps is the inculcation of the belief that they are all prepared to die at any moment. So long as the group holds together, no individual member of it dares to hold a contrary opinion on that basic point. Having convinced themselves that they are unafraid, they can then justify all crimes against

96

others. It's extremely simple and emotional and childlike on the most destructive level.'

The admiral's sneer was broader. 'Well, well,' he said, 'quite a philosopher, aren't you?' His keen eyes grew curious. 'Very interesting though. I had never thought of the bravery factor being so fundamental.'

He seemed about to speak again, but the roboperator interrupted. 'I am unable to get through to the destroyer Y-381907.'

Gosseyn-Ashargin hesitated. He was startled. He said, 'No contact at all?'

'None.'

He was recovering now. 'Very well, keep trying until the message is delivered, and advise me on Gorgzid.'

He turned, and shook hands with Paleol. A few minutes after that he pulled the lever of the Distorter cage which was supposed to take Ashargin back to Enro's palace.

XIII

Null-Abstracts

For the sake of sanity, be careful not to LABEL. Words like Fascist, Communist, Democrat, Republican, Catholic, Jew refer to human beings, who never quite fit any label.

GOSSEYN expected to wake up in his own body. Expected it because it had happened on such an occasion the first time. Expected it with such a will to have it so that he felt a pang of disappointment as he looked through the transparent door of the Distorter cage.

For the third time in two weeks, he saw the military control room of Enro's palace.

His disappointment passed swiftly. Here he was, and there was nothing he could do about it. He stepped to the door, and was surprised to see that the room outside the cage was empty. Having failed to get back to his own body, he'd taken it for granted that he would immediately be asked to explain the meaning of the message he'd sent to Captain Free. Well, he was ready for that, also.

He was ready for many things, he decided, as he headed for

the great windows at the far end of the room. The windows were bright with sunlight. Morning? he wondered as he looked out. The sun seemed higher in the sky than when he had come to Enro's palace the first time. It was confusing. So many different planets in different parts of the galaxy moving around their suns at different velocities. And then there was the loss of time factor of the so-called instantaneous Distorter transport.

He estimated that it was approximately 9:30 a.m., Gorgzid City time. Too late to have breakfast with Enro and Secoh—not that he was interested. Gosseyn started for the door that led to the outer corridor. He half expected to be told to halt, either by a command from a wall phone or by the appearance of someone with instructions for him. No one stopped him.

He had no illusions about that. Enro, who had a special personal gift for seeing and hearing distant sights and sounds, was not unaware of him. This was a deliberately granted opportunity, a withholding of control rooted in either curiosity or contempt.

The reason made no difference. Whatever it was, it gave him a breathing spell free of tension. That was important, to begin with. But even that was unimportant in the long run.

He had a plan, and he intended to force Ashargin to take any and every risk. That included, if necessary, ignoring direct orders from Enro himself.

The corridor door was unlocked, as it had been a week before. A woman carrying a pail was coming along the corridor. Gosseyn closed the door behind him, and beckoned the woman. She trembled, apparently at the sight of the uniform, and she acted as if she was not accustomed to being addressed by officers.

'Yes, sir,' she mumbled. 'The Lady Nirene's apartment, sir? Two flights down. Her name is on the door of the apartment.'

Nobody stopped him. The girl who answered the door was pretty, and looked intelligent. She frowned at him, then left him standing. He heard her farther inside the apartment hallway call, 'Ni, he's here.'

There was a muffled exclamation from inside. And then Nirene appeared in the hallway. 'Well,' she snapped, 'are you coming in? Or are you going to stand there like a nitwit?'

Gosseyn held his silence. He followed her into a tastefully furnished living room, and sat down in the chair to which she motioned him. There was no sign of the other woman. He saw that Nirene was studying him with bleak eyes. She said in a bitter voice, 'Speaking to you carries heavy penalties.'

'Let me reassure you,' said Gosseyn, 'you are in no danger of any indignity from the Prince Ashargin.' He spoke deliberately in the third person. 'He's not a bad sort, actually.'

'I have been ordered,' she said, 'ordered on pain of death.'
She was tense.

'You cannot help it if all your advances are refused,' said
Gosseyn.

'But then you risk death.'

'The prince,' said Gosseyn, 'is being used for a private purpose of Enro. You don't think Enro will leave him alive after
he's through with him.'

She was suddenly very pale. 'You dare to talk like that,'
she breathed, 'knowing that he might be listening.'

'The prince,' said Gosseyn, 'has nothing to lose.'

Her gray eyes were curious—and more. 'You speak of him
—as if he is someone else.'

'It's a way of thinking objectively.' He broke off. 'But I had
two purposes in coming to see you. The first is a question,
which I hope you will answer. I have a theory that no man can
subjugate a galactic empire in eleven years, and that four
million hostages held here in Gorgzid indicate tremendous un-
rest throughout the Greatest Empire. Am I right about that?'

'Why, of course.' Nirene shrugged. 'Enro is quite candid
about it. He is playing a game against time, and the game
interests him as much as the result itself.'

'It would. But now, question two.' Quickly, he explained
Ashargin's position in the palace, and finished, 'Has he yet
been assigned an apartment?'

Nirene's eyes were wide and wondering. 'Do you mean to
tell me,' she said, 'that you don't really know what has happened?'

Gosseyn did not answer. He was busy relaxing Ashargin,
who had suddenly become tense. The young woman stood up,
and he saw that she was regarding him in a less unfriendly
manner. She pursed her lips, and then looked back with a
searching, puzzled gaze.

'Come with me,' she said. She walked swiftly to a door that
opened on to another corridor. She passed through a second
door at the far end, and stepped aside for him to enter. Gosseyn saw that it was a bedroom.

'Our room,' she said. Once again the tone was in her voice,
and her eyes watched him questioningly. She shook her head
finally. 'You really don't know, do you? Very well, I'll tell
you.'

She paused, and tensed a little, as if putting the fact into
words gave it a sharper reality, then: 'You and I were married
this morning under a special decree issued by Secoh. I was
officially notified a few minutes ago.'

99

Having spoken the words, she slipped past him, and was gone along the corridor.

Gosseyn closed the door after her and locked it. How much time he had he didn't know, but if the Ashargin body was ever to be reorientated, then moments like this must be utilized.

His plan was very simple. He would remain in the room until Enro ordered him to do some specific thing. Then he would disobey the order.

He could feel Ashargin quivering at the deadliness of such an idea. But Gosseyn held out against the weakness, and thought consciously for the benefit of the other's nervous system, *Prince, every time you take a positive action on the basis of a high-level consideration, you establish certainties of courage, self-assurance and skills.*

All that was oversimplified, of course, but a necessary preliminary to higher level Null-A training.

Gosseyn's first act was to go into the bathroom and turn on the hot water. He set the thermostat, and then, before undressing, went out to the bedroom to look for a mechanical device that would give off a rhythmic sound. He failed to find one.

That was disappointing, but still there were makeshifts that would do. He undressed and, when the tub was full, turned off the faucet, but allowed a steady leak, not too fast and not too slow. He had to force himself to climb into the water. For Ashargin's thin body, it seemed hot to the point of scalding.

At first he breathed gaspingly, but gradually he grew accustomed to the heat, and he settled back and listened to the rhythmic sound of the leak.

Drip, drip, drip, went the faucet. He kept his eyes unblinkingly open, and watched a bright spot on the wall at a point higher than eye level. Drip, drip, drip. Steady sound, like the beat of his heart. Beat, beat, beat—hot, hot, hot, he transposed the meaning. So hot, every muscle was relaxing. Drip—drip—drip. Re-lax, re-lax, re-lax.

There was a time in the history of man on Earth when a drop of water falling rhythmically on a man's forehead had been used to drive him mad. This, of course, was not on the head; the position under the faucet would have been uncomfortable. But the principle was the same.

Drip—drip—drip. The Chinese torturers who used that method didn't know that behind it was a great secret, and that the man who went mad did so because he thought he would, because he had been told he would, because he had absolute faith that the system would produce madness.

100

If his faith had been that it would produce sanity, the effect was just as great in that direction. If his faith had been that it would make a thin, gangling body strong, the rhythm worked equally well in that direction. Drip, drip, drip. Relax, relax, so easy to relax. In hospitals on Earth, when men were brought in taut from emotional or physical ills, the warm bath was the first step in relaxation. But unless other steps were taken, the tension soon returned. Conviction was the vital ingredient, a flexible, empirical sort of conviction which could be readily altered to fit the dynamic world of reality, yet which was essentially indestructible. Gosseyn had it. Ashargin did not. There were too many unbalanced developments in his weak body. Years of fear had kept his muscles flabby, drained his energy and stunted his growth.

The slow minutes dragged rhythmically by. He felt himself dozing. It was so comfortable, so cozy, to lie in the warm water, in the womb of warm water from which all life had come. Back in the hot seas of the beginning of things, in the bosom of the Great Mother—and drift to the slow, pulsing rhythm of a heartbeat that still quivered with the thrill of new existence.

A knock on the outer door of the bedroom brought him lazily back to awareness of his surroundings. 'Yes?' he called.

'Enro,' came the strained voice of Nirene, 'has just called. He wants you to report to him immediately.'

Gosseyn felt the pang go through Ashargin's body. 'All right,' he said.

'Prince,' said Nirene, and her tone was urgent, 'he was very blunt about it.'

Gosseyn nodded to himself. He felt stimulated, and he could not completely fight off Ashargin's uneasiness. But there was no doubt in his mind as he climbed out of the bathtub.

The moment for him to defy Enro had arrived.

He dressed, nevertheless, without haste, and then left the bedroom. Nirene was waiting in the living room. Gosseyn hesitated at sight of her. He was acutely conscious of Enro's special power of hearing and seeing through solid walls. There was a question he wanted to ask, but not directly.

The solution occurred to him after a moment. 'Have you a palace directory?'

She walked silently to the videophone in one corner, and brought a glowing flexible plate, which she handed him with the explanation: 'Just pull that slide down. Each time it clicks it shows the floor of the person you want, and where his apart-

101

ment is. There's a list of names on the back. It's automatically kept up to date.'

Gosseyn didn't need the list. He knew what names he wanted. With a quick movement of his hand he slid the lever to Reesha, covering the action as much as possible.

Presumably, Enro could 'see' through a hand as readily as through walls, but there must be some limitation to his gift. Gosseyn decided to depend on speed.

One glance he took, had his information, and then he shifted the lever to the name of Secoh. That, also, required only an instant. He moved the lever casually but swiftly to zero position, and handed the plate back to Nirene.

He felt wonderfully calm and at ease. The Ashargin body was quiescent, accepting the violent positivities that were being forced upon it with an equanimity that promised well for the future.

'Good luck,' he said to Nirene.

He suppressed an Arshargin impulse to tell her where he was going. Not that Enro wouldn't know in a few minutes. But he had the feeling that if he named his destination an attempt would be made to divert him.

Out in the hall, he walked swiftly toward the stairway, climbed one flight of stairs, which brought him within one floor of Enro's apartments. He turned off to the right, and a moment later he was being admitted to the apartment of the woman he had once known as Patricia Hardie. He hoped that Enro would be curious as to what his sister and the Prince Ashargin had to say to each other, and that the curiosity would restrain him from immediate punitive action.

As Gosseyn-Ashargin followed the servant into a large reception room he saw that Eldred Crang was standing at the window. The Venusian Null-A detective turned as the visitor entered, and gazed thoughtfully at him.

There was silence as they looked at each other. It seemed to Gosseyn that he was more interested in seeing Crang than Crang could possibly be in the Prince Ashargin.

He could appreciate Crang's position. Here was a Null-A who had come into the heart of the enemy stronghold, who was pretending—with her connivance—that he was married to the sister of the warlord of the Greatest Empire, and on that tenuous basis—more tenuous even than he might realize, in view of Enro's belief in brother-sister marriage—was apparently prepared to oppose the dictator's plans.

Just how he would do it was a problem in strategy. But then there were people who might wonder how the Prince Ashargin could ever hope to set himself against the same tyrant. Gosseyn was trying to solve that problem by a bold defiance, based upon a plan that still seemed logical.

He had no doubt that Crang would be equally bold, if necessary—and that he would not have come at all if he had thought his presence would not have some effect.

It was Crang who spoke first. 'You wish to see the Gorgzin Reesha.' He used the feminine of the title of ruler on Enro's home planet.

'Very much.'

Crang said, 'As you possibly know, I am the Gorgzin's husband. I hope you don't mind telling me your business first.'

Gosseyn welcomed it. The sight of Crang had braced him immensely. The non-Aristotelian detective was so skillful an operator that his mere presence on this scene seemed partial proof at least that the situation was not as bad as it seemed.

Crang spoke again. 'What's on your mind, prince?' he said pleasantly.

Gosseyn launched into a frank account of what had happened to Ashargin. He finished, 'I am determined to raise the level of the prince's position here in the palace. So far he has been treated in an unforgivably debasing fashion. I should like to use the good offices of the Gorgzin to alter the attitude of his excellency.'

Crang nodded thoughtfully. 'I see.' He came away from the window, and motioned Gosseyn-Ashargin into a chair. 'I hadn't really estimated your position in this picture at all,' he said. 'From what I had heard, you were accepting the debasing role which Enro had assigned to you.'

'As you can see,' said Gosseyn, 'and as Enro must be realizing, the prince insists that so long as he is alive he be treated according to his rank.'

'Your use of the third person interests me,' said Crang, 'and I am also interested in the qualifying phrase "so long as he is alive." If you are able to hold firmly to the implications of that phrase, it seems to me the, uh, prince might obtain redress from the Gorgzid.'

It was approval of a kind. It was cautious and yet unmistakable. It seemed to assume that the dictator might be listening in on the conversation, and so the words were on a high verbal level. Crang hesitated, then went on:

It is doubtful, however, if my wife could be of much assistance to you as an intermediary. She has taken the position of being absolutely opposed to the war of conquest which her brother is waging.'

That was information indeed, and from the look on Crang's

face, Gosseyn realized that the man had imparted it to him deliberately.

'Naturally,' said Crang, 'as her husband, I also oppose the war without qualification.'

Briefly, it was dazzling. Here was their method of boldness, different from his own, yet rooted in the special reality of Patricia's relationship to Enro. Gosseyn grew critical. The method had the same inherent flaws as did the opposition he was developing at this moment. How were they overcoming the flaw? Gosseyn asked the question.

'It seems to me,' he said slowly, 'that in taking such a stand, you and the Gorgzin have greatly restricted your freedom of action. Or am I wrong?'

'Partly wrong,' said Crang. 'Here in this sun system, my wife's legal rights are almost equal to those of Enro. His excellency is greatly attached to the traditions, the customs and the habits of the people, and so he has made no effort to destroy any of the local institutions.'

It was more information. And it fitted. It fitted his own plan. Gosseyn was about to speak again, when he saw that Crang was looking past his shoulder. He turned, and saw that Patricia Hardie had entered the room. She smiled as her eyes met his.

'I was listening in the next room,' she said. 'I hope you don't mind.'

Gosseyn indicated that he didn't, and there was a pause. He was fascinated. Patricia Hardie, the Gorgzin Reesha of the planet Gorgzid, sister of Enro—the young woman who had once pretended to be the daughter of President Hardie of Earth, and who had later pretended to be the wife of Gilbert Gosseyn—with so great a career of intrigue behind her, she was unquestionably a personality to be reckoned with. And, best of all, she had never to his knowledge wavered in her support of the League and of Null-A.

She was, it seemed to him, becoming more beautiful, not less. She was not quite so tall as Leej, the Predictor woman, but she seemed more lithely built. Her blue eyes had the same imperious expression in them as was in Leej's gray eyes, and both women were equally good looking. But there the resemblance ended.

Patricia glowed with purpose. Perhaps it was a youthful purpose, but the other woman didn't have it. Possibly, he knew what Leej was like, and knew, also, Patricia's career. That could be very important. But Gosseyn thought it was more than that. Leej was a drifter. As long as she had been aware of her future, she had had no reason to be ambitious. And even if she should suddenly acquire a purpose, now that she could no longer depend on her prophetic gift, it would take a long time to change her habits and her basic attitude.

Crang broke the silence. 'Prince,' he said, and his tone was very friendly, 'I think I can clear up your puzzlement as to why you are married to Lady Nirene. My wife, knowing nothing of the conversation of last week, took it for granted that any relationship between Nirene and yourself would be legalized by the church.'

Patricia laughed softly. 'It never occurred to me,' she said, 'that there were undercurrents in the situation.'

Gosseyn nodded, but he was grim. He assumed that she was aware of Enro's past intentions for her, and that she regarded those intentions lightly. But she was missing additional undercurrents, it seemed to him. Enro must still hope for a legal marriage relationship with his sister, or he would not have tried to prevent her from learning that he regarded the relationship as unimportant where other people were concerned. His about-face gave a sharp insight into both his character and his purposes.

'Your brother,' Gosseyn said aloud, 'is a remarkable man.' He paused. 'I presume he can hear what we're saying here—if he so desires.'

Patricia said, 'My brother's gift has a curious history.' She paused, and Gosseyn, who was looking directly at her, saw from her expression that she intended to give him information. She went on, 'Our parents were either very religious or very clever. They decided that the male Gorgzid heir should spend his first year after birth in the crypt with the Sleeping God. The reaction of the people was hostile in the extreme, and so after three months Enro was removed, awakened, and thereafter his childhood was normal.

'He was about eleven when he began to be able to see and hear things in distant places. Naturally, father and mother immediately considered it a gift from the God himself.'

'What does Enro think?' asked Gosseyn.

He didn't hear her answer. A rush of Ashargin memories flooded into his consciousness about the Sleeping God, bits of things he had learned when he was a slave of the temple.

Every report he had heard was different. Priests were allowed to look at the God at their initiation rites. Not one of them ever saw the thing. The Sleeping God was an old man, a child, a youth of fifteen, a baby—the subsequent accounts had as little relationship as that.

Those details held Gosseyn's mind only flashingly. Whether those who looked were hypnotically deluded, or whether the illusion was mechanical seemed of incidental importance. The aspect of the picture that almost shocked Gosseyn out of his seat was the detail of the Sleeping God's daily existence—he was unconscious, but fed and exercised by a complicated system of machinery. The entire temple hierarchy was organized to keep that machinery running.

The light that broke upon Gosseyn at that moment was dazzling because—this was the way a Gosseyn body would be looked after.

His mind strained at the thought. For many seconds, the idea seemed too fantastic for acceptance. A Gosseyn body here at what was now the headquarters of the Greatest Empire. Here, and protected from harm by all the forces of a powerful pagan religion.

Crang broke the silence. 'Time for lunch,' he said. 'That's for all of us, I believe. Emro doesn't like to be kept waiting.'

Lunch! Gosseyn estimated that an hour had passed since Enro had ordered him to report. Long enough to set the stage for a crisis.

But lunch itself passed in virtual silence. The dishes were whisked off, and still Enro remained seated, thus holding the others to the table also. For the first time the dictator stared directly at Gosseyn-Ashargin. His gaze was bleak and unfriendly.

'Secoh,' he said, without looking around.

'Yes?' The lord guardian was quick.

'Have the lie detector brought in.' The steely gaze remained fixed upon Gosseyn's eyes. 'The prince has been asking for an investigation and I am happy to oblige him.'

Considering the circumstances, it was about as true a statement as Enro had made, but Gosseyn would have changed one word in the utterance. He had expected an investigation. And here it was.

Enro did not remain seated. As the lie detector knobs were fastened to Gosseyn-Ashargin's palms, he climbed to his feet and stood looking down at the table. He waved the others to remain in their chairs, and began.

'We have here a very curious situation,' he said. 'One week ago, I had the Prince Ashargin brought to the palace. I was shocked at his appearance and his actions.' His lips twisted. 'Apparently, he suffered from a strong sense of guilt, presumably as a result of his feeling that his family had failed the people of the Greatest Empire. He was nervous, tense, shy, almost tongue-tied and a pitiful spectacle. For more than ten years he had been isolated from interplanetary and local affairs.'

Enro paused, his face serious, his eyes glowing. He con-

106

tinued in the same intense tone.

'Even that first morning he showed one or two flashes of insight and understanding that were not in character. During his week on the flagship of Admiral Paleol, he behaved to some extent as his past history would have led us to expect. During his final hour aboard the ship, he changed radically once more and again showed knowledge that was beyond the possibilities of his position. Among other things, he sent the following message to the destroyer, Y-381907.'

He turned with a quick movement to one of the hovering secretaries, and held out his hand. 'The message,' he said. A sheet of paper was handed to him.

Gosseyn listened as Enro read the message. Every word seemed as incriminating as he had known it was. A dictator, the most powerful warlord in the galaxy, had turned aside from his many duties to give attention to an individual whom he had intended to use as a pawn in his own game.

Whether or not the unseen player who had similarized the mind of Gilbert Gosseyn into the brain of Prince Ashargin had foreseen such a crisis as this didn't matter. Gosseyn might be a pawn himself, subject to being moved at someone else's will, but when he was in charge events happened his way—if he could make them.

Enro was speaking again in his dark voice. 'It did not occur immediately to either Admiral Paleol or myself what mission that ship was on. I will say only this now. We identified the ship finally, and it seems incredible that Prince Ashargin should ever have heard about it. Its mission was secret and important, and though I will not mention the nature of the mission, I can inform the prince that his message was not delivered to the ship.'

Gosseyn refused to accept that. 'The roboperator on the flagship sent the message while I was there,' he said quickly.

The big man shrugged. 'Prince,' he said, 'it was not stopped by us. The message was not acknowledged by the destroyer. We have been unable to contact the Y-381907 for several days, and I am afraid that I shall have to ask you for some very straight answers. The destroyer is being replaced on Yalerta by a battleship, but it will require more than a month of flight for the replacement ship to reach that planet.'

Gosseyn received the two pieces of news with mixed feelings. It was a great victory that no more Predictors would be sent from Yalerta for an entire month. The destroyer was another matter.

'But where could it have gone?' he asked.

He thought of the Follower, and grew tense. After a

107

moment he rejected the more dangerous implications of that idea. It was true, apparently, that the Follower frequently was not able to predict events that were related to Gilbert Gosseyn. Yet that applied only when the extra brain was being used. It seemed reasonable, accordingly, to believe that he knew where Gosseyn was.

Right there that train of logic ended. There was no reason at all why the Follower should suddenly become secretive with Enro as to the whereabouts of the destroyer. Gosseyn gazed up at Enro with unflinching eyes. The time had come to deliver another shock.

'Doesn't the Follower know?' he asked.

Enro had parted his lips to speak again. Now, he brought his teeth together with a click. He stared at Gosseyn with baffled eyes. At last he said:

'So you know about the Follower. That settles it. It's time the lie detector gives us some idea of what goes on in your mind.'

He turned a switch.

There was silence at the table. Even Crang, who had been absently pecking at the food on his plate, stirred in his chair, and laid down his fork. Secoh was frowning thoughtfully. Patricia Hardie watched her brother with a faint curl to her lips. It was she who spoke first.

'Enro, don't be so stupidly melodramatic.'

The big man twisted towards her, his eyes narrowed, his face dark with anger. 'Silence,' he said harshly. 'I need no comments from a person who has disgraced her brother.'

Patricia shrugged, but Secoh said sharply, 'Your excellency, restrain yourself.'

Enro turned toward the priest, and for a moment, so ugly was the expression on his face, it seemed to Gosseyn that he was going to strike the lord guardian.

'Always were interested in her, weren't you?' he said with a sneer.

'Your sister,' said the priest, 'is co-ruler of Gorgzid and of the overlordship of the Sleeping God.'

Enro ran one hand through his red hair, and shook himself like a young lion. 'Sometimes, Secoh,' he said, and the sneer was broader, 'you give the impression that you are the Sleeping God. It's a dangerous illusion.'

The priest said quietly, 'I speak with authority vested in me by the State and the Temple. I can do no less.'

'I am the State,' said Enro coldly.

Gosseyn said, 'I seem to remember hearing that one before.'

Neither man seemed aware of his remark. And for the first

time it struck him that he was witnessing a major clash. Gosseyn sat up.

'You and I,' said Secoh in a singsong voice, 'hold the cup of life but for a moment. When we have drunk our fill, we shall go down into darkness—and there will still be a State.'

'Ruled by my blood.' Violently.

'Perhaps.' His voice sounded faraway. 'Excellency, the fever that has seized on you I shall feed until victory is achieved.'

'And then?'

'You will receive the Temple call.'

Enro parted his lips to say something. Then he closed them again. There was blank expression on his face, that slowly changed into a comprehending smile.

'Clever, aren't you?' he said. 'So I'll receive the Temple call, will I, to become an initiate. Is there anything significant, possibly, in the fact that you issue the calls?'

The priest said quietly, 'When the Sleeping God disapproves of what I say or do, I'll know.'

The sneer was back on Enro's face. 'Oh, you will, will you? He'll let you know, I suppose, and then you'll tell us?'

Secoh said simply, 'Your thrusts do not reach me, excellency. If I used my position for my own ends, the Sleeping God would not long tolerate such blasphemy.'

Enro hesitated. His face was no longer dark, and it seemed to Gosseyn that the powerful ruler of one-third of the galaxy felt himself on dangerous ground.

He was not surprised. Human beings had a persistent attachment for their own homes. Behind all Enro's achievements, inside the skin of this man whose word was law on nine hundred thousand warships, were all the impulses of the human nervous system.

In him they had become twisted until, in some cases, they were barely recognizable as human. Yet the man had once been a boy, and the boy a baby born on Gorgzid. So strong was the connection that he had brought the capital of the Greatest Empire to his home planet. Such a man would not lightly insult the pagan religion by the tenets of which he had been reared.

Gosseyn saw that he had read correctly the processes of the other's mind. Enro bowed sardonically to Patricia.

'Sister,' he said, 'I humbly beg your pardon.'

He turned abruptly toward Gosseyn-Ashargin. 'These two people on the destroyer,' he said. 'Who are they?'

The moment for the test had come.

Gosseyn answered promptly, 'The woman is a Predictor, of no particular importance. The man is called Gilbert Gosseyn.'

109

He glanced at Patricia and Crang casually as he spoke the name so familiar to them. It was important that they show no sign of recognition.

They took it, it seemed to Gosseyn, very well indeed. They continued intently watching his face, but there was not a trace of surprise in their eyes.

Enro was concentrating on the lie detector. 'Any comments?' he asked.

The pause that followed was of many seconds duration. Finally, cautiously, the detector said, 'The information is correct as far as it goes.'

'How much farther should it go?' Enro asked sharply.

'There is confusion,' was the reply.

'Of what?'

'Identity.' The detector seemed to realize the answer was inadequate. It repeated. 'There is confusion.' It started to say something else, but the sound must have been cut off, for not even the sense of a letter came through.

'Well, I'll be——,' said Enro explosively. He hesitated. 'Is the confusion in connection with the two people on the destroyer?'

'No,' said the detector briskly. 'That is'—it sounded uncertain again—'that is, not exactly.' It spoke up with determination, 'Your excellency, this man is Ashargin, and yet he isn't. He——' It was silent for a moment, then lamely, 'Next question, please.'

Patricia Hardie giggled. It was an incongruous sound. Enro sent her a terrible glance.

He said savagely, 'What fool brought this faulty detector in here? Bring a replacement at once.'

The second lie detector, when it had been attached, said in answer to Enro's question, 'Yes, this is Ashargin.' It paused. 'That is—he seems to be.' It finished uncertainly, 'There is some confusion.'

There was some confusion now in the dictator, also. 'This is unheard of,' he said. He braced himself. 'Well, we'll get to the bottom of it.'

He stared at Ashargin. 'These people on the destroyer—I gather from your message to Captain Free that they are prisoners.'

Gosseyn nodded. 'That's right.'

'And you want them brought here. Why?'

'I thought you might like to question them,' said Gosseyn.

Enro looked baffled again. ' I can't see how you expect to use anyone against me once they're here in my power.' He

110

turned to the machine. 'What about that, Detector? Has he been telling the truth?'

'If you mean, does he want them brought here? Yes, he does. As for using them against you—it's all mixed up.'

'In what way?'

'Well, there's a thought about the man on the ship being here already, and there's a thought about the Sleeping God—they all seem to be mixed up somehow with Ashargin.'

'Your excellency,' interposed Secoh, as the astounded Enro stood silent, 'may I ask a question of the Prince Ashargin?'

Enro nodded but said nothing.

'Prince,' said the priest, 'have you any idea as to the nature of this confusion?'

'Yes,' said Gosseyn.

'What is your explanation?'

'I am periodically possessed, dominated, controlled and directed by the Sleeping God.'

And, thought Gosseyn with deep satisfaction, *let the lie detectors try to disprove that.*

Enro laughed. It was the laughter of a man who has been keyed up and is suddenly confronted with something ridiculous. He sat down at the table, put his face in his palms, his elbows on the table, and laughed. When he looked up finally, there were tears in his eyes.

'So you are the Sleeping God,' he said, 'and now you have taken possession of Ashargin.'

The humor of it struck him anew, and he guffawed for a full half minute before once more controlling himself. This time he glanced at Secoh.

'Lord guardian,' he said, 'how many is this?' He seemed to realize that the question required explanation for the others at the table. He turned to Gosseyn. 'During the course of a year, about a hundred people on this planet alone come forward claiming to be possessed by the Sleeping God. Throughout the Empire about two thousand red-haired men pretend to be Enro the Red, and during the last eleven years approximately ten thousand people have come forward claiming to be Prince Ashargin. About half of these are over fifty years old.'

Gosseyn said, 'What happens when they appear before a lie detector?'

The big man scowled. 'All right,' he said, 'let's have it. How do you do it?'

Gosseyn had expected skepticism. Except for Crang, these were thalamic people. Even Patricia Hardie, friendly though she was to Venus, was not a Null-A. Such individuals would hold contradictory ideas, and even discuss the contradiction, without in any way being influenced by the reality. The important thing was that a seed had been planted. He saw that Enro was scowling.

'Enough of this farce,' said the big man. 'Let's get down to some facts. I admit you fooled me, but I don't see how you expect to gain anything by it. What do you want?'

'An understanding,' said Gosseyn. He spoke cautiously, yet he felt bold and determined. 'As I see it, you want to use me for something. Very well, I'm willing to be used—up to a point. In return, I want freedom of action.'

'Freedom of what?'

Gosseyn's next words took in the other people at the table. 'In launching this war,' he said, 'you endangered the life of every person in the galaxy, including the Greatest Empire. I think you should accept advice from those who will share your fate if anything goes wrong.'

Enro leaned forward, and drew his arm back as if to strike him in the face. He sat like that for a moment, tense, his lips compressed and his eyes bleak. Slowly, he relaxed, and leaned back in his chair. There was a faint smile on his face, as he said, 'Go on, hang yourself!'

Gosseyn said, 'It seems to me that you've concentrated so completely on the offensive part of the war that you have perhaps not taken into account some equally important aspects.'

Enro was shaking his head wonderingly. 'All this,' he said in amazement, 'from someone who has spent the last eleven years in a vegetable garden.'

Gosseyn ignored the comment. He was intent, and it seemed to him that he was making progress. His theory was simplicity itself. The Prince Ashargin had not been brought forward at this critical moment except for the most urgent reasons. He would not be lightly eliminated until the purpose for which he had been resurrected was accomplished.

Besides, this was a good time to obtain information as to just what Enro was doing about certain individuals.

'For instance,' Gosseyn said, 'there is the problem of the Follower.' He paused to let that sink in, then went on. 'The Follower is a virtually indestructible being. You don't think that, when this war is won, a man like the Follower will allow Enro the Red to dominate the galaxy.'

Enro said grimly, 'I'll take care of the Follower if he ever gets any ideas.'

'That's easy to say. He could come into this room at this moment, and kill everybody in it.'

The big man shook his head. He looked amused. 'My

friend,' he said, 'you've been listening to the Follower's propaganda. I don't know how he makes that shadow shape of his, but I decided long ago that all the rest was based on normal physics. That means Distorters and, in case of weapons, energy transmission. There are only two Distorters in this building not in my control, and I tolerate them. I defy anyone to build machines in my vicinity that I don't know about.'

Gosseyn said, 'Still, he can predict your every move.'

The smile faded from the other's face. 'He can make any prediction he pleases,' he said harshly. 'I have the power. If he he tries to interfere with it, he'll quickly find himself in the position of a man who has been sentenced to hang. He knows the exact day and hour, but there is nothing he can do about it.'

Gosseyn said, 'In my opinion you haven't thought that through the way you ought to.'

Enro was silent, his gaze fixed on the table. He looked up finally. 'Anything else?' he said. 'I'm waiting for these conditions you mentioned.'

It was time to get down to business.

Gosseyn could feel the gathering strain on Ashargin's body. He would have liked to ease up a little on the tense nervous system of the prince. He thought of glancing at Crang, Patricia or Secoh to see how they were reacting to the developing situation. It would give Ashargin a moment of relaxation.

He suppressed the impulse. Enro had practically forgotten that there was anyone else present. And it would be unwise to distract his concentrated attention. He said aloud:

'I want to have permission to make a call anywhere in the galaxy at any time of the day or night. Naturally, you can listen in—you or your agent, that is.'

'Naturally,' said Enro sarcastically. 'What else?'

'I want to have the authority to use the Distorter transporter anywhere in the Greatest Empire at will.'

'I'm glad,' said Enro, 'you're restricting your movements to the Empire.' He broke off. 'Continue, please.'

'I want authority to order any equipment I please from the Stores Department.' He added quickly, 'No weapons, of course.'

Enro said, 'I can see that this could go on and on. What do you offer in exchange for these fantastic demands?'

Gosseyn spoke his answer, not to Enro, but to the lie detector. 'You've been listening to all this—have I been speaking frankly so far?'

The tubes flickered ever so faintly. There was a long hesitation. 'You mean everything up to a point. Beyond that there

113

is confusion involving——' It stopped.

'The Sleeping God?' asked Gosseyn.

'Yes—and then again, no.'

Gosseyn turned to Enro. 'How many revolutions are you fighting,' he asked, 'on planets of the Greatest Empire, where vital war equipment is being manufactured?'

The dictator stared at him sourly. He said finally, 'More than twenty-one hundred.'

'That's only three percent. What are you worried about?' It was a negative statement for his purposes, but Gosseyn wanted information.

'Some of them,' said Enro frankly, 'are important technologically out of proportion to their numbers.'

That was what he had wanted to hear. Gosseyn said, 'For what I have asked, I'll make radio speeches in support of your attack. Whatever the name of Ashargin is worth in controlling the empire, I place at your disposal. I'll co-operate until further notice. That's what you want of me, isn't it?'

Enro stood up. 'Are you sure,' he said savagely, 'that there isn't anything else you want?'

'One more thing,' said Gosseyn.

'Yes?'

Gosseyn ignored the sneer in the big man's voice. 'It has to do with my wife. She will no longer appear at the royal bathtub.'

There was a long pause. And then a powerful fist smashed down on the table.

'It's a deal,' said Enro, in a ringing voice, 'and I want you to make your first speech this afternoon.'

XIV

Null-Abstracts

For the sake of sanity, use QUOTATIONS: For instance, 'conscious' and 'unconscious' mind are useful descriptive terms, but it has yet to be proved that the terms themselves accurately reflect the 'process' level of events. They are maps of a territory about which we can possibly never have exact information. Since Null-A training is for the individuals, the important thing is to be conscious of the 'multiordinal'—that is the many valued—meaning of the words one hears or speaks.

I T was late afternoon when Gosseyn returned to Nirene's apartment. The young woman was sitting at the table writing a letter. She laid down her pen when he entered, climbed to her feet, and went over to a big chair. From its depths she gazed at him, her gray eyes steady.

'So we've all got about two months to live,' she said at last.

Gosseyn-Ashargin pretended to be surprised. 'That long?' he said.

He made no further comment. Just what she had heard about the luncheon incident or where she had heard it didn't matter. He felt sorry for her, but her destiny was not yet actually in his hands. When a ruler could order a woman to become the mistress or wife of a stranger because she had paused for half a minute to speak to him, that was a fact that defied normal expectations. She had made the mistake of being born a member of the old nobility, and she existed beside the abyss of Enro's suspicions.

It was Nirene who once more broke the silence. 'What are you going to do now?'

Gosseyn had been asking himself the question, aware that it was greatly complicated by the possibility that at any moment he might be back in his own body.

But suppose he wasn't? Suppose he remained here for several days longer. What then? Was there anything he could do that would be of value now or later to either Ashargin or Gosseyn?

There was Venus. Were any Venusians out in space yet? Did they even know what was going on?

And he really ought to have a look at the Sleeping God. That involved obtaining permission from Secoh.

His mind paused as he came to item number three on his list. Train Ashargin. He looked at Nirene.

'I've been driving the prince rather hard,' he said, 'and I think I'd better let him have a rest for about an hour.'

'I'll call you when the time is up,' said Nirene, and her voice was so gentle that Gosseyn glanced at her, startled.

In the bedroom Gosseyn rigged up a wall recorder to repeat a three-minute relaxation pattern. Then he lay down. During the hour that followed he never quite went to sleep. There was always the voice in the background, the monotone of Ashargin's voice repeating the few phrases over and over.

Lying there, he allowed his mind to idle around the harsher

115

memories of Ashargin's prison years. Each time he came to an incident that had made a profound impression, he talked silently to the younger Ashargin. He made it as real as that, as if the fifteen, sixteen or twenty year old Ashargin heir was in each case a living entity inside him. The older Ashargin talked to the younger at a moment when the latter was undergoing a traumatic experience.

From his greater height of understanding, he assured the younger individual that the affective incident must be looked at from a different angle than that of a frightened youth. Assured him that fear of pain and fear of death were emotions that could be overcome, and that in short the shock incident which had once affected him so profoundly no longer had any meaning for him. More than that, in future he would have better understanding of such moments, and he would never again be affected in an adverse fashion.

It was one more Null-A training make-shift, as had been all the others. But it was a system of self-therapy that was scientifically sound, and which would bring definite benefits.

'Relax,' the voice soothed on. And because of what he was doing, every word meant, 'Relax the tensions of a life time. Let all those past fears and doubts and uncertainties be discharged from the nervous system.'

The effect did not depend on any belief that something would happen, though conviction made it more powerful. But it would take time. There were many suppressed memories that would have to be skillfully brought out in the open, before the therapy could be used on them.

Prince Ashargin was not going to be relaxed in one day.

Nevertheless, by the time Nirene knocked softly on the door, he had had not only the equivalent of an hour's sleep, but a psychoanalytic reorientation that under the circumstances he could have secured in no other way.

He stood up refreshed, feeling himself ready for the evening and the night.

The days stepped by, and the question was, how was he going to find out about Venus?

He had several possibilities. All of them required a hint as to what he wanted to know. Enro might be as quick at seeing the meaning in such a hint as the person to whom it was directed.

That was a risk he could not take until he had exhausted every other means.

At the end of four days, Gosseyn was a badly worried man. He saw himself isolated here in the body of the Ashargin heir, in spite of his so-called freedom of action, prevented from doing the only things that mattered.

Venusian Null-A's alone could stop Enro and the Predictors. That was his assumption, based on his observations and his knowledge of things as they were. But as far as he knew, they were cut off, unable to act. They could be easily destroyed by a dictator who had already ordered hundreds of planets pulverized.

Each day he hoped to be returned to his own body. He tried to help. He used Distorter elevators whenever possible to move from one building to another. Four times in four days he took trips to distant planets and back. But his mind remained in the body of Prince Ashargin.

He waited for a call informing him that the Y-381907 had been contacted. No call came.

What could be happening?

On the fourth day he went personally to the Interplanetary Communications Department. It occupied a building ninety stories high and ten blocks wide. The building information section had one hundred roboperators redirecting calls to the proper sector centers. He identified himself to one of them.

'Oh, yes,' it said. 'Prince Ashargin. We have received instructions about you.'

Gosseyn made his inquiry, turned away and then came back. He was curious about small things. 'What kind of instructions?' he asked.

The answer had the frankness of Enro behind it. The roboperator said, 'You can call anywhere but transcriptions of every conversation must be sent to the Intelligence Center.'

Gosseyn nodded. He could expect no more than that. He took a Distorter cage to the sector center he wanted, and seated himself at the videophone. Presently, he was saying, 'I want to speak to Captain Free, or anyone aboard the Y-381907.'

He could have made the call from Nirene's apartment, but here he could see the Distorter that carried the message. He could watch the contact attempt being made, as the roboperator dialed the pattern which, according to the foot-thick transparent plate that listed destroyers, belonged to the Y-381907.

All this he could see with his own eyes. If it was possible for him to prevent interference in the attempt to contact the destroyer, then this was one of the methods.

Another was to call from a planet visited at random. He had done that twice, without result.

Now, a minute passed. Then two minutes. Still there was no answer. After about four minutes the roboperator said,

'One moment, please.' At the end of ten minutes, the operator's voice came again. 'The following situation exists. When Similarity was raised to the known mechanical limit of twenty-three decimal places, a faint response was achieved. This was, however, an automatic process. It is evident that the pattern at the other end is still partly similarized, but that deterioration is continuous. Clearly, no attempt is being made by those on the ship to hold to the pattern.'

Thank you,' said Gosseyn-Ashargin.

It was hard to imagine that his body was out there somewhere while his reasoning self was here attached to the nervous system of the Ashargin heir.

What could be happening?

On the sixth day, Enro went on the public videophone with a message. He was visibly jubilant, and his voice rang with triumph as he reported:

'I have just been informed by Grand Admiral Paleol, commander of our forces in the Sixth Decant area that the capital city of Tuul was destroyed a few hours ago by our invincible fleet. This is but one of an unending series of victories won by our men and our weapons against a fiercely resisting enemy.

'Fight on, admiral. The hearts of the people and the confidence of your government are with you.'

Tuul? Gosseyn remembered the name with Ashargin's memory. Tuul was the stronghold of the most powerful State of the League group. It was one more planet out of thousands, but the fact that it was labeled 'capital' would be symbolic to the unintegrated minds to whom a map, in a semantic sense, was the territory, and the word the event itself.

Even for Gilbert Gosseyn, the destruction of Tuul was a turning point. He dared not wait any longer.

After dinner he invited Nirene to go with him to see Crang and Patricia. 'I hope,' he said pointedly, 'that the Gorgzin and you can find a great deal to talk about.'

She looked at him in momentary surprise, but he did not enlarge on his words. His idea for partially overcoming Enro's gift of clairvoyance could not be openly stated.

Nirene did her best. Gosseyn had no idea what she suspected was going to happen. But at the beginning her voice hardly stopped.

Patricia's answers were halting at first. She looked distinctly taken aback by the machine-gunlike voice that fired at her so steadily. And then suddenly, she must have caught on. She walked over and sat on the edge of Crang's chair, and began to talk back.

118

Nirene, ten feet away, hesitated, and then came over and sat on Ashargin's lap. The conversation that followed was the most active that Gosseyn had ever heard between two women. There was scarcely a moment during the rest of that evening when his own cautious words were not spoken against the background trill of wifely chatter.

Gosseyn first stated one of his lesser purposes. 'Know anything about training extra brains?' he asked. It was the first time he had mentioned the word to Crang.

The slim man's fine, yellow-tinged eyes studied him thoughtfully. Then he smiled. 'A little. What is it you want to know?' 'It's a problem of time, I think,' said Gosseyn. 'The first photograph is too slow, somehow. Slower than a chemical photographic plate, and the most complex of electronic tubes are chain lightning compared to it.'

Crang nodded, and said, 'It's notorious that specialized machines can perform any particular function much faster and frequently better than a given human appendage or organ. That is the price of our virtually unlimited adaptability.'

Gosseyn said quickly, 'You think the problem unsolvable?'

The other shook his head. 'It's a matter of degree. It's possible the original training followed a wrong pattern, and that a different approach might bring better results.'

Gosseyn knew what Crang meant. A pianist who learned the wrong system of fingering could not become a virtuoso until he laboriously taught himself the proper method. The human brain and body as a whole could be educated to achieve results in many different ways. Some of those ways were heartbreaking in the results they achieved, and some were so remarkable that the ordinary individual who had been properly conditioned came to be regarded as a genius.

The question was, how could his understanding of that general truth be utilized to re-train his extra brain when he returned to his own body?

'I would say,' said Crang, 'that it's a matter of setting up correct ideas.'

They talked around that for a while. For the moment Gosseyn was not worried about what Enro might hear. Even if the dictator could tune out the almost unending vibration of sound from Nirene and Patricia, this part of the conversation would not mean anything to him.

He lost none of his caution, but he was preoccupied with a desire to find out what the nature of such an idea would be. Crang made several suggestions, but it seemed to Gosseyn that the non-Aristotelian detective was still striving to estimate the extent of Ashargin's knowledge.

Thàt decided him finally. He turned the conversation to the problem of possession of one mind by another. He pointed out that it might be done by an extra brain, and that the similarization process involved could be a contact on a high level between a full grown extra brain and the vestigial of such a brain present in all human beings. Thus the greater would still come to the lesser.

Crang was watchful. 'What puzzles me,' he said, 'is what would the extra brain be doing while it was in possession of the vestigial? Would it dominate both bodies at the same time, or would the greater be in a state of relaxation?'

'Relaxation, definitely,' said Gosseyn.

It was a point he had been wanting to put over, and he was pleased. In spite of handicaps, he had managed to inform Crang that the Gosseyn body was unconscious.

Since Crang already knew that Gosseyn was aboard the Y-381907, his picture of the situation must be clearing up considerably.

'There was a time,' Gosseyn went on, 'when I took it for granted that such a position could only be maintained by some third party enforcing the interchange. It seems hard to believe'—he hesitated—'that the Sleeping God would leave his mind in a body so circumscribed as that of Ashargin if he had a way of preventing it.'

He hoped Crang got the point, that Gilbert Gosseyn was not actually in control of his own destiny.

'And, of course,' he went on, 'Ashargin is only a puppet who has now done about as much as he can.'

'I wouldn't say that,' said Crang, deliberately.

So abruptly did they arrive at the main purpose of their intent and cautious interchange.

At least, Gosseyn reflected as he eyed the other, it was his main purpose. Crang's position in all this frankly puzzled him. The man seemed to be doing nothing. He had taken the risk—the terrific risk in view of what he had done on Venus— of coming to Enro's headquarters. And now here he sat day after day, doing nothing.

His plan, if he had any, would have to be important indeed to justify his inaction while the battle of the Sixth Decant moved relentlessly to a final decision.

Crang resumed briskly: 'As I see it, prince, these mystical discussions can only lead so far. There comes a time when men act. Now, Enro is an outstanding example of a man of action. A military genius of the first order. His like will not be seen again in the galaxy for centuries.'

It was strange praise, coming from the lips of Eldred

120

Crang. And since it was false to facts—any Venusian Null-A trained in military tactics could equal Enro's 'genius'—it obviously had a purpose.

He shifted Nirene to a more comfortable position on his lap, and started to settle back.

At that moment he saw the opportunity for himself in what Crang had said. He interposed quickly:

'It seems to me that men like yourself will leave their mark on the military history of the galaxy. It should be interesting to follow the developments, and to know something about them.'

Crang laughed. 'Time will tell,' he said, and changed the subject. He went on, 'It's unfortunate that Enro is not yet recognized as the greatest military genius who ever lived.'

Gosseyn nodded glumly. He recognized that something was coming. But his own question had been evaded. He was positive that Crang had understood what he had tried to say.

And he won't answer, he thought grimly. *Well, if he's really got a plan, it had better be good.*

'I feel sure,' said Crang, 'that after his death even the people of the League group will recognize and acclaim the consummate skill of the attack that is being launched against the central powers.'

And now Gosseyn saw the plan. 'Greatest . . . who had lived.' 'After his death——'

Crang was proposing that an attempt be made to kill Enro.

After a moment Gosseyn was amazed. There was a time when the idea of using Ashargin to kill Enro had seemed the only possible use to which so powerless an individual could be put. All that was changed. The Ashargin heir had already been used to influence billions of people. He was known to be alive. At the proper moment his influence might be decisive.

To sacrifice him now in an attempt to assassinate the dictator was comparable to throwing away a queen in a game of chess. Even at that moment he had thought of it as a sacrifice. Now, with what he knew of Enro, he felt convinced that Ashargin would give up his life futilely.

Besides, the death of Enro would not stop the fleet. Paleol was there, gaunt and grim and determined. Paleol, and his thousands of officers who had put themselves beyond the laws of the League, would seize control of the Government against any group that tried to take over the Greatest Empire.

Of course, if Ashargin were killed while trying to murder Enro, presumably Gilbert Gosseyn would be back in control of his own body. For him, who was still convinced that he would be able to return normally, that was something to consider a week hence. And—just in case—the plan *could* be started now. Preparations ought to be made.

Grudgingly, with many reservations, Gosseyn nodded his acceptance of the plot.

That ended the evening. He had expected that details would be discussed, but Crang stood up and said, 'We've had a pleasant and amiable talk. I'm glad you were able to drop in.'

At the door the Null-A detective added, 'You might try to imitate the reflex that makes for good vision.'

It was a possible method of training that had already occurred to Gosseyn. He nodded. 'Good night,' he said curtly.

His impression of the visit as he walked with a silent Nirene back to her apartment was one of intense disappointment.

He waited till Nirene was out of the apartment, and then called Madrisol of the League on the videophone.

He waited tensely while the call was put through. For this could be interpreted as treason. He had asked Enro for the right to phone anyone he pleased, but unauthorized individuals did not contact the enemy in time of war. He was wondering how close a watch the Intelligence Department kept on him, when the operator's voice came:

'The League secretary agrees to speak to the Prince Ashargin, but only under the condition that it is clearly understood that he is a legal authority speaking to an outlaw.'

Gosseyn saw instantly the legal implications for Ashargin if he accepted such a ruling. He intended to do everything in his power to help the League win this war. If victory did result, then Ashargin would be in a dangerous position.

He felt annoyed, but after a moment he thought of a way out. 'The Prince Ashargin,' he said, 'has imperative reasons for speaking to Madrisol, and therefore accepts the condition but without prejudice.'

He had not long to wait after that. The lean ascetic looking face of Madrisol came into the screen. The man's face seemed even thinner than when he had last seen it with the eyes of Gilbert Gosseyn's body. The League secretary snapped, 'Is this a surrender offer?'

The question was so unrealistic that Gosseyn was pulled from his own purposes. Madrisol continued in a sharp tone, 'You understand there can be no compromise with principle. All individuals in the ruling hierarchy of the Greatest Empire must submit themselves to trial by the League Tribunal.'

A fanatic. In spite of his own complete opposition to Enro, Gosseyn's voice held a note of irony as he said, 'Sir, don't you think you are making a hasty assumption? This is not, nor am I in a position to make, a surrender offer.'

He went on quickly, 'The reason for my call will probably surprise you. It is of vital importance that you do not refer by name to the matter about which I am going to talk. What I intend to say will presently be reported to Enro, and any indiscretion on your part could have disastrous effects.'

'Yes, yes, go on.'

Gosseyn did not let it go at that. 'Have I your word?' he asked. 'Your word of honour?'

The answer was cold. 'Honour does not enter into any relationship between a League authority and an outlaw. But,' continued Madrisol, 'I shall certainly not make any revelations that would be dangerous to a friendly planet.'

It was the promise he wanted. Yet, now that it had been made, Gosseyn hesitated. Ashargin's memory of entire sun systems being destroyed put a restraint on his tongue.

If Enro made a wild guess as to the planet involved, he could be counted on to act. A single suspicion would be sufficient. At the moment, Venus was an incident to the dictator. As long as it was kept in that status, the Venusians would probably be safe.

Madrisol's voice came impatiently, 'I must ask you to come to the point.'

Once more Gosseyn went over in his mind the words he had prepared—and took the plunge. He explained about the call that Gilbert Gosseyn had made several weeks before to Madrisol, and the request he had made at that time. 'Did you ever do anything about that?'

Madrisol was frowning. 'I seem to recall the matter vaguely. I believe that one of my technician staff tried to put a call through.'

'What happened?' Tensely.

'Just a second. I'll check to see if the call was actually made.'

'Careful,' cautioned Gosseyn.

Madrisol's lips pressed more tightly together, but he nodded. He came back in less than a minute. 'No,' he said, 'the call has not yet been made.'

Gosseyn stared at the man wordlessly for a moment. He was not absolutely convinced. It was expecting a lot of a man in Madrisol's position to reveal any information to the Prince Ashargin. But he remembered how curt the other had been when he had phoned him up from Venus. And this fitted. How it fitted.

He found his voice. 'I urge you,' he said, 'to establish contact at once—personally.'

He broke the connection, depressed. It was beginning to look as if Crang's desperate plan was not a last resort at all, but the only resort. And yet—no! Paleol would execute every person in the palace, Nirene, Patricia, Crang. . . .

Gosseyn grew calm. No use thinking about such things. Unless some decisive action was taken Nirene and Crang and Ashargin—at least—would die shortly anyway. He must remember the great role that Crang had played on Venus, and trust that the Null-A detective was being as skillful now as he had been then.

He would attempt to kill Enro if Crang advised it.

It required more than an hour to figure out the pattern that he wanted. The actual words took only four and a quarter minutes to say into the recorder.

It was an intricate process that he began then, intricate in the sense that he wanted to set up responses on the unconscious level of the mind, and actually change the reactions of the autonomic nervous system.

What he attempted then was old in human history. The superb legions of Julius Caesar defeated vaster armies of the barbarians because the nervous systems of Roman soldiers had been trained to co-ordinated fighting. The legions of Caesar would have stood little chance against the armies of the Eastern Roman Empire of the Sixth Century.

There had been only a slight change in weapons, but the training of the men had been improved.

In 1940, the dictator Hitler had trained the nervous systems of his men in a new and different type of mechanical warfare. He was not defeated until superior numbers of men and machines adopted his methods. The machines existed before the blitzkrieg, but the nervous systems of the men who operated them had to be trained to the new integration. When that training was complete, superiority existed automatically.

In the days that followed the fumbled peace of World War II, more and more people began to accept the conclusions which the new science of General Semantics was laboriously deriving from the mass of available evidence. One of these conclusions was, 'The human nervous system is uniquely capable of unlimited training, but the method is the determining factor.'

Gosseyn's—and Crang's—idea was based on a principle of vision. A relaxed eye sees best. The normal eye remains relaxed when it shifts steadily. When, for any reason, an eye capable of good vision begins to stare, the image blurs. Unlike a camera, the eye sees clearly only on the instant following the relaxing shift.

It seemed to Gosseyn that if he could, while in Ashargin's body—while he was waiting—discover an automatic way for his extra brain to relax, then he would attain a quicker and sharper 'photograph' for similarity purposes. How could an extra brain be relaxed? An obvious approach would be the associative relaxation of the surrounding tissue.

So he set about relaxing the blood vessels of the cortex, the thalamus, and the sub-cortex—where the embryo extra brain of Ashargin would be located.

By association, all the cells around the blood vessels would automatically relax, also. That was the theory, and it had been proven many times.

Each time the voice on the recorder made the suggestion, he imitated the method he used with his extra brain in his own body to obtain a 'memorized' area. Two hours went by. He reached the point where he could follow the pattern and think of other things.

'Relax—look . . . relax—look . . .' The assassination plan would have to be very carefully worked out if it were true that Enro had guards watching him from peepholes in the walls. 'Relax—look . . . relax—look . . . relax—look . . .' There were several possibilities, of course. Since Ashargin was supposed to make the attack, the whole of the prince's position had to be considered. Suppose that both Ashargin and Gosseyn were dead a week hence, would that revive automatically the nearest Gosseyn replacement body, in this case the Sleeping God of Gorgzid?

'Relax—look . . . relax—look . . .' If it were the latter, then Gosseyn could see merits in the plan. He tried to imagine the effect if the Sleeping God should rise up to confront Enro and Secoh. 'Relax—look . . . relax—look . . . relax—look . . .' It seemed to Gosseyn that there was one preliminary which he must take care of personally.

If the sequence of events actually followed the pattern he had pictured, then he must make an investigation. He was assuming that the Sleeping God was a Gosseyn body.

That would have to be checked.

Enro did not turn up for lunch. Secoh, who arrived late, explained, 'He has gone to see Admiral Paleol.'

Gosseyn studied the priest as he settled himself at the table.

At forty, the other's face was marked with an intricacy of the passions that had impelled him to strive for the great rank he held. But there was more than that. After the way Secoh had talked to Enro on the day the lie detector was used on Ashargin, it seemed probable that the lord guardian was a man who believed what he taught.

Was this the moment to broach the subject of an interview? Gosseyn decided that it was. How should he bring the matter up? His method, when he finally spoke, was frankness. When he had finished, Secoh stared at him thoughtfully.

Twice, he parted his lips to speak. Twice, he stirred in his chair as if he intended to get up and leave. At last, he said mildly, 'The privilege of seeing the Sleeping God is granted only to members of the Order.'

'Exactly,' said Gosseyn.

Secoh looked startled, and Gosseyn hoped that there was a picture in his mind of what it would mean to have it publicly known that the Ashargin heir was a convert to the pagan religion that he cherished. Did he have a vision of an entire galaxy worshipping before the videophone image of the crypt of the Sleeping God? Gosseyn hoped so.

Secoh put down his fork and knife, and placed his hands on the table. They were slim and delicate looking hands, but there was firmness in them, also. He said at last in a kindly voice:

'My boy, I don't wish to discourage you. Your position is an anomalous one. I would be happy to personally give you the lower order instruction, and by an extension of my discretionary powers I think that could be made to include the Ceremony of the Beholding.'

So that was what it was called.

'I must warn you, however,' Secoh went on, 'the usual protection assured novices and initiates would not be accorded to you. We are in process of creating a universal state and our great leader has found it necessary to make hard decisions regarding individuals.'

He stood up. 'Tomorrow morning,' he said, 'be ready at six to go to the Temple. In view of your claims last week to be possessed, it had been my intention to take you into the presence of the Sleeping God. I am curious to know whether or not there will be an omen.'

He turned and walked away from the table, and out of the room.

In Gosseyn's case, the lower order instruction was part of the Ceremony of the Beholding. It was a history of the Sleeping God, and fascinating in its own way after the manner of folk tales.

The Temple of the Mound had existed before men were on Gorgzid. In the misty past, after he had created the universe, the god had chosen the planet Gorgzid for his resting place. There, guarded by his chosen people, he slept from his arduous labors. A day would come when, waking at last from his brief slumber—brief in the cosmic sense—he would rise and carry on his work.

To his people of Gorgzid had been given the task of making

126

the world ready for his awakening. On that bright day he would want a universe united.

As the rites proceeded, and the picture unfolded, Gosseyn realized many things for the first time. This was the justification for Enro's conquests. If you accepted the initial assumptions, then all the rest followed.

Gosseyn was shocked. He was making an assumption of his own, that this was a Gosseyn body. If such was the madness that built up around Gosseyn bodies, then he who was immortal by means of a series of such bodies, would have to reconsider the whole problem of his immortality.

It was about nine o'clock when he was dressed in a long white robe, and the Parade of the Beholding began. It was a curious route they took, down steps that fitted into a curved metal wall. They came to a depth in which was an atomic pile drive—and Gosseyn had his second shock.

A spaceship! The Temple of the Mound was a ball-like spaceship buried in the soil drift of centuries, perhaps for thousands of years.

They were climbing now, up the opposite curved wall. They came to the central floor, and turned into a room that hummed with the faint undercurrents of sounds. Gosseyn suspected the presence of many machines, but he didn't have his extra brain to verify the suspicion. The far wall curved into the room. From each corner arched a columned pylon. The four curved pilasters ended on a narrow buttress about twenty feet out from where the wall should have been.

It could have been the head of a coffin. The inner wall was translucent and glowed with an all-pervading light. Little steps led from it to the top of the buttress. Secoh climbed one of the staircases, and motioned to Gosseyn to climb the one that led up from the other side. As he reached the top, a panel slid open in the upper portion of the crypt.

'Kneel,' said Secoh sonorously, 'and behold!'

From the kneeling position Gosseyn could see the shoulders, part of the arms and chest, and the head of the man who lay inside. The face was lean and very lax, the lips slightly parted. It was the face of a man of about forty. The head was large and the face had a strangely blank look. It was a good-looking countenance, but only because of its symmetry and line of cheek and bone. It was the face of a moron. There was not even a faint resemblance to Gilbert Gosseyn.

The Sleeping God of Gorgzid was a stranger.

They arrived back at the palace in time for lunch, and at first Gosseyn did not realize that the great crisis was upon him.

There were two guests in the salon in addition to Enro,

127

Patricia, Crang and Nirene—altogether eight people at the table. The visitors wore uniforms complete with the insignia of the rank of marshal. The conversation at the table was dominated by Enro and the two military men.

Their conversation had to do with a Board of Inquiry that had investigated what was called a revolution. Gosseyn gathered that the revolution had been successful for reasons that were still obscure. The two officers were the Board.

He watched them curiously. They both seemed, in their manners and expressions, ruthless men. Before they announced their recommendations, he decided that two such coldly intellectual individuals would inevitably solve any such problem by recommending the destruction of the rebel planets.

He glanced at Crang and saw that the Null-A detective was impassive, but that, beside him, Patricia was showing signs of agitation. He realized that there must have been mention of the Board's work before his arrival in the salon. The two of them were definitely interested in what was going on. Abruptly, Patricia broke into the conversation.

'Gentlemen,' she said sharply, 'I sincerely hope that you have not chosen the easy way out in coming to your decision.'

The two officers turned and glanced at her, and then, as of one accord, looked questioningly at Enro. The Gorgzid studied his sister's face, a faint smile on his lips.

'You may be sure,' he said suavely, 'that Marshals Rour and Ugell will have considered only the evidence.'

'Naturally,' nodded Rour. Ugell merely gazed at Patricia with his ice-blue eyes.

'I want to hear the recommendations,' said Patricia curtly, 'before I make up my mind as to that.'

The faint smile remained unchanged on Enro's face. He was enjoying himself. 'I seem to remember a rumor,' he said, 'that my sister once took a special interest in the system under discussion.'

To Gosseyn the realization of the truth had come many seconds before. Venus! This was the Board of Inquiry that had been appointed to investigate the defeat of Thorson in the solar system.

'Well, gentlemen,' said Enro amiably, 'I see that we are all interested in hearing what you have to say.'

Ugell took a paper from an inner pocket, and put on a pair of glasses. He looked up. 'Are you interested in the reasons for our decision?'

'Most certainly,' said Enro. 'What I want to know is, what happened? How did Thorson, one of the great trouble

128

shooters of the empire, fail on a mission that was to be a mere incident in his career?'

Rour was silent. Ugell said, 'Your excellency, we questioned more than a thousand officers and men. Their stories made the following picture. Our armies successfully captured the cities of the rebels. Then, on the death of Marshal Thorson, the new commander ordered that Venus be abandoned. Naturally, these orders were carried out. So you see it is no disgrace to our armies, but the action of one man for reasons which we have not been able to discover.'

The picture was reasonably accurate. It failed to mention that Venusian Null-As had successfully defended their planet against the attacking forces. The investigation had not ferreted out the role that Gilbert Gosseyn had played in the death of Thorson, but, still, the facts that had been discovered were a part of the reality.

Enro was frowning. 'Was Thorson murdered by his successor?' he asked.

'There is no evidence pointing in that direction,' said Rour, as Ugell failed to answer. 'Marshal Thorson was killed during an attack which he personally led against a rebel stronghold on the planet, Earth.'

Enro exploded into anger. 'The incredible fool,' he said savagely. 'What was he doing leading any force in person?' With an effort the dictator controlled himself. 'However, gentlemen, I am very glad to have heard this account. It fits in with some information which I already have, and with some theories of mine. At the moment I am troubled in my own palace here by people who are foolishly plotting against my life, and so I should like you to give me the name of the officer who succeeded Thorson as commander of our forces on Venus.'

Ugell read from the paper: 'His name is Eldred Crang. We have been unable to find any trace of this traitor.'

Enro stared straight ahead. 'And, gentlemen, what are your recommendations?' Ugell read in a monotone, 'That the habitable parts of the system be sprayed with any one-year radioactive isotope that is available in the region, and that the system be rendered uninhabitable.'

He looked up. 'Marshal Rour is rather taken with a new idea that a young woman psychologist has been urging upon him recently. That is, that some planet be populated solely with criminally insane people. It seemed to us, though this notion was not incorporated in the text of our findings that it might be an interesting experiment to carry out as soon as the planets in question become habitable again.'

He handed the document to Enro, who took it without a word. There was a pause while he read it.

So Enro had known all the time. That was the thought that Gosseyn held in his mind. Their silly little plot—which had never really got beyond the embryo stage—had probably amused him even as he pondered the most devastating answer he could make to all their hopes.

It seemed clear, also, that he had known for some days who Eldred Crang was.

Enro was passing the document to Patricia. Without looking at it, she started to tear it up.

'That, gentlemen, is what I think of your recommendations.'

She climbed to her feet. Her face was colorless. 'It's just about time, Enro,' she said, 'that you and your executioners stop this mad murder of every one who has the courage to oppose you. The people of the planets Venus and Earth are harmless.'

'Harmless?' said Rour involuntarily. 'If they're so harmless, how is it that they were able to defeat our armies?'

She turned on him, her blue eyes flashing. 'Your report has stated—just now—that there was no defeat. That the action to retreat was taken at the command of the officer who succeeded Thorson.'

She leaned towards him. 'Is it possible that you are trying to cover up a defeat for our forces by a false statement, an appeal to the vanity of my brother?'

She was beside herself, in a thalamic fury. With a gesture she waved aside his effort to speak, and answered her own question.

'Never mind,' she said, 'your facts are reasonably accurate. I'll vouch for them. Because I gave the order to the officer who succeeded Thorson. He had no recourse but to obey the sister of his ruler. He sits here beside me as my husband.'

'His price was high,' sneered Enro.

He turned to the military men. 'Gentlemen, I have known for several days the identity of Eldred Crang. I am unable to act against him as a traitor because here on Gorgzid my sister's authority is very similar to my own, and I am bound by my religious faith to uphold her rights. I am trying to persuade the lord guardian to . . . uh . . . grant her a divorce, and he has taken the request under advisement.'

The words were earnestly spoken. It was hard to believe that behind the apparent logic and integrity of them was Enro's determination to use that religion to compel his sister to follow the ancient Gorgzid custom of brother-sister marriage. And that all the rest was fabrication.

130

Patricia was speaking again, earnestly. 'The people of the solar system have developed an educational system of the highest order, a culture which I should like to see modeled throughout the galaxy.'

She turned to look down at her brother. 'Enro,' she said, 'there can be no point in destroying a system which had devoted itself to education. If at any time it should be necessary to take over those planets, it could probably be done without bloodshed.'

Enro laughed. 'An educational system, eh?' He shrugged cynically. 'Secoh will be only too happy to tell you the plans the Temples have for subjugated planets.'

He turned to the marshals and there was a savage note in his voice as he said: 'Gentlemen, I must apologize for my sister's ill-tempered rudeness. She has a tendency to forget that her rule as Gorgzin does not extend beyond the planetary system where she and I are joint heirs. In ordering Lieutenant General Crang to withdraw our forces from Venus, she forgot that the Greatest Empire is a private achievement of my own. In marrying him, and permitting him and'—he hesitated, and glared for an instant at Gosseyn-Ashargin—'other upstarts to plan against me under her protection, she forfeited any right which she might have had to appeal to the softer side of my nature.'

His teeth snapped decisively. He said grimly: 'You may be sure that I do not appoint Boards of Inquiry, and then ignore their recommendations. And, as a precaution, to insure that the Gorgzin does not place herself in jeopardy by going to Venus, I shall immediately issue an order that no galactic Distorters can be used by her until after the destruction of the population of the solar system has been carried out as recommended. Thank you, gentlemen. You have my best wishes.'

Gosseyn noticed that the negating order did not extend to Prince Ashargin. He said nothing, but immediately the meal was over, he headed for the public 'Distorter' system of the palace. He didn't know if it was possible to go to Venus in a Distorter cage; by ship, yes, but he couldn't get hold of a ship —and so his only recourse was to make the attempt.

He took the torn segments of the Venusian report from his pocket and quickly pieced them together. He still had to admire the way Crang had removed them from Patricia's plate, studied them briefly, and then casually passed them on to Ashargin.

The galactic co-ordinates of the position in space of Sol were printed right across the top of page one. He read, *Decant Eight, r36,400 theta 272° Z1800——*

131

Thirty-six thousand, four hundred light-years from the galactic axis, at an angle of 272° from the standard line—which was based on some remote galaxy—and eighteen hundred light-years on the minus side of the galactic plane. And his very first task must be to get to Decant Eight.

As he pulled the lever in the cage, Gosseyn felt the change. Felt himself return to his own body—free of Ashargin.

He wakened in the swift fashion of the change, sat up abruptly, and then lay back with a groan as every stiff muscle in his body shrieked in protest against the sharp movement.

There was a feminine exclamation from near the bed. Leej came into the line of vision of his smarting eyes.

'You're awake,' she said, and her voice was little more than a whisper. 'I thought something was going to happen, but I couldn't be sure.'

Tears came into her eyes. 'I've got to tell you,' she said. 'We're cut off. Something has happened to the Distorter system. The ship is marooned. Captain Free says it will take us five hundred years to get to the nearest base.'

The mystery of the lost destroyer, Y-381907, was explained.

XV

Null-Abstracts

A few of the operational principles of general semantics are as follows: (1) Human nervous systems are structurally similar one to the other, but are never exactly the same. (2) Any human nervous system is affected by events—verbal or nonverbal. (3) An event—that is a happening—affects the body-and-mind as a whole.

GOSSEYN did not try to move again immediately. His eyes were watering from the sudden flood of light, but his vision was better. His body ached. Every joint and muscle seemed to be protesting the one attempt he had made to sit up.

He recognized what had happened. Allowing for the passage of time during the Distorter transport, he had been away from the destroyer for about a month. During the whole time his body had been lying unconscious.

Compared to the attention the Gosseyn bodies must receive from their automatic 'incubators,' the care he had been given during the month just past, however well meaning, had probably been on a level only slightly higher than primitive.

He grew aware again of Leej. She was sitting on the edge of the bed, watching him with eyes that glowed emotionally. But she said nothing, and so, favoring his stiff muscles, he looked around the room.

It was a rather nicely furnished bedroom with twin beds. The other bed had been slept in, and he surmised that it had been occupied by Leej. He passed instantly on to the thought that they were probably imprisoned together.

That was an assumption that he intended to check on as soon as possible.

His gaze came back to her, and this time she spoke. 'How are you feeling? The pictures I have are not clear on that point.'

He managed a reassuring smile for her. He was just beginning to realize what a disastrous month it must have been for a woman of her position. In spite of what the Follower had tried to do to her, she was not really accustomed to danger or reverses.

'I think I'm all right,' he said slowly. And his jaw ached from the effort of speaking.

Her delicate face showed concern. 'Just a moment,' she said. 'I'll get some ointment.'

She disappeared into the bathroom, and emerged almost immediately with a small plastic tube. Before he could realize her intention, she drew the bedclothes from him. For the first time he realized that he was completely undressed. She squeezed a fine slick of oil onto her palm, and began to rub it vigorously into his skin.

'I've been doing this all month,' she smiled. 'Just imagine.'

Oddly enough, he knew what she meant. Imagine Leej, a free Predictor, who had servants for every purpose, actually performing such menial labor herself. Her amazement at herself made the intimacy of the act subtly right and normal. He was no Enro, requiring the soft feel of women's hands to make him happy, but he settled back and waited while she rubbed the ache out of his legs, arms and back. She stepped away finally and watched his hesitant attempts to sit up.

To Gosseyn, his helplessness was a startling condition. Not really unexpected, but a reality which somehow he would have to take into account in the future. While he experimented with

133

exercising his muscles, Leej brought his clothes out of a drawer.

'I had everything cleaned,' she said, 'in the ship's cleaning plant, and I bathed you about two hours ago, so you just have to get dressed.'

The fact that she had managed to secure the services of the laundry department interested Gosseyn, but he did not comment on that mundane level. 'You knew I was going to wake up?'

'Naturally.'

She must have seen the questioning expression of his face, for she said quickly:

'Don't worry, the blurs start soon enough, now that you're awake.'

'When?' He was tense at the thought of action.

'In about fifteen minutes.'

Gosseyn began to dress more swiftly.

He spent five of the fifteen minutes slowly walking around the room. Then he rested for a minute, and for two minutes walked faster, swinging his arms with a free rhythm. He paused finally and looked down at Leej where she had sat down in a chair.

'What's all this about being lost in space?' he asked.

The eagerness went out of her eyes. 'We're cut off,' she said somberly. 'Somebody set up a relay that destroyed the Distorter Matrix for the nearest base. That happened at the moment when you became unconscious, after the matrix had been used once.'

The technical words sounded strange coming from her lips, but presently only the meaning remained. In that first moment after his awakening, when his alertness had been subnormal, he had only partially grasped the implications of what she had said. It wasn't that he hadn't understood. He had. But his mind had leaped to the related but comparatively unimportant idea that this explained why the destroyer had for so long failed to answer videophone calls.

Now, he felt a chill.

Cut off, Leej had said. Cut off four hundred light-years from the nearest base. If the ship's Distorter transport system had really been put out of commission, then they would be dependent on atomic drive with all the speed limitations of ordinary space-time travel.

He parted his lips to speak. Leej knew virtually nothing of science. The words she used must have been picked up during the past month, and they probably meant very little to her.

He had better find out as quickly as possible from more

134

authoritative quarters the full extent of the catastrophe.

He turned and looked at the door, annoyed at the idea of being imprisoned. These people couldn't possibly suspect what he could do with this extra brain. And, therefore, locked doors were childish barriers, irritating when there were so many things to do. He turned to question Leej.

She said quickly, 'It's not locked. We're not prisoners.'

Her words anticipated his question. It made him feel good to be back again where such things were possible. He walked to the door; it opened effortlessly. He hesitated, and then stepped across the threshold and out into the corridor. It was silent and deserted.

He took a photograph of the floor just outside the door, and because he was intent, a second passed before he realized that he must have used his extra brain automatically at just about the time predicted by Leej.

He returned into the room, and stood looking at her. 'Was that it?' he said. 'Was that the moment?'

She had climbed to her feet to watch him. Now, with a sigh, she sank back into her chair. 'What did you do?'

Gosseyn had no objection to telling her—except for one thing. 'If you should ever be captured,' he explained, 'a lie detector might obtain information from you that would be dangerous for us all.'

He shook his head at her, smiling. From the expression on her face, he knew that she knew what he was going to say. But he said it anyway. 'How did you do it?'

'I snatched your blaster.'

'You had a vision of the month ahead?'

She shook her head. 'Oh, no. The blur that started then continued throughout the month. But it was I who saw you slump to the floor.' She stood up. 'It was all very easy, I assure you.'

Gosseyn nodded. He could see what she meant. Captain Free and Oreldon would have stood blank for a second, not realizing what was happening.

'They offered no resistance,' said Leej. 'And I had them carry you to our room. But just a moment now. I have some soup for you.'

Our room, thought Gosseyn. It was a point which he had intended bringing up as gently as possible. He watched her as she walked swiftly out of the room. She came back a moment later, carrying a tray on which was a steaming bowl of soup. She was so friendly, so helpful; she took their relationship so completely for granted, that he changed his mind about speaking to her just then.

He ate the soup, and felt much better. But when he gave her

135

back the tray, his thoughts were already turning back to their deadly situation.

'I'd better go and see Captain Free,' he said.

As he walked along the empty corridor, Venus and all the mighty events of the galaxy seemed very far away.

Captain Free opened the door of his room, and Gosseyn's first impression was that he was ill. The stocky commander's face was very pale, and there was a feverish look in his brown eyes. He stared at Gosseyn as if he were seeing a ghost. The color rushed abruptly into his cheeks.

'Gosseyn,' he said, and his voice was a croak, 'what's been the matter with you? We're lost.'

Gosseyn stared at him, wondering if this exhibition of the emotion of fear explained the inefficiency which had enabled him to capture the destroyer. He said finally, quietly, 'We've got work to do. Let's do it.'

They walked side by side along the silent corridors of the ship to the control room. In an hour he had the picture. Extra circuits had been built into the matrixes that were in the three similarity slots of the control board. They were so interconnected that if any one of them was used once on a 'break,' the pattern in all three would be disorganized.

The break had occurred during the similarization which had also resulted in his becoming unconscious a month before. The disarranged matrixes had been tuned to the patterns of the three nearest bases. Since they no longer worked, it was impossible to get to base by similarity means.

Gosseyn saw that Captain Free believed every word of his explanation of the operation of the system, and that was enough for him. He believed it, also, but in a more qualified fashion.

Somebody, he told himself, *set up those circuits. Who?*

The problem was more subtle than it might at first appear. It was reasonable to assume that the Follower was responsible. And yet the shadow-thing had admitted to Janasen when the two of them were on Venus that he was not mechanically minded.

The statement was not necessarily fact. But, still, people who used the products of the machine age did not automatically know how to set up relays to interfere with the operation of intricate machines.

Gosseyn walked over to the captain's desk and sat down. He was more tired than he cared to think about. But he dared not slacken his effort. In far-off space a fateful order had been given. Destroy Venus! Or rather, destroy the people of the solar system.

Commands like that probably took time to carry out. But the time was running short.

After two minutes rest, he climbed to his feet. There was only one quick, logical method of solving their immediate problem. It seemed to him that he was ready to make it.

He memorized a number of key points aboard the ship as well as several power sources. And then he pressed the button that opened one of the sliding doors to the lower section of the ship. He motioned Captain Free to go ahead of him.

Wordlessly, they headed down the stairway.

It was a different world they came to. Here was the laughter of men, the shouts and the sounds of many movements. For Gosseyn it meant a confusion of perception of neural flow.

The dormitory doors were open, and men stood along the corridors. They stiffened to attention as Captain Free came up, but relaxed after he had passed. Gosseyn said:

'Do the men know the truth?'

The commander shook his head. 'They think they're making a trip between two planets. I've been in daily touch with the noncommissioned officers in charge, and everything is fine.'

'They didn't even worry about the connecting doors being locked for a month?' Sharply.

'They only go upstairs when ordered, and that usually means work. So I don't think they'll be worried.'

Gosseyn made no comment on that. His theory was that somebody had gone up without orders, and worked hard indeed. He could possibly have located the guilty man by questioning four hundred and eighty separate individuals with a lie detector. But while he did so, laboriously, Enro's fleet would arrive in the solar system, radioactive isotopes would be sprayed down upon the misty skies of Venus and Earth, and three billion people would die horribly without having received a single advance warning.

The prevision was without benefit of Predictors, but it was nightmarishly realistic none the less. Gosseyn shuddered, and swiftly put his attention back to the job at hand. At his suggestion, Captain Free ordered a general return to dormitories.

'Shall I have the doors locked?' he asked.

Gosseyn shook his head.

'There are several exits to this place,' the commander persisted. 'I presume you're down here for a purpose. Shall I have guards posted at the doors?'

'No,' said Gosseyn.

The captain stared at him uneasily. 'I'm worried,' he said. 'There's no one up there who's free except the Predictor woman. It'd be unpleasant if someone slipped up the stairway and closed the connecting doors between the two sections.'

Gosseyn smiled grimly. The other wasn't even close in his estimate of the situation. That wasn't the danger. 'It's a point I've considered,' was all he said.

They went into each dormitory in turn. While the non-commissioned officers and Captain Free made a roll call, Gosseyn talked to individuals. He made a pattern out of the task. 'What's your name? How are you feeling? Worried about anything?' With each question he watched not only the man's facial responses but the neural flow that came from him like an aura.

He made a fast job of it, particularly as the crew members began to answer. 'Feeling all right, Doc.' 'Yes, Doc.' Gosseyn did not discourage the assumption that he was a psychiatrist.

He was in the third dormitory when a relay closed in his extra brain. Somebody was climbing the stairway that led to the upper section of the ship. He turned to speak to Captain Free, but the commander was not in sight. A noncommissioned officer stepped forward smartly.

'The captain went to the washroom. He'll be right back.'

Gosseyn waited. It would take, he estimated, one and a half minutes for the Follower's agent to go from the stairway to the control room from which the Predictors had been sent to their assigned stations. Since all such subsidiary Distorters operated through the main matrix, the control room must be first.

He would have liked to talk to Leej, but to bring her down by similarity would be too startling. And, besides, there wasn't time. He said something about being right back, stepped out into the corridor, crouched down, and in that position similarized himself behind the captain's desk in the control room.

Cautiously, he peered over the top of the desk, but for a while he made no effort to move, simply knelt there and watched. The man was removing the panel of the Distorter board directly over the similarity slots. He worked swiftly, and every little while looked over his shoulder toward one or the other of the two entrances. And yet Gosseyn had no impression of frantic haste. It was not surprising; traitors such as this always had some extra quality of nerve or boldness that set them apart from their fellows. Such a man would have to be handled very carefully.

As he watched, the other lifted down one of the metal panels. Swiftly, he drew out the matrix in the slot, laid it on the floor, and came up immediately with a curved, glowing shape. Because of its shininess, it was so different from the other that a moment passed before Gosseyn recognized it. A

Distorter matrix, not dead, but energized.

He stepped out of his hiding place, and walked toward the control board. He was about ten feet from it when the man must have heard him coming. He stiffened and then slowly turned.

'I beg your pardon, sir,' he said, 'but I was sent up here to do some work on this——' He stopped the lie. Relief flooded his face. He said, 'I thought you were one of the officers.'

He seemed about to turn back to the board when Gosseyn's expression must have warned him. Or perhaps he was taking no chances. His hand moved convulsively, and a blaster appeared in it.

Gosseyn similarized him thirty feet from the control board. He heard the hiss of the blaster, and then a cry of amazement, behind him. He turned swiftly, and saw that the other was poised rigid in every muscle, facing away. In the man's tense hand he caught the glint of the blaster's stock. Swiftly, he photographed it, and as the other swung jerkily around, he similarized the weapon into his own hand. He was deliberate now.

He got the maniacal terror he wanted, but he got something more also. Snarling like an animal, the man made an attempt to reach the Distorter switches. Three times Gosseyn similarized him back to his starting point. The third time, abruptly, the other ceased his mad effort. He stopped. He snatched a knife from an inner pocket, and before Gosseyn could realize his intention, plunged the blade into his own left breast.

There were sounds of running footsteps. Captain Free, followed an instant later by Leej, came darting into the control room. 'What happened?' Captain Free asked breathlessly.

He stopped short, and he stood by wordlessly as the traitor grimaced at them, shuddered—and died.

The commander identified him as an assistant to the communications engineer. He verified that the matrix the fellow had put into the similarity slot was for the base four hundred light-years away.

There was time, then, for explanations. Gosseyn offered the main points of his rationalization that had led him to set his trap.

'If it was an agent of the Follower, then he must still be aboard. Why? Well, because no one was missing. How did I know that? You, Captain Free, kept in touch with the non-commissioned officers in charge of dormitories, and they would surely have reported it if a man were missing.

'So he was still aboard. And for a whole month he waited in the lower part of the ship, cut off from the control room.

You can imagine the ferment he was in, for he surely hadn't planned on waiting so long before making his escape. Why would he have a way of escape? I think it'd be because a man would always include a way of escape when making his plans, and would only accept the idea of death if he felt himself trapped.

'With all those pressures working on him, he wasted no time getting upstairs when the doors opened.

'Of course, the new matrix would also have a wrecking circuit in it, which would operate the moment he used it to escape. But there's one little point about that which puzzles me. Captain Free tells me we'll have to stop at a base about eighteen thousand light-years from here, and pick up the matrixes that will take us to Venus at r36000 theta 272 Z1400, and when we get there, we're going to have to have our papers in order.

'My little point is this: How did a mechanic expect to turn up at base without release papers of some kind? Crew members of warships usually have to explain why they are not with their ships. You might say the Follower would protect him, but that isn't really logical. I don't think the Follower would care to have Enro know that he was responsible for cutting off Predictors from the fighting fleets for a whole' month.'

He looked up. 'As soon as you've fixed up that circuit, captain, come and see me. I'll be in my room.'

XVI

Null-Abstracts

For the sake of sanity, learn to evaluate an event in terms of total response. Total response includes visceral and nervous changes, and emotional reaction, the thought about the event, the spoken statement, the action repressed, the action taken, et cetera.

As soon as he reached the bedroom, Gosseyn took off his shoes and lay down on top of the bed. He had been feeling the nausea coming on for more than an hour. The great effort of trapping the saboteur had been a strain almost too much for him to maintain.

He was anxious not to show weakness. And so it was pleasant to feel the strength flowing back into his body. After twenty minutes of lying with closed eyes, he stretched, yawned, and opened his eyes.

He sat up with a sigh. It was like a signal. Leej came in carrying another bowl of soup. The timing of it obviously indicated prevision. Gosseyn ate the soup thinking about that, and he was just finishing it when Captain Free came into the room.

'Well,' he said, 'we're all set. Give the signal and we'll start.'

Gosseyn glanced at Leej, but she shook her head. 'You can't expect anything from me,' she said. 'As far as I can see, there's nothing wrong, but I can't see as far as we're going.'

Captain Free said, 'We're lined up to go through the remainder of Decant Nine to the nearest marginal base in Decant Eight. There, of course, we have to stop.'

'Approach that base with a break,' Gosseyn said, 'and then we'll talk some more.'

Eighteen similarity jumps and slightly more than ten minutes later, according to the time that seemed to have passed, Captain Free came back into the cabin.

'We're six and three quarter light-years from the base,' he said. 'Not bad. That puts us within eleven thousand light-years of Venus.'

Gosseyn climbed off the bed and walked stiffly to the control room. He sank into the lounge in front of the transparent dome. The question in his mind was, should they flash straight into the base? Or should they make their approach overland? He glanced questioningly at Leej.

'Well?' he said.

The young woman walked over to the control board. She settled into the circular chair, turned, and said, 'We're going in.' She pulled the lever.

The next second they were inside the base.

There was dimness all around. As his eyes became accustomed to the lesser light, Gosseyn saw that the enormous metal cave was much larger than the base of the Greatest Empire on Venus.

Gosseyn turned his attention to Captain Free. The commander was giving instructions over the videophone. He came over to Gosseyn just as Leej also walked up. He said:

'An assistant of the port captain will come aboard in about half an hour. Meanwhile I've given orders for the new equipment to be brought into the ship. They accept that as routine.'

Gosseyn nodded, but he was thoughtful as he studied the

officer. He was not worried to any extent as to what Captain Free might be able to do against his interests. With Leej and himself co-ordinating to frustrate a threatening danger before it was scheduled to happen, risks from men and machines need scarcely be thought about.

Still, the man seemed to be co-operating not as a prisoner but as an open partner. He had no desire to call the other's attention to his neglect of duty as an officer of the military forces of the Greatest Empire, and yet, some understanding seemed essential.

He decided to be frank. After he had finished, he had to wait for nearly a minute. Finally, Captain Free said:

'Gosseyn, a man in your position, with your special power, can scarcely have any idea of what hundreds of thousands of officers in the Greatest Emipre went through when Enro took over. It was very skillfully done, and if the others were like me, then they must have felt trapped.

'It was virtually impossible to know what to do. There were spies everywhere, and the overwhelming majority of the crews were for Enro. When he was war minister he had his oppor-tunity to place his traitors in key positions everywhere.'

Captain Free shrugged. 'Very few of us dared show resist-ance. Men were being executed right and left ; the dividing line seeming to be whether or not you made open comment. As a result of a lie detector test, I was listed as a doubtful person, and warned. But I was allowed to live because I had not re-sisted in any way.'

He finished, 'The rest was simple enough. I rather lost in-terest in my career. I was easily wearied. And when I realized what this trip to Yalerta meant, I'm afraid I let discipline go by the board. It seemed to me that the Predictors would insure an Enro victory. When you came along, I was shocked for a few minutes. I saw myself courtmartialed and executed. And then I realized you might be able to protect me. That was all I needed. From that moment I was your man. Does that answer your question?'

It did indeed. Gosseyn held out his hand. 'It's an old custom of my planet,' he said, 'in its highest form a method of sealing friendships.'

They shook hands. Briskly, Gosseyn turned to Leej.

'What's on the time horizon?' he asked.

'Nothing.'

'No blurs?'

'None. The papers of the ship show that we are on a special mission. That mission is vaguely stated, and gives Captain Free considerable authority.'

'That means we get out of the base without the slightest thing going wrong?'

She nodded, but her face was serious. 'Of course,' she said earnestly, 'I'm looking at a picture of the future that you could alter by some deliberate interference. For instance, you could try to make a blur just to prove me wrong. I really have no idea what would happen then. But my picture says there is no blur.'

Gosseyn was interested in experiments, but not at the moment. Still, there were other aspects of the situation.

The whole problem of prevision seemed to become more puzzling the further he looked into it. If Enro, the Predictors and Gilbert Gosseyn himself were all products of the same kind of training, then why couldn't he who had been in an 'incubator' thirty times as long as a Predictor, and more than a hundred times longer than Enro—why couldn't he see across distance as Enro did, and into the future like the Predictors?

Training, he thought. His. For they had received none. But he had been given flawed training, for a purpose which later had to be changed.

As soon as he had warned the Venusians, he'd have to consult Dr. Kair and the other scientists. And this time they'd work on the problem with a new understanding of its possibilities.

It was just a few minutes less than an hour after their arrival that they flashed out of the base. Ten jumps and ten thousand light-years brought them near Gela.

Next stop, Venus.

At Gosseyn's suggestion, Leej set the 'break' needles. Rather, she spent several seconds setting them. Then abruptly she leaned back, shook her head, and said, 'There's something wrong.'

'It's beyond my range, but I have a feeling that we won't get as close to the planet as we did when we went into that base. I have a sense of interference.'

Gosseyn did not hesitate. 'We'll phone them,' he said.

But the videophone and plate were silent, lifeless.

That gave him pause, but not for long. There was really nothing to do but take the ship through to Venus.

As before, the similarity jump seemed instantaneous. Captain Free glanced at the distance calculators, and said to Leej:

'Good work. Only eight light-years from the Venusian base. Can't do much better than that.'

There was a clatter of sound, a bellowing voice: 'This is the roboperator in charge of communications—an emergency!'

143

XVII

Null-Abstracts

For the sake of sanity, be aware of SELF-REFLEXIVE-NESS. A statement can be about reality or it can be about a statement about a statement about reality.

GOSSEYN took five quick steps toward the control board, and stood behind Captain Free, tense and alert. He shifted his gaze steadily from one to the other of the rear, side and front video plates. The roboperator spoke again in its 'emergency' voice.

'Voices in space,' it roared. 'Robots sending messages to each other.'

'Give us the messages,' Captain Free commanded loudly. He glanced around and up at Gosseyn. 'Do you think Enro's fleet is here already?'

Gosseyn wanted more evidence. I was released, he thought, from Ashargin's brain within a few minutes after Enro gave the order. It probably took about forty hours for me to get back to the destroyer, two hours more to get the ship moving, less than an hour at the base, and then just under eighty hours to get here to Venus—about a hundred and twenty-two hours, only three of which could be considered wasted.

Five days! The assigned fleet, of course, could have been detached from a base much nearer to Venus, in fact, probably had been. That was one trouble with his expectations. Similarity videophone communications involved the movement of electrons in a comparatively simple pattern. Electrons were naturally identical to eighteen decimal places, and so the 'margin of error' in transmission was only fourteen seconds for every four thousand light-years—as compared to ten hours for material objects for the same distance.

Enro's fleet could be here ahead of them on the basis of time saved by the use of telephone orders. But attacks on planetary bases involved more than that. It would take time to load the equipment for the type of atomic destruction that was to be rained down on Earth and Venus.

And there was another point, even more important. Enro had plans of his own. Even now, he could be delaying his orders to destroy the people of the solar system in the hope that the threat of such an attack would force his sister to marry him.

The roboperator was bellowing again. 'I am now,' it shouted, 'transmitting the robot message.' Its tone grew quieter, more even. 'A ship at CR-94-687-12 . . . bzzz . . . similarize . . . Converge and attack . . . five hundred human beings aboard . . . bzzz . . . zero 54 seconds . . . Capture——'

Gosseyn spoke in a hushed voice:

'Why, we're being attacked by robot defenses.'

The relief that came had in its excitement and pride as well as caution. Scarcely more than two and a half months had passed since the death of Thorson. Yet here already were defenses against interstellar attacks.

The Null-A's must have sized up the situation, recognized that they were at the mercy of a neurotic dictator, and concentrated the productive resources of the system on defense. It could be titanic.

Gosseyn saw that Captain Free's fingers were quivering on the lever that would take them back to the star Gela, the base a thousand light-years behind them.

'Wait!' he said.

The commander was tense. 'You're not going to stay here?'

'I want to see this,' said Gosseyn, 'for just one moment.'

For the first time, Gosseyn glanced at Leej. 'What do you think?'

He saw that her face was tense. She said, 'I can picture the attack, but I can't see its nature. There's a blur a moment after it starts. I think——'

She was interrupted. Every radar machine in the control room stammered into sound and light. There were so many pictures on the viewplates that Gosseyn could not even glance at them all.

Because, simultaneously, something tried to seize his mind.

His extra brain registered a massively complex energy network, and recorded that it was trying to short circut the impulses that flowed to and from the motor centers of his brain. Trying? Succeeding.

He had a swift comprehension of the nature and limitations of this phase of the attack. Abruptly, he made the cortical-thalamic pause.

The pressure on his mind ended instantly.

Out of the corners of his eyes, he saw that Leej was standing stiffly, a distorted expression on her face. In front of him Captain Free sat rigid, his fingers contracted like marble claws less than an inch from the lever that would take them back to Gela.

Above him, the roboperator transmitted: 'Unit CR- . . . bbzzzz . . . incapacitated. All personnel aboard but one seized —concentrate on the recalcitrant——'

With one flick of his finger, Gosseyn pushed the lever which was set to break near the base a thousand light-years away.

There was blackness.

The destroyer Y-381907 poised in space, safe, slightly more than eight hundred light-years from Venus. In the control chair Captain Free began to lose that abnormal rigidity.

Gosseyn whirled, and raced for Leej. He reached her just in time. The stiffness that had held her on her feet let go. He caught her as she fell, limply.

As he carried her to the lounge in front of the transparent dome, he visualized the happenings elsewhere on the ship. Men by the hundreds must be falling or had already fallen to the floor. Or if they had been lying down throughout the crisis, then now they were sagging, loose muscled, as if every tension in their bodies had suddenly let go.

Leej's heart was beating. She had hung so lax in his arms that for a moment the thought had come that she was dead. As Gosseyn straightened, her eyelids flickered and tried to open. But it was nearly three minutes before she was able to sit up and say, wanly, 'Surely, you're not going back?'

'Just a minute,' said Gosseyn.

Captain Free was stirring, and Gosseyn had a vision of the commander convulsively tugging at switches, levers and dials in a frantic belief that the ship was still in danger. Hurriedly, he lifted him out of the control chair.

His mind was busy as he carried the man to the lounge beside Leej, thinking about what she had said. Now, he asked, 'You see us returning?'

She nodded reluctantly. 'But that's all. It's outside my range.'

Gosseyn nodded, and sat staring at her. His sense of elation was dimming. The Venusian method of defense was so unique, so calculated to catch only people not Null-A trained, that, once they engaged, only his presence had saved the ship.

Briefly, it had seemed as if the Venusians had an invincible defense.

But if he hadn't been aboard, then there would have been no blur to confuse Leej. She would have foreseen the attack in ample time for the ship to escape.

In the same way, Enro's fleet, with its Predictors, would escape the first onslaught. Or perhaps the predictions could be so accurate that the fleet could keep on breaking toward Venus.

It was possible that the entire Venusian defense, marvelous though it was, was worthless. In building their robots, the Venusians had failed to take the Predictors into their calculations.

The fact was not surprising. Even Crang had not known about them. It might be, of course, that there'd be no Predictors on the fleet Enro was sending. But that surely could not be counted on.

His mind reached that far, and then circled back to what Leej had said. He nodded, visualizing the situation. Then he said:

'We'll have to try again, because we've got to get through those defenses. It's as important as ever.'

In a way it was more important. Already there was in his mind a picture of robot defense forces like this opposing Enro's titanic fleet in the Sixth Decant. And if a method could be found to make them react a little faster, so that the attack came in one second and not in fifty-four, then even the prevision of the Predictors might be too slow.

Gosseyn considered several possibilities, then carefully explained the nature of the cortical-thalamic pause to Leej and the captain. They went through the routine several times, a mere brushing on the edge of the subject, but it was all there was time for.

The precautions might not work, but they were worth trying.

The preliminaries completed, he seated himself in the control chair, and looked around. 'Ready?' he asked.

Leej said in a querulous tone, 'I don't think I like being out in space.' That was her only comment.

Captain Free said nothing.

Gosseyn said, 'All right, this time we're going through as far as we can.'

He pushed the lever.

The attack came thirty-eight seconds by the clock after the blackness ended. Gosseyn watched the nuances of its development, instantly nullified the assault on his own mind. But this time he took a further step.

He tried to superimpose a message upon the complex force. 'Order attack to end!' He repeated that several times.

He waited for the command to be echoed by the robo-operator, but it continued to transmit messages between the robotic brains outside the ship. He sent a second message. 'Break all contacts!' he ordered firmly.

The ship's robovoice said something about all but one of

the units being incapacitated, and, without a single reference to his command, added, 'Concentrate on the recalcitrant——'

Gosseyn pressed the similarity lever, and broke after five light-minutes.

In sixteen seconds, the attack resumed. He sent a quick glance at Leej and the commander. They were both sagging in their seats. Their brief Null-A training hadn't proved very effective.

He forgot them, and watched the viewplates, waiting for a blaster attack. When nothing happened, he jumped a light-day nearer Sol. A glance at the distance gauges showed that Venus was still slightly more than four light-days away.

This time the attack resumed after eight seconds.

It was still not fast enough. But it helped to fill out the picture that was forming in his mind. The Venusians were trying to capture ships and not destroy them. The devices they had developed for that purpose would have been marvelous in a galaxy of normal human beings. And they were wonderful in their ability to distinguish between friend and foe. But against extra brains or Predictors they had a limited value. Gosseyn suspected that they had been rushed through the assembly lines in the belief that time was short.

Since that was truer every minute, he tried one more test. He sent a message to the unit that was still trying with a blind, mechanical obstinacy to capture him: 'Consider me and everyone aboard captured.'

Again, there was no response to show that anybody had heard. Once more Gosseyn pushed the similarity lever, the needle controls of which had been set so accurately by Leej. *Now,* he thought, *we'll see.*

When the momentary blackness ended, the distance indicators showed ninety-four light-minutes from Venus. In three seconds the attack came, and this time it was on a different level entirely.

The ship shuddered in every plate. On the view plate the defensive screen was a bright orange in color. The robo-radar spoke for the first time, a whining howl: 'Atomic bombs approaching!'

With the flip of his finger, Gosseyn moved the similarity lever back, and jumped nine hundred and eleven light-years towards Gela.

The second attempt to penetrate the Venusian defenses had failed.

Gosseyn, his mind already intent on the details of the third attempt, revived Leej. She came to consciousness, and shook her head.

'It's out of the question,' she said. 'I'm too tired.'

He started to say something, but instead he studied her face. The lines of weariness in it were unmistakable. Her body drooped noticeably.

'I don't know what those robots did to me,' she said, 'but I need a rest before I can do what you want. Besides,' she went on, 'you haven't got the energy either.'

Her words reminded him of his own weariness. He rejected the obstacle, and parted his lips to speak. Leej shook her head.

'Please don't argue with me,' she said in a tired voice. 'I can tell you right now that there's slightly more than a six-hour pause to the next blur, and that we spend the time in much-needed sleep.'

'You mean, we just sit out here in space?'

'Sleep,' she corrected. 'And stop worrying about those Venusians. Whoever attacks them will withdraw and look the situation over, as we did.'

He supposed she was right. The logic behind her remark was Aristotelian, and without evidence to support it. But her general argument was more plausible. Physical weariness. Slow reflexes. An imperative need to recuperate from the friction of battle.

The human element had entered the list of combatants.

'This blur,' he said finally, 'what's it about?'

'We wake up,' said Leej, 'and there it is.'

Gosseyn stared at her. 'No advance warning?'

'Not a word——'

Gosseyn woke up in darkness, and thought, 'I've really got to investigate the phenomenon of my extra brain.' He felt immediately puzzled that he should have had such a thought during the sleep hour.

After all, his idea—a sound one—had been to leave the problem until he reached Venus.

There was a stirring in the next bed. Leej turned on the light. 'I have a sense of continuous blur,' she said. 'What's the matter?'

He felt the activity then, within himself. His extra brain working as it had when an automatic process was reacting to a cue. It was a sensation only, stronger than his awareness of the beating of his heart or the expansion and contraction of his lungs, but as steady. But this time there was no cue.

'When did the blur start?' he asked.

'Just now.' Her tone was serious. 'I told you there'd be one at this time, but I expected it to be the usual kind, a momentary block.'

Gosseyn nodded. He had decided to sleep up to the moment of the blur. And here it was. He lay back, closed his eyes, and deliberately relaxed the muscles of the blood vessels of his brain, a simple suggestive process. It seemed the most normal method of breaking the flow.

Presently, he began to feel helpless. How did a person stop the life of his heart or lungs—or the interneuronic flow that had suddenly and without warning started up in his extra brain?

He sat up and looked at Leej, and parted his lips to confess his failure. And then he saw a strange thing. He saw her appear to get up from her bed, and go to the door fully dressed. And then she was sitting at a table where Gilbert Gosseyn also sat, and Captain Free. Her face flickered. He saw her again, farther away this time. Her face was vaguer, her eyes wide and staring, and she was saying something he didn't catch.

With a start he was back in the bedroom, and Leej was still there, sitting on the edge of the bed gazing at him in amazement. 'What's the matter?' she said. 'It's continuing. The blur is continuous.'

Gosseyn climbed to his feet and began to dress. 'Don't ask me anything just now,' he said. 'I may be leaving the ship, but I'll be back.'

It took a moment, then, to bring back into his mind one of the areas he had 'memorized' on Venus two and a half months before.

He could feel the faint, pulsing flow from his extra brain. Deliberately, he relaxed as he had on the bed. He felt the change in the memory; it altered visibly. He was aware of his brain following the ever changing pattern. There were little jumps and gaps. But each time the photographic image in his mind would come clear and sharp, though changed.

He closed his eyes. It made no difference; the change continued. He knew that three weeks had passed, a month, then the full elapsed time since his departure from Venus. And still his memory of the area remained on a twenty decimal level.

He opened his eyes, shook himself with a shuddering muscular movement, and consciously forced himself to become aware again of his surroundings.

It was easier the second time. And still easier the third time. At the eighth attempt the jumps and gaps were still there, but when he returned his attention to the bedroom, he realized that the uncontrolled phase of his discovery was over.

He no longer had the sensation of flow inside his extra brain.

Leej said, 'The blur has stopped!' She hesitated, then: 'But there's another one due almost immediately.'

Gosseyn nodded. 'I'm leaving now,' he said.

Without the slightest hesitation, he thought the old cue word for that memorized area.

Instantly, he was on Venus.

He found himself, as he had expected, behind the pillar he had used as a point of concealment on the day he arrived on Venus from Earth aboard the President Hardie.

Slowly, casually, he turned around to see if perhaps his arrival had been observed. There were two men in sight. One of them was walking slowly toward a partly visible exit. The other one looked directly at him.

Gosseyn walked toward him, and simultaneously the other man started forward, also. They met at a halfway mark, and the Venusian had a faint frown on his face.

'I'm afraid I'll have to ask you to remain here,' he said, 'until I can call a detective. I was watching the spot where you'—he hesitated—'materialized.'

Gosseyn said, 'I've often wondered what it would seem like to an observer.' He made no effort to conceal what had happened. 'Take me to your military experts at once.'

The man looked at him thoughtfully. 'You're a Null-A?'

'I'm a Null-A.'

'Gosseyn?'

'Gilbert Gosseyn.'

'My name is Armstrong,' said the man, and he held out his hand with a smile. 'We've been wondering what had happened to you——' He broke off. 'But let's hurry.'

He did not head for the door, as Gosseyn had expected. Gosseyn slowed, and commented. Armstrong explained, 'I beg your pardon,' he said, 'but if you want fast contact you'd better come along. Does the word Distorter mean anything to you?'

It did indeed. 'Just a few as yet,' Armstrong amplified. 'We've been building vast numbers, but for other purposes.'

'I know,' said Gosseyn. 'The ship I was on ran into some of the result of your labors.'

Armstrong stopped as they came to the Distorter. His gaze was intent, and his face slowly whitened. 'You mean,' he said, 'that our defenses are no good?'

Gosseyn hesitated. 'I don't know yet for certain,' he said, 'but I'm afraid they're not.'

They went through the Distorter blackness in silence. When Armstrong opened the cage door, they were at the end of a corridor. They walked rapidly, Gosseyn slightly behind, to where several men were sitting at desks poring over piles of documents. Gosseyn was not particularly surprised to discover that Armstrong was unacquainted with any of the men. Null-A Venusians were responsible individuals, and could go at will into factories where the most secret work was carried on.

Armstrong identified himself to the Venusian nearest the door, and then he introduced Gosseyn.

The man who had been sitting down stood up and held out his hand. 'Elliott is my name,' he said. He turned toward a nearby desk, and raised his voice. 'Hey, Don, call Dr. Kair. Gilbert Gosseyn is here.'

Gosseyn did not wait for Dr. Kair to arrive. What he had to say was too urgent for any delays. Swiftly he explained about the attack that Enro had ordered. That caused a sensation, but of a different kind than he expected.

Elliott said, 'So Crang succeeded. Good man.'

Gosseyn, on the point of continuing his account, stopped and stared at him. The light of understanding that broke over his mind then was dazzling for a moment. 'You mean,' he said, 'that Crang went to Gorgzid for the purpose of somehow persuading Enro to launch an attack on Venus——' He stopped, thinking of the still-born plot to assassinate Enro. Explained now. It had never been intended to succeed.

His brief exhilaration faded. Soberly, he told the group of Venusians about the Predictors. He finished with the utmost earnestness:

'I haven't actually tested my idea that Predictors can get through your cordons, but it seems logical to me that they can.'

There was a brief discussion, and then he was taken over to a videophone where a man had been pressing buttons and talking in a low tone to a roboperator. He looked up now. 'This is a hook-up,' he said. 'Tell your story again.'

This time Gosseyn went into greater detail. He described the Predictors, their culture, the predominantly thalamic natures of individuals he had met, and he went on to give a picture of the Follower and his estimate of what the shadow-shape was. He described Enro, the court situation of Gorgzid, and the position of Eldred Crang.

'I have just now discovered,' he went on, 'that Crang went out into space for the purpose of tricking Enro into sending the fleet to destroy Venus. I can tell you that he has accomplished this mission, but unfortunately he didn't know that Predictors existed. And so, the attack which is now about due, will be fought by the enemy under more favorable con-

152

ditions than anyone could have imagined who knew the nature of the defense forces which have been developed here on Venus and Earth.'

He finished quietly, 'I leave these thoughts with you.'

Elliott sat down in the chair he had vacated. He said earnestly, 'Send in your comments to Robot Receiver in the usual manner.'

Gosseyn learned upon inquiry that the usual method was for small groups of individuals to discuss the matter and come forth with as many reasonable suggestions as they could think of. Then one of their number joined in a similar discussion with other delegates like himself. The recommendations moved from level to level as each group of delegates in turn appointed delegates to still more broadly based groups. Thirty-seven minutes after Elliott asked for comments, Robot Receiver called him, and gave him four principle suggestions, in the order of priority:

(1) Draw a line on the star Gela, the base from which ships from the central mass of the galaxy would come, and concentrate all defenses along this line, so that the robot reaction to the appearance of warships would take place within two or three seconds.

Since the alternative was complete destruction, their hope must be that such a line defense, catching the enemy by surprise, would be able to capture the entire first fleet, Predictors or no.

(2) Have Leej bring in the destroyer, and see what a Predictor could do knowing the nature of the defense.

(3) Abandon the plan to operate secretly against Enro in favor of the League, and offer the League all available weapons in the full knowledge that the information might be misused and that a vindictive League peace would be hard to distinguish from an unconditional victory by Enro. In return, require the acceptance of Venusian emigrants.

(4) Abandon Venus.

Gosseyn returned to the destroyer, and the arrangements for the third attempt to break through the defenses were made. He would have liked to remain aboard, but Leej herself rejected his presence.

'One blur, and we'd be lost. Can you guarantee there won't be any?'

Gosseyn couldn't. He had control to some extent of his new ability to predict the future in so far as blurs were concerned.

'But suppose there's a blur while I'm on the ground?' he asked. 'It's in your range.'

'But you're not concerned,' Leej pointed out. 'All these things have their limitations, as I've told you.'

Her ability didn't look limited when at one minute to two the Y-381907 materialized three miles above the galactic base on Venus, and plunged off at an angle through the atmosphere. It was followed a moment later by a line of torpedoes. It darted like a shooting star in and out of the atmosphere of the planet, out of sight most of the time except for the videoplate picture they had of its spasmodic flight.

A dozen times atomic torpedoes exploded where it had been an instant before, but each time it was gone beyond the farthest reach of the explosion. At the end of an hour of fruitless chase, Central Robot Control ordered all robot units to discontinue the chase.

Gosseyn similarized himself aboard the destroyer, took the controls away from a weary Leej, and brought the ship down in the yards of the Military Industrial Branch.

He made no comment to any of the Venusians. The ship's break-through spoke for itself.

Predictors could get through robotic mind control defenses.

It was more than three hours later when they were having dinner that Leej suddenly stiffened. 'Ships!' she said.

For seconds she sat rigid, then slowly relaxed, 'It's all right,' she said, 'they're captured.'

It was nearly fifteen minutes before Robot Control confirmed that a hundred and eight warships, including two battleships and ten cruisers had been seized by a concentrated force of fifteen million mind-controlling robots.

Gosseyn accompanied a large boarding party that investigated one of the battleships. As swiftly as possible the officers and crew were removed. Meanwhile Null-A scientists studied the controls of the ship. In that department Gosseyn proved helpful. He lectured to a large group of prospective officers on the information he had gained as to the operation of the destroyer.

Afterwards, he made several attempts to utilize his new ability to foresee events, but the pictures jumped too much. Whatever relaxation he had achieved must still be incomplete. And he was too busy to more than discuss the problem with Dr. Kair, briefly.

'I think you're on the right track,' the psychiatrist said, 'but we'll have to go into that thoroughly when we have more time.'

Time became a watchword during the days that followed. It was discovered on the basis of interviews—Leej foresaw the discovery by twenty-four hours—that there were no Predictors with the fleet.

It made no difference to the Venusian plan. A survey of Venusian opinion indicated the general belief that there could be a second fleet within a few weeks, that it would have Predictors aboard, and that it might be captured despite the presence of the prescient men and women from Yalerta.

It made no difference. Venus would still have to be abandoned. Action groups of scientists worked in relays on a twenty-four-hour basis, setting up auxiliary Distorters in each of the captured ships, similar to those which had been used to send the Predictors from Yalerta to the fleet in the Sixth Decant.

The capture of the warships of the Greatest Empire made it possible to set up a chain of ships stretching to within eight hundred light-years of the nearest League base, which was just over nine thousand light-years distant. From that near point videophonic communication was established.

The arrangement with the League proved surprisingly easy. A planetary system that would shortly be attaining a daily peak production of twelve million robotic defense units of a new type made a surprising amount of sense to the rigid-minded Madrisol.

A fleet of twelve hundred League ships used the chain of captured warships to break toward Gela. The four planets of that sun were overwhelmed in four hours, and so further attacks by future Enro forces were cut off until he could recapture his base.

It made no difference. To the Venusians, the League members were almost as dangerous as Enro. So long as the Null-As were on one planet, they were at the mercy of people who might become afraid of them because they were different, people who would shortly be justifying the execution of millions of other neurotics like themselves, and who would also presently discover that the new weapons which they were being offered were not invincible.

The reaction to such a discovery could not be guessed. It might not mean anything. And then again, all the benefits derived from the defense units might be dismissed as unimportant if they failed to achieve that absolute perfection so dear to the hearts of the unintegrated.

The Null-As did not bring up the possible weaknesses of their offerings during the conferences which decided that two hundred to two hundred thousand individuals would be

155

allotted immediately to each of some ten thousand League planets.

Even as the details were discussed, the movement of families got under way.

Gosseyn watched the migration with mixed emotions. He did not doubt the necessity of it, but having made the concession, logic ended and feeling began.

Venus abandoned. It was hard to believe that two hundred million people would be scattered to the far distances of the galaxy. He did not doubt that in scattering there would be collective safety. Individuals might meet with disaster as still more planets were destroyed in the war of wars. It was possible, though only vaguely so, that some would be harmed on planets here and there. But that would be the exception and not the rule. They were too few to be considered dangerous, and each Null-A would swiftly size up the local situation and act accordingly.

Everywhere now there would be Null-A men and women at the full height of their integrated strength, never again to be cut off in one group on an isolated star system. Gosseyn selected several groups going to comparatively nearby planets, and went with them through the Distorters, and saw them safely to their destinations.

In each case the planets where they arrived were democratically governed. They were absorbed into the population masses that, for the most part, didn't even know they existed.

Gosseyn could only follow groups at random. More than a hundred thousand planets were receiving these very special refugees, and it would have taken a thousand lifetimes to follow them all. A world was being evacuated except for a small core of one million who would remain behind. The role of those who stayed was to act as a nucleus for the billions on Earth who knew nothing of what had happened. For them the Null-A training system would carry on as if there had been no migration.

The rivers of Null-A travelers flowing toward the Distorter transmitters became a stream, then a trickle. Before the last of the migrants were finally gone, Gosseyn went to New Chicago where a captured battleship, renamed the *Venus*, was being fitted out to take him, Leej, Captain Free and a crew of Null-A technical experts into space.

He entered a virtually deserted city. Only the factories, which were not visible, and the Military Center were flamboyantly active. Elliott accompanied Gosseyn into the ship, and gave him the latest available information.

'We haven't heard anything from the battle, but then our

156

units are probably just going into action.' He smiled, and shook his head. 'I doubt if anybody will bother to give us the details of what happens. Our influence is waning steadily. The attitude toward us is a mixture of tolerance and impatience. From one hand we get a pat on the shoulder for having invented weapons which, for the most part, are regarded as decisive, though they aren't. From the other hand we get a shove and an admonition to remember that we are now just a tiny, unimportant people, and that we must leave the details in the hands of those who are the experts in galactic affairs.'

He paused, amused but grave.

'Whether they know it or not,' he said, 'almost every Null-A will try to affect the ending of the war. Naturally, the direction we want events to take are peaceful rather than warlike. It may not show immediately, but we don't want the galaxy divided into two groups that violently hate each other.'

Gosseyn nodded. The galactic leaders had yet to discover—though actually they might never do so; the process would be so subtle—that what one Null-A like Eldred Crang had done, would shortly be multiplied by two hundred million. Thought of Eldred Crang reminded Gosseyn of a question he had been intending to ask for many days.

'Who developed your new robot devices?'

'The Institute of General Semantics, under the direction of the late Lavoisseur.'

'I see.' Gosseyn was silent for a moment, thinking out his next question. He said finally, 'Who directed your attention to the particular development that you've used so successfully?'

'Crang,' said Elliott. 'Lavoisseur and he were very good friends.'

Gosseyn had his answer. He changed the subject. 'When do we leave?' he asked.

'Tomorrow morning.'

'Good.'

The news brought a sense of positive excitement. For weeks he had been almost too busy to think, and yet he had never quite forgotten that such individuals as the Follower and Enro were still forces to be reckoned with.

And there was the even greater problem of the being who had similarized his mind into the nervous system of Ashargin.

Many vital things remained to be done.

XVIII

Null-Abstracts

For the sake of sanity, remember: 'The map is not the territory, the word is not the thing it describes.' Wherever the map is confused with the territory, a 'semantic disturbance' is set up in the organism. The disturbance continues until the limitation of the map is recognized.

THE following morning the powerful battleship sped out through the interstellar darkness. In addition to its all Null-A crew, it was loaded with a hundred thousand robotic mind control units.

They stopped the ship at Dr. Kair's request after the first break.

'We've been studying you at odd intervals,' he told Gosseyn, 'though you were about as elusive as anyone could be. But still, we got something.'

He brought some photographs out of his brief case, and handed them around. 'This picture of the extra brain was taken a week ago.'

The area glowed with millions of fine interlacing lines. 'It's alive with excitation,' Dr. Kair said. 'When you consider that at one time its only contact with the rest of your body and brain tissue appeared to be the blood vessels that supply it and the nerve connections that affect the blood stream directly—when you consider that, then the present condition of the extra brain is, by comparison, one of enormous activity.'

He broke off. 'Now,' he said, 'about further training. My colleagues and I have been thinking about what you told us, and we have a suggestion to make.'

Gosseyn interrupted. 'First, a question.'

He hesitated. What he had to say was in a way irrelevant. And yet, it had been pressing on his mind ever since his talk the day before with Elliott.

'Who,' he asked, 'gave the direction to the training I received under Thorson?'

Dr. Kair frowned. 'Oh, we all made suggestions but in my opinion the most important contribution was made by Eldred Crang.'

158

Crang again! Eldred Crang, who knew how to train extra brains; who had transmitted messages from Lavoisseur before the death of that earlier, older Gosseyn body—the problem of Crang was thus suddenly and intricately again to the fore.

Briefly, objectively, he outlined the cases of Crang to the group. When he had finished, Dr. Kair shook his head.

'Crang came to me for an examination just before he left Venus. He was wondering if the strain was telling on him. I can tell you he is a normal Null-A without any special faculties, though his reflexes and integration were on a level that I have seen only once or twice before in my entire career as a psychiatrist.'

Gosseyn said, 'He definitely had no extra brain?'

'Definitely not.'

'I see,' said Gosseyn.

It was another door closing. Somehow, he had hoped that Eldred Crang would be the player who had similarized his mind into the body of Ashargin. It wasn't eliminated from the picture but a different explanation seemed to be required.

'There's a point here,' said the woman psychiatrist, 'that we discussed once before, but which Mr. Gosseyn may not have heard about. If Lavoisseur gave Crang his knowledge of how to train extra brains, and yet now it turns out that the method is not a very good one, are we to believe that Lavoisseur-Gosseyn bodies were only trained in what now seems to be an inefficient method?' She finished quietly, 'The death of Lavoisseur seems to indicate that he had no ability at pre-vision, and yet already you are at the edge of that and other abilities.'

Dr. Kair said, 'We can go into those details later. Right now I'd like Gosseyn to try an experiment.'

When he had explained what he wanted, Gosseyn said, 'But that's nineteen thousand light-years away.'

'Try it,' urged the psychiatrist.

Gosseyn hesitated, and then concentrated on one of his memorized areas in the control room of Leej's skytrailer. He swayed as with vertigo. Startled, he fought a sense of nausea. He looked at the others in amazement. 'That must have been a similarity of just under twenty decimals. I think I can make it if I try again.'

'Try,' said Dr. Kair.

'What'll I do if I get there?'

'Look the situation over. We'll follow you as far as the nearby base.'

Gosseyn nodded. This time he closed his eyes. The changing picture of the memorized area came sharp and clear.

When he opened his eyes, he was on the skytrailer.

He did not move immediately from the area of his arrival, but stood gathering impressions. There was a quiet, neural flow from the near reaches of the ship. The servants, he decided, were still on duty.

He walked forward, and looked out. They were over open countryside. Below was a level plain. Far to his right he caught the shimmer of water. As he watched, and the ship moved on, he lost sight of the sea. That gave him an idea.

He bent over the controls, and straightened again almost immediately as he saw how they were set. The trailer was still following the circular route that he had set for it just before he made his successful effort to seize the destroyer.

He made no attempt to touch the controls or alter them. The ship could have been tampered with in spite of its appearance of being exactly as he had left it.

He probed for magnetic current flow, but found nothing unusual. He relaxed his mind, and tried to see what was going to happen. But the only picture of the control room that he could get showed no one in it.

That brought up the question, 'Where am I going next?'

Back to the battleship? It would be a waste of time. He had an impulse to know how long it had taken him to come to Yalerta, but that was something he could check on later.

Great events were transpiring. Men and women for whose safety he felt partially responsible were still in danger areas: Crang, Patricia, Nirene, Ashargin. . . .

A dictator must be overthrown, a great war machine brought to a halt by any possible means.

Abruptly, he made his decision.

He arrived at the Follower's Retreat at his memorized area just outside the door of the power house. He reached the upper floor without incident, and paused to ask a man the way to the Follower's apartment.

'I'm here for an appointment,' he explained, 'and I must hurry.'

The servant was sympathetic. 'You came in the wrong way,' he said, 'but if you will follow that side corridor you'll come to a large anteroom. They'll tell you there where to go next.'

Gosseyn doubted if anyone would tell him what he wanted to know. But he came presently to a room that was not as large as he had expected, and so ordinary that he stared at it, wondering if he had come to the right place.

A number of people sat in lounges, and directly across from him was a little wooden fence inside which were eight desks. A man sat at each desk, apparently doing clerical work.

Beyond the desks was a glass inclosed office with one large desk in it.

As he passed through the gate, and into the little fenced area, several of the clerks rose up from their chairs in a half protest. Gosseyn ignored them. He was shifting the wire in the control room of the skytrailer again, and he wanted to get inside the glass office before letting Yanar become aware of him.

He opened the door, and he was closing it behind him when the Predictor became aware of him. The man looked up with a start.

There was another door beyond Yanar, and Gosseyn headed straight for it. With a jump, Yanar was on his feet and barring his way. He was defiant.

'You'll have to kill me before you can go in there.'

Gosseyn stopped. He had already penetrated with his extra brain the room beyond the door. No impulse of life came. That was not final proof that it was unoccupied. But his sense of urgency dimmed considerably.

He frowned at Yanar. He had no intention of killing the man, particularly when he had so many other ways at his disposal of dealing with the Predictor. Besides, he was curious. Several questions had bothered him for some time. He said:

'You were aboard Leej's ship as an agent of the Follower?'

'Naturally,' Yanar shrugged.

'I suppose you mean by that, how else would the ship have been waiting for us?'

Yanar nodded warily. His eyes were watchful.

'But why allow any means of escape?'

'The Follower considered you too dangerous to be left here. You might have wrecked his Retreat.'

'Then why bring me to Yalerta?'

'He wanted you where Predictors could keep track of your movements.'

'But that didn't work?'

'You're right. That *didn't* work.'

Gosseyn paused at that point. There was an implication in the answers that startled him.

Once more now, more sternly, he stared at the Predictor. There were several other questions he had in mind, particularly about Leej. But actually they didn't matter. She had proved herself to his present satisfaction, and the details could wait.

That settled it. He similarized Yanar into the prison cell which Leej and Jurig and he had occupied weeks ago.

Then he opened the door and stepped into the room he

believed to be the Follower's private office.

As he had sensed, the place was unoccupied.

Curiously, Gosseyn looked around him. An enormous desk faced the door. There were built-in filing cabinets against the wall to the left, and an intricate system—it looked intricate and somewhat different—of Distorter mechanisms and controls to his right.

Feeling both relieved and disappointed, Gosseyn considered his next move. Yanar was out of the way. Not that that meant much one way or the other. The man was a nuisance, but not a danger.

Gosseyn headed for the filing cabinets. They were all magnetically locked, but it was the work of a moment to open each circuit with his extra brain. Drawer after drawer slid outward at his touch. The files were of the plastic variety, similar to the palace directory which Nirene had shown him when he was in Ashargin's body.

The equivalent of scores of pages of print were impressed on successive layers of molecules. Each 'page' showed up in turn as the index slide at the edge was manipulated.

Gosseyn searched for and found a plate with his own name on it. There were four printed pages in the file. The account was very objective, and for the most part detailed what had been done in connection with him. The first item read.

'Transferred name from GE-4408C.' It seemed to indicate another file elsewhere. There followed a reference to his training under Thorson with the notation, 'Have been unable to find any of the individuals who participated in the training, and discovered it too late to prevent it.'

There were several references to Janasen, then a description of the Distorter relay system that had been used to transport Gosseyn from Janasen's apartment on Venus. 'Had this device built by the same people who made F. for me, so that it would actually seem to be an ordinary cooking table.' That was printed, but there was a notation in longhand on the margin: 'Very cunning.'

Gosseyn read the four pages with a sense of disappointment. He had expected to find an overtone of reference that would fill in his own picture of what had happened between the Follower and himself. But the account was too brief and too matter-of-fact. At the bottom of the fourth page was a note: 'See Ashargin.'

Gosseyn secured Ashargin's file. That was longer. In the early pages the writer dealt principally with Ashargin's life from the time he arrived at the Temple of the Sleeping God. It was not until the last page that there was any cross reference to Ashargin's 'file'. The comment was brief. 'Under lie detector questioning by Enro, Ashargin made several references to Gilbert Gosseyn.' Besides the item, in longhand, was written: 'Investigate.'

The final paragraph on Ashargin said:

'The forced marriage of the Prince and Princess Ashargin seems to have developed into a relationship of fact as well as name. The change in this man calls for an urgent inquiry, although Enro is coming around to the idea that a co-operative Ashargin will be valuable even after the war. The Predictors find his conduct exemplary during the next three weeks.'

There was no indication as to when the three weeks had begun, no mention of the trip to Venus on which Gosseyn-Ashargin had started, nor any definite statement that he was back at the palace.

Gosseyn put the file back in its drawer, and continued his examination of the room. He found a narrow door skillfully built into the Distorter panels. It led into a tiny bedroom that contained one piece of furniture, a neatly made up bed.

There was no clothes closet, but there was a very small bathroom with toilet and wash basin. A dozen towels hung on a plain metal towel rack.

The Follower, if this was indeed his inner sanctum, did not coddle himself.

It took most of the day to explore the Retreat. The building had no unusual features. There were servants' quarters, several entire sections devoted to a busy clerical staff, the power plant in the basement, and a wing made up of prison cells.

The clerks and power attendants lived in cottages along the coast line farthest from the main building. Yanar and five other Predictors had apartments on one corridor. There was a hangar in the rear of the structure large enough to house a dozen skytrailers. When Gosseyn looked into it, there were seven large machines and three small planes. The latter were of the type that had attacked him during his escape from the prison.

No one interfered with him. He moved at will through the buildings and around the island. Not a single person seemed to have the authority or the inclination to bother him. Such a situation had probably never existed before on the island, and apparently they were all waiting for the Follower to come to do something about it.

Gosseyn waited also, not without some doubts, but with a strong determination not to depart. He had a will to action, a sense that events were moving to a head much faster than his almost passive existence at the Retreat indicated.

163

His plans were made, and it was only a matter of waiting till the battleship arrived.

He slept the first night in the little bedroom adjoining the Follower's office. He slept peacefully with his extra brain cued to respond to any operation of the Distorter equipment. He had not yet established that the Follower manipulated his curious shadow-shape by means of Distorter relays, but the available evidence pointed in that direction.

And he knew just what he intended to do to prove or disprove the theory.

The next morning he similarized to Leej's skytrailer, ate breakfast with three waitresses hovering around him, anxious to do his slightest bidding. They seemed puzzled by his politeness. Gosseyn didn't have time to train them in self-respect. He finished his meal and set to work.

First, he laboriously rolled up the drawing room rug. And then he began to cut free the metal floor plates as near as he could remember to the point where the Follower had materialized on the ship.

He found the Distorter within inches of where he expected it to be.

That was fairly convincing. But he had another verification in the cell where he had been imprisoned when he first arrived on Yalerta. A wild-eyed Yanar watched him through the bars as he broke open the seemingly solid metal cot, and there, also, found a Distorter.

Surely, the picture was becoming clearer, sharper. And the crises must be near.

The second night passed as uneventfully as the first. Gosseyn spent the third day going through the files. There were two pages on Secoh that interested him, because the information in them had not been a part of Ashargin's memory. The forty-seven pages on Enro were divided into sections, but they merely confirmed what he had already heard, with many added details. Madrisol was listed as a dangerous and ambitious man. Grand Admirel Paleol was depicted as a killer. 'An implacable character,' the Follower had written, which was quite a tribute from a person who had some fairly implacable characteristics himself.

He investigated only names that he knew, and a few cross references. It would take a staff of experts to go through the tens of thousands of files and make a comprehensive report.

On the fourth day he left the files alone, and worked out a plan for himself and the battleship to follow. It was uneconomical in terms of time wasted for the ship to trail him over the galaxy, when his purpose, as well as the purpose of

Elliott and the others, was to get through to Gorgzid.

He wrote, 'Enro has safeguarded his home planet by a system of doling out matrixes for the Gorgzid base under such a strict system that it is highly improbable that any could be secured by normal methods.

'But a man with an extra brain should be able to secure a matrix. . . .'

He reached that early point in his summing up when the long expected relay closed in his brain, and he knew that the battleship had similarized to a break halt near the base eleven hundred light-years away.

Gosseyn made the jump back to the *Venus* instantly.

'You must have similarized yourself from the ship to Yalerta in a little over an hour,' Dr. Kair estimated.

They couldn't figure it out exactly. But the speed was so much greater, the margin of error so very small compared to the ninety-odd hours the battleship had required for the journey, that the time involved scarcely mattered.

One hour plus. Awed, he walked a hundred feet to the towering transparent dome of the battleship's control room. He was not exactly a man who had to have the vastness of space explained to him, and that made the new potential of his extra brain seem even more impressive.

The blackness pressed against the glass. He had no particular sense of distance with the stars that he could see. They were tiny bright points a few hundred yards away. That was the illusion. Nearness. And, now, for him they were near. In five and a half hours he could similarize himself across the hundred thousand light-year span of this spinning galaxy of two hundred thousand million suns—if he had a memorized area to which he could go.

Elliott came up beside him. He held out a matrix which Gosseyn took.

'I'd better be going,' he said. 'I won't feel right until those filing cabinets are aboard the *Venus*.'

He checked to make sure the matrix was in the sheath, and then similarized himself to the Follower's office.

He took the matrix out of its protective sheath, and carefully laid it on the desk. It would be too bad if the battleship actually similarized to the matrix, but Leej was aboard to make sure that the ship's break toward Yalerta fell short of a complete jump.

As he had expected, the *Venus* arrived successfully above the island just under three hours later. Study units were landed, and Gosseyn went aboard for a conference.

To his surprise, Dr. Kair planned no experiments and no training.

'We're going to use a work therapy,' the psychiatrist explained. 'You will train yourself by doing.'

He amplified briefly. 'Frankly, Gosseyn, training would take time, and you're doing all right. The advantage that you appear to have had over Lavoisseur is that you found out that there were other things that could be done, and you tried to do them. It seems certain that he knew nothing of the Predictors, or he would have mentioned them to Crang. Accordingly, he never had any reason to believe that he could train himself to foresee the future.'

Gosseyn said, 'That means I go back immediately and go through the Distorter in the Follower's office.'

There was one other thing he had to do, and he did it the moment he was down in the Retreat again. He similarized Yanar to his one memorized area on the island of Crest.

That humane duty performed, he joined the group investigating the Follower's private Distorter system. Already the results were interesting.

'That is the most advanced setup we've seen to date,' one of the Null-As told him. 'More intricate. Some of the printed circuits inside that paneling will take time to trace.'

They had already decided to work on the assumption that the Follower's Distorters operated on a better than twenty decimal similarity basis.

'So we're going to remain on Yalerta for a while, and give you a chance to come back. Besides, we have to wait for that battleship of Enro's which you mentioned. It's due any day now.'

Gosseyn agreed that the final purpose at least was important. It was vital that no more Predictors be sent to Enro's fleet.

He was not so sure about waiting for his return. The action he was about to take could become involved, and might require a prolonged effort. Still, if the Distorter was really fast, only the journey through it would take time. He could now be sure of similarizing himself back to the ship with minimum time error, and then back again to wherever he had been.

It was the opinion of all that there was no time to waste, and that a thorough investigation of the instruments would take quite a while.

Once again Gosseyn agreed. His own examination had shown him that the paneling was divided into two sections. In one division were three Distorters, the controls of which could be adjusted to any patterns.

The second division had in it only one instrument. It had as its control a single protruding tube, which could be pulled or pushed by a tiny lever. In the past he had discovered that such single control Distorters were similarizable to any one destination to which they had a permanent matrix. He hoped that this one was tuned to the Follower's real headquarters in the galaxy.

He pulled the lever without hesitation.

Gosseyn did not move immediately after the blackness ended. He was in a large, book-lined room. Through a half open door he could see the edge of a bed.

He let his extra brain become aware of the life in the building. There was a great deal, but it seemed on a quiet and peaceful level. As far as he was able to make out, there was no one in the adjoining room.

His gaze was moving around swiftly now. He saw that the Distorter to which he had been similarized was one of two set at right angles to each other in a corner.

That seemed to complete the general picture.

He memorized a floor area at his feet, then walked over and picked one of the books out of the bookcase. It was printed in the Gorgzid language.

That gave him a moment of exhilaration, but as he was turning to the flyleaf he thought: *It doesn't necessarily mean I'm on Gorgzid. Many people in the Greatest Empire will have books printed in the language of the capital planet.*

At that instant his thought poised. He stared down at the name in the flyleaf, shook his head, and put the book back on the shelf.

But five other volumes he selected at random had the same name in them.

It was the name of Eldred Crang.

Gosseyn walked slowly to the bedroom door. He was puzzled, but not very worried. As he moved across the bedroom, he sensed the presence of people in the room beyond. Cautiously, he opened the door a crack. A corridor. He opened the door wider, slipped through and closed it behind him.

If necessary, he could make a retreat at the speed of similarity. But he wasn't sure yet whether he was going to retreat.

He reached the end of the corridor and stopped. From where he stood he could just see the back of somebody who looked like Patricia Hardie. She spoke then, and the identification was complete.

Her words had no importance, nor had the answer Crang

gave her. What mattered about them was that here they were, and in the library adjoining their bedroom was a Distorter that connected with the Follower's Retreat on Yalerta.

It was a bewildering discovery, and Gosseyn decided against confronting the couple until he had discussed the matter with Elliott and the others.

But he was not yet ready to leave Gorgzid. He returned to the library, and stood contemplating the second Distorter. Like the one which he had already used in the Retreat, it was a single control affair.

It seemed logical to find out where it would take him. He pressed the lever.

He emerged in what seemed to be a small storeroom. There were piles of metal cases in one corner, and several shelves. A single, closed door seemed the only normal entrance.

There was no Distorter except the one through which he had come.

Swiftly, Gosseyn memorized a floor area, and then tried the door. It opened out upon a rather bare office. A desk, two chairs and a rug completed the picture.

Beyond the desk was another door.

Gosseyn paused on his way across the room and tried the drawers of the desk. They were locked with key locks, and could not be opened by an extra brain without the use of power.

The office door opened onto a corridor about ten feet long, at the end of which was another door. Gosseyn pushed it wide without hesitation, stepped through, and stopped.

The large chamber that spread before him hummed with faint undercurrents of sound. A narrow buttress extended twenty feet from one wall. It was so skillfully integrated that it seemed to be a projection of the wall itself, a prolonged curving out instead of the flat surface which the wall normally should have been.

The nearer curve of the jutting wall was translucent, and glowed with an all-pervading light. Tiny stairways led from the floor to the top of the crypt of the Sleeping God of Gorgzid.

The effect of it upon him was different than when he had seen it through the eyes of Ashargin. Now, with his extra brain, he sensed the pulsing currents of energy that operated the invisible machines. Now, there came a faint sense of life force, a human neural flow, slight, steady, and with scarcely any variation in intensity.

Gosseyn climbed the steps without benefit of the Ceremony of the Beholding, and looked down at the Sleeping God of

168

Gorgzid. His examination of the face and of the crypt was different from that of Ashargin, sharper, more alert. He saw things to which the duller senses of the prince had been blind.

The 'coffin' was a structure of many sections. The body was held by a series of tiny, viselike arms and hands. He recognized their purpose. They were designed to exercise the muscles. If the Sleeping God ever wakened from his long sleep, he would not find himself stiff and weak, as Gilbert Gosseyn had after a month of being unconscious on the destroyer Y-381907.

The sleeper's skin was healthy. His body looked firm and strong. Whoever had planned his diet had had more equipment than had been available to Leej on the destroyer.

Gosseyn came down the steps, and examined the base of the coffin. As he had expected, the stairs were movable, and the base panels could slide back.

He slid them out of the way, and stood looking down at a machine.

Almost immediately he realized that he had come to the end of a trail. On all his journeyings, on the mightiest ships of the Greatest Empire, he had never seen a machine quite like this one.

After he had gazed at it a while, he shook his head in wonder. The circuits were printed in intricate designs, but he was able to identify more than a dozen purposes.

He recognized a Distorter circuit, a lie detector, a robot relay, and other more simple devices. But that electronic brain had no less than one hundred and forty-seven main circuits, each one of which was a unit in depth, the surface and interior of which was interlaid with many thousands of smaller circuits.

Even the almost human robot weapons which Lavoisseur had turned over to the Venusians had only twenty-nine main sections.

Intent now, Gosseyn studied the artificial brain. On that closer examination, several of the wires seemed burned out. The discovery alerted him, and in quick succession he saw several other damaged segments. How so well-built and protected an instrument could have been damaged was not easy to understand, but the end result was unmistakable.

It would take an immense amount of skill to repair the machinery and awaken the Sleeping God.

It would probably not be his job. He was in the front line, and not in the technical department. It was time he went back to the battleship.

He similarized himself, and arrived on the *Venus* to hear the alarm bells ringing.

Elliott explained that the battle was over. 'When our robots

169

acted, I don't think they even knew what hit them. We captured the entire personnel.'

It was a very satisfying victory, for more reasons than one. The captured battleship was the one Enro had sent more than a month before to replace the Y-381907. It had come to start a new flow of Predictors to the fleet of the Greatest Empire. It would take time for another ship to replace it. That was one result.

The second result, it seemed to Gosseyn, was the more important when properly considered. The *Venus* was free to follow him to Gorgzid.

No Null-A had any explanation to offer for the mystery of Eldred Crang. Elliott said: 'We can only assume that he did not know about the Predictors, and therefore made no statements on a concrete predictable level. Your discovery seems to indicate that Crang is more aware of what is going on than we suspected.'

A short time later Gosseyn was given another matrix, and Elliott told him, 'We'll leave at once, and we'll see you in about three days.'

Gosseyn nodded. He intended to explore the Temple of the Sleeping God in more detail. 'I want to see if the atomic drive is still in working order. Maybe I can take the whole temple out to space.' He grinned. 'They might take that as an omen that the god disapproves of their aggression.'

He finished more seriously. 'Except for that, I'll lie pretty low until you people arrive.'

Before leaving the ship, he sought out Dr. Kair. The psychiatrist motioned him to a chair, but Gosseyn rejected the offer. He stood frowning, then said:

'Doctor, there's something at the end of this trail we're following that's going to be different from anything we expected. I've had some hazy pictures——' He paused, then: 'Twice, now, my mind has been similarized into the body of Prince Ashargin. On the surface it looks as if someone was helpfully giving me a look at the larger scene of events, and I'm almost willing to accept that as the motive.'

'But why through Ashargin's eyes? Why is he necessary?'

'You see, it comes down to this: If it's possible to put my mind into other people's bodies, why wasn't it put into the body of Enro? With Enro under my control, I think I could end the war like that.'

He snapped his fingers.

'The logic of that seems so inescapable that I can only conclude we are looking at the picture from the wrong angle.

170

There must be another answer, possibly an answer bigger than the war itself.

He stood frowning, then held out his hand. Dr. Kair shook it silently. Gosseyn stepped away, and, still holding on to the matrix, similarized himself to the little storeroom in the Temple of the Sleeping God on Gorgzid.

Even as he came out of the blackness, he realized with a thalamic sense of frustration that he was going to wake up in the body of the Prince Ashargin—for the third time in as many months.

XIX

Null-Abstracts

For the sake of sanity, remember: First is the event, the initial stimulus; second is the nervous impact of the event, via the senses; third is the emotional reaction based on the past experience of the individual; fourth comes the verbal reaction. Most individuals identify the first and fourth steps, and are not aware that the second and third exist.

'IT'S dinner time,' said Nirene.

Gosseyn-Ashargin climbed to his feet, and they walked in silence along the corridor. Her face was thoughtful, and when she tucked her fingers lightly under his arm, it looked like an automatic gesture. But the very unconscious nature of it emphasized for Gosseyn what he had already realized from Ashargin's memory, that this marriage had indeed developed into an affectionate relationship.

'I'm not so sure,' said Nirene, 'that the privilege of being at the royal dinner table is one that I enjoy. I can't decide whether I've been promoted or not.'

Gosseyn-Ashargin did not reply. He was thinking of the body of Gilbert Gosseyn lying in the storeroom in the Temple of the Sleeping God. At any moment, Secoh might walk in and find it.

Beside that fact, the private life of the Prince and Princess Ashargin faded into insignificance.

Neither Enro nor Secoh were present for dinner, which did not make Gosseyn feel any better. He had a vision of the

Lord Guardian deciding to spend this night of all nights at the Temple. There was no question of what he himself must do, but the details occupied his attention for most of the meal.

So it was with a sense of something wrong that he looked up suddenly and saw that the two women were very pale. Patricia was saying:

'. . . I didn't think I'd feel this way, but the possibility of a complete League victory makes me almost as uneasy as I used to be when I thought of my brother winning unconditionally.'

Nirene said: 'The terrible thing about being pulled into a war against your will is that, no matter how little you had to do with it, you discover finally that your own fate is bound up with the fortunes of your side.'

Briefly, Gosseyn was drawn aside from his urgent private purposes. He knew what they were thinking, and there must have been a real reverse to shock them so violently.

Defeat would be a personal disaster for everyone in the Greatest Empire. There would be humiliation, armies of occupation, a ruthless search for war criminals, vengefulness that would show little or no comprehension of the possible effects on the nervous systems of both victors and vanquished.

He parted his lips to speak, and then closed them again, struck by a sudden thought. *If the situation was really serious, then this might be the explanation for the dictator's absence from dinner.*

Before he could say anything, he had confirmation. Patricia said:

'Enro's with the fleet. They lost four divisions without a trace, and the battle of the Sixth Decant is stopped while they plan counter measures.'

'And where is Secoh?' Gosseyn asked.

Nobody knew, but Crang gave him a sharp questioning look. All he said, however, was: 'It's important, of course, that there be no complete victory. Unconditional surrender is an illusion.'

Gosseyn did not hesitate. They might as well know the facts. Briefly, succinctly, without giving his source of information, or describing the robotic weapons and their effect, he told them what the possible result would be in the war.

He finished: 'The sooner Enro realizes that he's got a long war of attrition on his hands, and makes or accepts overtures of peace, the more quickly he'll insure that no accident of fate brings about complete ruin.'

He stood up. 'If Enro comes back before I do, tell him I want to see him.'

He excused himself, and walked rapidly out of the room.

Arriving in the outer corridor, he headed for the roof. Several planes were parked near the stairway from which he emerged. As he seated himself in the front seat of the nearest one, the plane's electronic brain spoke to him through a loud-speaker.

'Where to?'

'Over the mountain,' said Gosseyn, 'I'll tell you where to go from there.'

They took off swiftly over the city. To the impatient Gosseyn, it seemed as if the spread of lights below would never end. Finally, however, the blackness began, and soon it was general except for vagrant spots of light that dotted the horizon.

Once more the roboplane spoke. 'We're over the mountains. Where to?'

Gosseyn looked down. He could see nothing. The sky was cloud-filled, the night like pitch.

'I want you to land on a little road about half a mile this side of the Temple of the Sleeping God,' he ordered.

He described it in detail, estimating the distance of various clumps of trees, and picturing the curving of the road on the basis of Ashargin's sharp memory of the scene.

The flight continued in silence. They came down in darkness, and bumped to a stop.

Gosseyn's parting admonition was: 'Come back every hour.'

He stepped down onto the road, walked a few feet, and stopped. He waited then for the plane to make its almost silent take off—a rush of air and a slight hiss of power—and then he started off along the road.

The night was hot and still. He met no one, but that was expected. This was a road that Ashargin knew of old. A thousand and more nights like this he had tramped from the potato fields back to his cot in one of the work huts.

He reached the even deeper shadows of the temple itself and paused again. For a long minute he listened for sounds that would indicate activity.

There was no sound.

Boldly, yet with care, he pushed open the metal door, and started down the same metal stairway which had been his route during the Parade of the Beholding.

He reached the door of the inner chamber without incident, and to his surprise it was unlocked. The surprise lasted only a few moments. He had brought along an instrument for picking locks, but it was just as well not to have to make Ashargin's poorly coordinated fingers cope with it.

He slipped inside, and closed the door softly behind him.

173

The now familiar scene of the crypt spread before him. Swiftly, he walked to the small corridor that led to the private office of the Lord Guardian.

At that door he paused again and listened. Silence. Safely inside, he headed for the storeroom door. He held his breath as he peered into the dim interior, and sighed with relief as he saw the body lying on the floor.

He was in time. But the problem now was to get the unconscious body to safety.

First, he hid the matrix under a metal box on an upper shelf. Then, quickly, he knelt beside the still form, and listened for life in it. He heard the heartbeat, and felt the pulse, and felt the warmth of the slow, measured breathing of the unconscious Gosseyn. And it was one of the strangest experiences of his existence to be there watching over his own body.

He climbed to his feet, bent down, and slipped his hands under the armpits. He drew a deep breath, and jerked. The limp body moved about three inches.

He had expected difficulty in moving the body, but not that much. It seemed to him that if he could get it started that would be the important thing. He tried again, and this time he kept going. But his muscles began to ache as he crossed the little den, and he took his first rest at the door.

His second rest, somewhat longer, came at the end of the short corridor. When he reached the middle of the chamber of the crypt nearly twenty minutes later, he was so worn out that he felt dizzy.

He had already decided on the only possible place in the temple where he could hide the heavy body. Now, he began to wonder if he would have the strength to put it there.

He climbed the steps to the top of the crypt. From that vantage point, he studied the mechanism of the covering; not the transparent plates near the head of the sleeper, but the translucent sections farther along the twenty-foot length of the coffin.

They slid back. It was as simple as that. They slid back, and revealed straps and tubes and holding devices for three more bodies. Two of them were on a slightly smaller scale than the other. At the sight, understanding dawned on Gosseyn. The smaller ones were for women.

This spaceship was designed to take two women and two men across the miles of interstellar space and the years of time between star systems that had not had similarity travel established between them.

He wasted no time pondering the implications, but bent his muscles to the enormous task of dragging the Gosseyn body up the steps and into the crypt.

How long it required he had no idea. Again and again he rested. A dozen times it seemed to him that Ashargin was being driven beyond all the resources of his thin physique. But at last he had the body tied in place. Tied because there must be a mechanism for disposing of dead bodies. Parts of this machine were so faulty that they probably had no operating function that would tell them when a body was alive. That might explain why the women and one of the men had not been replaced.

It was as well to take precautions.

He slid the panel back in place, moved the steps back into position, and he was standing on top of them making sure that there was no sign that they had been tampered with, when he heard a sound from the direction of the storeroom. He turned, tense.

Eldred Crang came in.

The Null-A detective stopped short, and put one finger to his lips in a warning fashion. He came forward swiftly, pushed the other stairway toward the rear of the crypt, and climbed up it.

With a gesture he slid back the panels where Gosseyn-Ashargin had put the Gosseyn body. For several seconds he gazed down at the body, and then he pulled the panels shut, climbed to the floor, and pulled the stairway back where it had been.

Ashargin meanwhile had returned to the floor also. Crang took his arm.

'Sorry,' he said in a low voice, 'that I didn't get a chance to help you cart it up there. But I wasn't in my apartment when the machine first sent a warning to me. I came as soon as I could to make sure'—he smiled—'that you hid it where it ought to go.'

'But now, quick, come along.'

Gosseyn followed him without a word. There was not a Null-A aboard the *Venus* who had questioned Crang's motives, and he was not going to start now. His mind bubbled with questions, but he was prepared to accept the implications of Crang's words that there was need for haste.

Through the little office and into the storeroom they hurried. Crang stepped aside when they came to the Distorter. 'You first,' he said.

They emerged in Crang's library. Crang started forward as urgently as ever, and then, halfway across the floor, he paused and turned. He indicated the Distorter through which Gosseyn had originally come from Yalerta.

'Where does that lead?' he asked.

When Gosseyn told him, he nodded. 'I thought it was something like that. But I could never be sure. Going through from here depends upon the operation of remote controls, which I've never been able to locate.'

Crang asking a question about something he didn't know was a new experience for Gosseyn. Before Gosseyn could ask any questions of his own, Crang said:

'Enro has been away for eight days, but he's due back any minute. That's according to word we received shortly after dinner. So go to your room as fast as you can'—he hesitated, evidently considering his next words—'and sleep,' he finished finally. 'But quick now.'

In the drawing room, Patricia said, 'Good night!' quietly.

At the outer door Crang said earnestly, 'Have a good night's rest. And I mean sleep!'

Gosseyn headed sedately along the corridor. He felt strangely blank, and he had a feeling that too many things had happened too swiftly. Why had Crang assured himself that the Gosseyn body was in the right place, after having first been warned by a machine? What machine? There was only one that had any relevancy, so far as Gosseyn could make out. And that was the damaged electronic brain under the crypt.

Had Crang established some control over that machine? It sounded as if he had.

But what did he mean, sleep?

He was two floors down, starting along the corridor to Nirene's and Ashargin's apartment, when a Venusian robotic weapon snatched at his mind.

He had time for one startled realization: This couldn't be the Null-A manned battleship *Venus*. There hadn't been time for it to arrive.

It could only be that this was a major League attack. But how had they got through?

The thought ended. He was fighting desperately to save Ashargin's body from being controlled.

XX

Null-Abstracts

For the sake of sanity, each individual should break down the blockages in his own nervous system. A blockage is a semantic disturbance in which adequate response is inhibited. Blockages can often be eliminated by the proper use of the thalamo-cortical 'delayed reaction,' by self-analysis, or by heteroanalysis.

ALMOST, he was overwhelmed before he could think. The feel of the complex force was so much stronger than when he had felt it in his own brain, its effect so swiftly paralyzing that he stopped involuntarily.

It was possible that that was what saved him then. He had to stand there, and he thought back to the old, simple version of establishing the famous cortical-thalamic pause, the method used to condition trainees:

'I am now relaxing,' he told himself, 'and all stimuli are making the full circuit of my nervous system, along my spinal cord, to the thalamus, *through* the thalamus and up to the cortex, and *through* the cortex, and then, and only then, back through the thalamus and down into the nervous system.

'Always, I am consciously aware of the stimulus moving up to and through the cortex.'

That was the key. That was the difference between the Null-A superman and the animal man of the galaxy. The thalamus—the seat of emotions—and the cortex—the seat of discrimination—integrated, balanced in a warm and wonderful relationship. Emotions, not done away with, but made richer and more relaxed by the association with that part of the mind —the cortex—that could savor unnumbered subtle differences in the flow of feeling.

All through the palace, men would be struggling in a developing panic against the powerful force that had struck at them. Once that panic began it would not stop short of hysteria. And instant by instant it would grow. The stimulus flashing down from the fearful thalamus, quickening the heartbeat, speeding up the breathing process, tensing the muscles, stimulating the glands to more violent production—and each

177

overexcited organ in its turn sending a new stimulus to the thalamus. Quickly, the cycle gained in speed and intensity.

Yet all that the individual had to do was to stop for an instant, and think: *The stimulus is now going through my cortex. I'm thinking and feeling, not just feeling.*

And so he achieved for Ashargin a full cortical-thalamic pause.

The complex force continued to struggle against him, and he realized that he would have to be alert to make sure that Ashargin was not overwhelmed by a surprise emotional shock.

He ran without hindrance to the apartment, and headed for the bedroom. He knew in what condition he'd find Nirene. He let the thought of it come consciously into his mind, so that Ashargin would know, also, and not be surprised. As he expected, Nirene was in bed rigid and unconscious. She had apparently wakened at the moment of attack, for there was a twisted look of amazed horror on her face.

It was her expression that sent a shock through Ashargin. Anxiety, alarm, fear ; like lightning the emotion ran its gamut.

Like lightning, the complex force pressed in and seized his mind.

In a desperate effort Gosseyn threw himself across the bed, so that he would be able to relax. It did no good. His muscles stiffened. He lay tautly sprawled at the foot of the bed.

He had wondered what it would be like, what a controlled person thought and felt. And it really wasn't very complicated at all. He slept.

And he dreamed a strange dream.

He dreamed that the body of Gosseyn in the crypt was now receptive as it had never been before, and that only in that unconscious position, and inside the memory crypt was it possible in its comparatively untrained state to achieve the tremendous rapport that had at last been established.

The thought came not from Gosseyn but through him.

'I am the memory of the past.' The thought reached to his mind through the unconscious body of Gosseyn. 'In me, the machine beneath the crypt, is the only memory of the Migration that has survived, and my memory is the result of an accident.

'All the machines were damaged to some extent in passing through great clouds of matter, the nature of whose basic energy was not suspected. As a result the memories of most of them were lost. What saved mine was that a key circuit was burned out before the greater damage could be done.

'In spite of their injuries, most of the machines that succeeded in making the journey were able to revive the bodies

178

they carried, for that is a simple mechanical function. I could also revive the one body still in my care, but unfortunately he would not be able to survive. And I am not allowed willfully to destroy a body until it is dead. Those who have tended me in recent years have forgotten that their ancestors came to this planet in the same way as the human being they worshipped, and still worship, as the Sleeping God.

'The ancestors arrived memoryless, and quickly forgot the manner of their arrival. The struggle for existence was fierce and demanding. The ships in which they came lie buried and forgotten in the soil drift of the ages. I arrived late, so my ship has not yet been covered.

'Everywhere their descendants have built up false pictures of their evolution on the basis of studying the fauna of their new homes. They do not yet realize that all life seeks movement, and that macrocosmic movement is limited to certain forms, and that the struggle to stand erect is part of the will to movement of particular species.

'The Great Migration was undertaken on the basis of an assumption not necessarily true, but true as far as was and is known. The assumption that the human nervous system with its cortical and higher developments is unique in time-space. It has never been imitated, and, when considered in all its intricate aspects, probably never will be——'

Two bodies, two nervous systems interacting, the greater to the lesser in the similarity fashion. The first picture came then, of men watching a bright point as it moved nearer the edge of a shadowed substance.

What that substance was neither the man in the crypt nor the machine whose vibrations were suffusing him knew.

A bright point that moved sedately, and men thoughtfully watching it. Men who had lived and died many million years before. The bright point hovered at the edge of the shadowed substance, poised for a moment, and then slipped over the edge.

It was gone instantly.

The pattern of surrounding space altered slightly. There was a sudden strain, a tension that brought a break in a basic rhythm. Matter began to change.

An entire galaxy shifted its time balance, but long before the physical crisis the decisive moment came for the inhabitants. The alternatives were bleak. To remain and die, or go to another galaxy.

They knew that the time required for such a journey would be vast beyond all the powers of mechanical and human ingenuity. As the years passed, even electronic patterns would alter radically, and would in many instances become meaningless.

More than ten thousand million ships started out, each with its crypt, each with its intricate machine designed to control the life cycles of two men and two women for a million or more years. Those ships were wonderfully made. Through the darkness they sped at three quarters the speed of light. For this was no Distorter-swift journey. There were no set matrixes where they were going, no memorized areas to which men and their machines could flash with the speed of thought. All that must yet be laboriously built up.

Once more, the dream changed. It grew more relaxed, more personal, though the thoughts that came were still not particularly directed at either Ashargin or Gosseyn.

'I similarized the mind of Gosseyn into the body of Ashargin. Gosseyn possesses the only extra brain in the galaxy, besides that of the Sleeping God—which does not count. The "god" could probably be awakened now, but certain mechanical processes necessary to his development have long been out of operation, so he could not remain alive more than a few minutes.'

'Why did I choose Ashargin? Because he was a weakling. From experience, I know that a stronger personality could have fought Gosseyn's control consciously. His being nearby was also a factor.

'After the first time, after the channel had been established, it didn't matter of course where he was.

'But there was another more important reason why Ashargin was the logical person. Because of the intricate Imperial plans of Enro, the prince could be in a position to do more than any other individual to bring Gosseyn to the crypt. And, naturally, it was reasonable to believe that he would also be valuable to Gosseyn himself.

'How tremendous this achievement is you may guess from the fact that I have now for the first time been able to tell the story of the Migration to a direct survivor of the expedition. Many times I have tried to maneuver a Lavoisseur-Gosseyn body into this crypt in the way that Gosseyn is there now. But I succeeded only in making successive generations of the Gosseyn body wary of me. The attempt previous to this one had extremely dangerous repercussions.

'I succeeded in similarizing the mind of old Lavoisseur into the body of the work priest whose duty it was to sweep out this inner chamber. My purpose was to give Lavoisseur an opportunity to repair the damage that had been done to the vital elements in my structure. The plan proved impossible, for

180

two reasons. First, the priest was not in a position to obtain the necessary equipment. And, secondly, he resisted being possessed.

'At first the resistance was not too great, and so some work was done, and some investigation made by Lavoisseur into the nature of the machinery of the crypt. As it turned out, it was unfortunate that even this brief opportunity existed. For Lavoisseur repaired a device over which I have no control, an instrument for initiating the matter change which caused the destruction of the other galaxy. The device was sent along in one of every ten thousand ships for study purposes only, and it interested Lavoisseur because there was nothing like it on the ship in which he had come.

'Although Lavoisseur did not know it, this device automatically attuned itself to the body of the priest, a result of precaution taken by the builders to insure that the instrument would always be under the control of a human being.

'Naturally, they intended the human being to be one of themselves.

'The priest need now merely think himself out of phase in time, and the change, fortunately limited, occurs. By using Distorter transport, he can direct the nebular substance to any point in the galaxy where he has a Distorter.

'When the priest's resistance to Lavoisseur's control grew too strong, it was necessary to break the contact. What followed was something I admit I did not foresee. After the priest recovered from his fright at what had happened, he came to believe that he had been possessed by the Sleeping God.

'His ability to assume the shadowshape seemed to confirm this analysis, and in a sense, of course, it is true that he gains his power from the Sleeping God. But only in the same way that I am the Player who has been manipulating your mind. The real gods and the real Players have been dead nearly two million years.

'But now, you are about to waken. Your position is a difficult one, but you have one duty. You must kill the priest who possesses this power. How you can do this once he is in his shadow shape I do not know.

'Yet kill him you must.

'And now, there is not much left to tell. Ashargin need merely transmit himself through a Distorter, and I will free him from Gosseyn's control, and Gosseyn will immediately awaken. Or Ashargin could be killed, and Gosseyn's mind would automatically return to his own body. Those are the only two methods.

'Eldred Crang was a confidante of Lavoisseur, and some years ago as a result of information he secured from Lavoisseur he came here and did some work on my damaged structure. At that time he was unsuccessful in making adequate repairs. More recently, he succeeded in setting up a relay by which I could send him warnings with sound and light signals —the kind of warning by which I called him here when Ashargin was hiding the Gosseyn body.

'One last warning. The attack which has captured the palace only seems to be a League attack. Actually, the priest chose that method to strike for power in order to discredit Enro——'

The 'dream' began to fade. He tried to pull it back, but it retreated even further. Then he grew aware that he was being physically shaken.

Gosseyn-Ashargin opened his eyes, and stared up at Nirene. Her face was white, but she was calm.

'Darling, Secoh is here to see you. Please get up.'

There was a sound at the bedroom door. Nirene drew back slowly, and Gosseyn had a clear view of the bedroom doorway.

Secoh, the Lord Guardian of the Sleeping God, stood just inside the bedroom, staring at him with unsmiling eyes. *Secoh,* Gosseyn was thinking, *the work priest who had once been sweeper in the inner chamber of the temple.*

Secoh—the Follower.

XXI

Null-Abstracts

It is not enough to know about Null-A training techniques. They must be learned on the automatic, that is, the 'unconscious' level. The 'talking-about' stage must give way to the 'doing' stage. The goal is flexibility of approach below the verbal level to any event. General semantics is designed to give the individual a sense of direction, not a new set of inflexibilities.

HE had a flash glimpse now of the whole picture. Entirely aside from the dream, so many things fitted. That mechanic on the destroyer killing himself rather than taking a chance on being questioned. What private emotional

182

reason could have driven him to it? Religious, of course.

And who would be in a better position than Secoh for finding out when a new planet like Yalerta had been discovered? As a chief adviser of Enro, he would have the resources of an empire at his disposal.

Millions of bits of information would be catalogued, condensed and organized for him to pass on to Enro—if he chose. Scientific information of every kind would be submitted to him for submission to the dictator. And so, radically new and different Distorter instruments had come to the attention of a man who knew little or nothing about any of the sciences, and who needed just such a development to give galactic-wide scope to his private wanderings.

A man who called himself the Follower, a name with religious meaning.

The rest of the scene, the motivation for everything, could be a growth based on the religion itself. It seemed natural that the Lord Guardian of the Sleeping God should have spurred the ambitions of a planetary emperor like Enro, driving him to conquer the Greatest Empire, then consolidating the galaxy in order to spread the religion farther.

The picture was not complete in all its parts, but in that flash moment it seemed logical to Gosseyn that he adopt it as the assumption on which he must base his actions now.

Secoh was the Follower. Secoh was a sincere believer in the religion of the Sleeping God. Secoh was a fanatic, sharp and alert on almost every level of thought—except his religious belief. And even there his very conviction must give him a flexible way of looking at things.

But if there was a weakness in this man, that was it. Gosseyn-Ashargin sat up slowly as Secoh approached the bed and sat down facing him. The priest said in a rich tone:

'Prince, you are about to be given an opportunity to win back for your family a measure of your former position.'

Gosseyn guessed then what was coming. He was not mistaken. He listened to the offer, which was in effect a vice regency with, as Secoh carefully put it, 'Only the Sleeping God himself above you.'

Meaning himself. And yet he undoubtedly believed what he said.

There was no pretense that League forces had captured Gorgzid. The Lord Guardian was frank. 'It seemed to Crang it might be a good bargaining point if the League appeared to have captured the capital.'

He waved a hand, dismissing that aspect of the subject.

'I can tell you,' he said sincerely, 'that Enro was no longer

183

satisfactory to the Sleeping God, and I need hardly say that the calls you have received from the Temple are an indication of where the God is trying to point my attention.'

He meant it. This man believed in his curious religion. His eyes glowed with honest purpose. Gosseyn studied him, and was only too conscious of how unsane the man was.

He wondered then: *Was Enro dead?* He asked the question.

Secoh hesitated, but only for a moment. 'He must have suspected something,' he confessed. 'I went to his apartment last night after his return to the palace, hoping to hold him in conversation until it was too late for him to get away. We had rather an explosive conversation.'

He scowled. The sacrilegious scum! In the past he has dissembled his hatred of the Sleeping God, but last night he was in a state of anxiety, and so he forgot himself, and actually threatened to destroy the temple.

'Then, just as the attack began, he similarized himself to Paleol's flagship.'

Secoh paused. Some of the fire went out of his eyes. He said thoughtfully, 'Enro is a very able man.'

It was a grudging admission, but the fact that Secoh could make such a statement was a measure of his own ability. His failure to capture Enro was clearly a major defeat, and yet he had already adjusted to it.

'Well,' said Secoh, 'are you with me or against me?'

It was a bald way of putting it, especially as there was no indication of what refusal might mean. Gosseyn decided against a direct question about that. He said instead:

'What would you have done with Enro if you had caught him?'

The Lord Guardian smiled. He stood up and walked over to the bedroom window. He beckoned Gosseyn-Ashargin, who came without hesitation.

Gosseyn stood beside the priest, and looked down on a courtyard that was changed. Gallows were going up. More than a dozen were already in position, and there were silent shapes hanging from nine of them. Gosseyn stared at the dead men thoughtfully. He was neither shocked nor impressed. Wherever men acted thalamically there usually would be found a full quota of hangmen. Beside him, Secoh said:

'Enro managed to get away but I did seize a number of his uncompromising supporters. Some of them I am still trying to persuade.' He sighed. 'I am easy to please, but in the final issue I must have cooperation. Accordingly, such scenes as that'— he pointed downward—'are necessary concomitants to the elimination of evil forces.' He shook his head. 'One can have no mercy on recalcitrants.'

Gosseyn had his answer. This was what happened to people who were 'against' instead of 'for'.

He knew now what crisis he must try to arrange. But it would be staking a great deal—Ashargin's life, among other things—on the intensity of Secoh's beliefs.

It was surprisingly easy to say the nonsense words. It took a moment to realize why: Ashargin's nervous system would have established channels for false to fact verbalisms about the Sleeping God—a point he'd have to remember in his final plans for the prince, who was obviously not yet trained in general semantics.

But he spoke the necessary words about having received a summons from the Sleeping God to the effect that a great honor was planned for Secoh. He must come to the temple, bringing with him Ashargin and a Distorter circuit. Gosseyn watched tensely for the Lord Guardian's reaction to the inclusion of the Distorter, since that would be a deviation from long established rituals. But apparently Secoh accepted any direct command of his god, regardless of past formalisms.

And so the first and simplest step was accomplished.

XXII

Null-Abstracts

General semantics is a discipline, and not a philosophy. Any number of new Null-A oriented philosophies are possible, just as any number of geometrical systems can be developed. Possibly, the most important requirement of our civilization is the development of a Null-A oriented political economy. It can be stated categorically that no such system has yet been developed. The field is wide open for bold and imaginative men and women to create a system that will free mankind of war, poverty and tension. To do this it will be necessary to take control of the world away from people who identify.

SECOH decided to make a pageant of it. In three hours, lines of planes, loaded with troops and priests from the capitol, dotted the sky on the route over the mountain to the Temple of the Sleeping God.

Gosseyn-Ashargin had hoped that they would make the journey through the Distorter in Crang's and Patricia's apartment. But when that didn't happen, he requested that Crang be in the same machine as he himself.

They sat down together.

There were many things Gosseyn wanted to know. He assumed, however, that there might be listening devices. So he began gravely, 'I have only gradually realized the nature of the friendship between yourself and the Lord Guardian.'

Crang nodded, and said with equal wariness, 'I am honored by his confidence.'

To Gosseyn, the fascinating aspect of the relationship so suddenly revealed was that Crang had, four years before, unerringly chosen Secoh instead of Enro as the person to whom he should attach himself.

The conversation went on in that polite fashion, but gradually Gosseyn obtained the information he wanted. It was an amazing picture of a Null-A Venusian detective, who had secretly gone out to space from Venus to discover the nature of the threat against Null-A.

It was Secoh, as Enro's adviser, who had put Crang in charge of the secret Enro base on Venus. Why? So that the Gorgzin Reesha would be beyond the reach of her brother's determination to make her his wife.

At that point Gosseyn had a sudden memory of Enro accusing Secoh. 'You always were taken with her!' the dictator had said.

He had a vision then of a work priest aspiring to the hand of the highest lady on the planet. And because such emotions became set on the unconscious level, all his triumphs since then meant nothing beside the potent early love feeling.

Another phrase of Crang's brought him a vivid picture of how the marriage of Crang and Patricia had been presented to Secoh as not a true marriage, but as another protection for her. They were saving her for the day when the Follower could claim her for his own.

A subsequent statement of Crang's made later, and seeming to have no connection with what had gone before, justified the dangerous deception. 'When a person has put away the fear of death,' the detective said quietly, 'he is free of petty fears and petty tribulations. Only those who want life under any conditions suffer bad conditions.'

Clearly, if the worst came to the worst, Mr. and Mrs. Eldred Crang would take death.

But why the attack driving out Enro? The explanation for that required even more caution in the telling. But the answer was dazzling. It was important that the dictator be put in a frame of mind where he would consider, or even initiate, negotiations for ending the war. Enro, driven from his home planet, his sister in the control of his enemy, would have a reason for making outside peace, so that he could concentrate on restoring his position in his own empire.

The amazing Crang had actually found a way that might end the war.

Crang was hesitating. And there was the faintest note of anxiety in his voice as he added carefully: 'It will be a great privilege to be present at the temple on so great an occasion, but isn't it possible that some of those who will be there are so delicately balanced emotionally that the very nearness of their god will upset them?'

'I'm sure,' said Gosseyn-Ashargin firmly, 'that the Sleeping God will personally insure that everything will take place as it should.'

That was as near as innuendo would take them to his plan.

Brilliant lights shone from hidden sources. Priests lined each side wall, holding glittering scepters of power and banners of rich cloth. Thus the preliminary ritual ended in the great chamber of the Sleeping God.

At the moment of crisis, Gosseyn-Ashargin put his hand lightly on the control lever of the Distorter. Before activating it, he took a final look around through the eyes of Ashargin.

He had an inexorable will to action, but he forced himself to examine the environment in which he intended to make his moves.

The guests were clustered near the door. There were priests there, also, headed by Yeladji, the Lord Watcher, arrayed in his gold and silver cloak of office. He had a frown on his plump face, as if he was not altogether happy about what was taking place. But apparently he knew better than to say anything.

The others were equally subdued. There were court functionaries whom Gosseyn-Ashargin knew by sight, and others whom he did not know. And there were Nirene, Patricia and Crang.

They would be in danger if Secoh tried to use energy, but that was a risk that would have to be taken. This was the showdown. Vast issues were at stake, and no danger could be considered too great.

Secoh stood alone in front of the crypt.

He was naked, a humble state which he had decreed years ago for all important ceremonials in the inner chamber, par-

ticularly those where robes of office were subsequently be-
stowed on the honored individual. His body thus revealed was
slender but firmly fleshed. His black eyes glowed with a
feverish light of expectancy. There seemed little likelihood
that he would grow suspicious at this final hour, but Gosseyn
decided to take no chances.

'Most noble Lord Guardian,' he began, 'after I have similarized myself from this Distorter to the one near the door, there
must be complete silence.'

'There will be silence,' said Secoh. And he put a threat into
the words for everyone present.

'Very well—*now!*' said Gosseyn-Ashargin. As he spoke he
activated the Distorter.

He found himself, as the machine had promised him in the
dream, back in the crypt in his own body. He lay quiet, aware
of the nearness of the 'god'. Then he directed a thought.

'Machine.'

'Yes?' The answer came swiftly into his brain.

'You indicated that henceforth you and I could communicate at will.'

'That is correct. The relationship, having been established,
is permanent.'

'You said, also, that the Sleeping God could now be awakened, but that he would die very quickly.'

'Death would come within a few minutes,' was the reply.
'Due to damage to the equipment, the endocrine glands are
atrophied, and I have been replacing their functions artificially.
The moment the artificial supply is cut off, the brain will begin
to deteriorate.'

'Do you think the body would be physically able to respond
to my commands?'

'Yes. This body, like all the others, has received a pattern of
exercises that were designed to enable it to function when the
ship arrived at its destination.'

Gosseyn drew a deep breath, and then he gave his next
order. 'Machine, I am going to similarize myself into the storeroom at the rear of this chamber.

'When I do that, put my mind into the body of the Sleeping
God.'

At first there was only blankness. It was as if his consciousness had been blotted by an all-absorbing material.

But the pressures driving him were too strong for that state
to last long. He had a sense, finally, of time passing swiftly,
and that brought his first thought in his new body.

Get up!

No. Not that first. Slide the lid. The lid must come first.

188

Action must follow an orderly pattern. Sit up, and slide the lid.

There was a blur of light, and a vague awareness of movement. And then, filling his ears and seeming to echo through his head, a cry of wonder from many throats.

I must have moved. The lid must be sliding. Push harder. Harder.

He was conscious of pushing, and of his heart beating rapidly. His body ached with an all-embracing pain.

Then he stood up. That was a sharper sensation, for there was more vision with it. He saw blurred figures in the mist before him, and a bright room.

Still the pressure to act and move and think faster grew inside him. He thought in anguish, *This body has only minutes to live.*

He tried to mutter the words he wanted, and to force the stiff larynx to movement. And, because sound like vision is in the mind and not the organ only, he was able presently to form the words that he had planned.

For the first time, then, he wondered how Secoh was taking the awakening of his 'god.'

The effect should already be tremendous. For this was a peculiarly unsound and dangerous religion for a man to have. Like the old idol worship of Earth which it resembled, it was based upon symbol identification, but unlike its counterparts elsewhere in space and time, it was subject to a special kind of disaster because the 'idol' was a living though unconscious human being.

Such a religion's continued acceptance by individuals depended on the god remaining asleep.

Its temporary acceptance by Secoh, if an awakening should occur, depended on the god taking it for granted that his chief guardian was above reproach.

This awakened god stood up before a throng of notables, pointed an accusing finger straight at Secoh, and said quickly:
'Secoh—traitor—you must die.'

In that instant, the innate will to survival of Secoh's nervous system demanded that he reject his religious belief.

He couldn't do it. It was too deeply ingrained. It was associated with every tension in his body.

He couldn't do it—which meant that he must accept his god's sentence of death without question.

And he couldn't do that.

All his life he had balanced himself precariously like a tight-rope walker; only, instead of a balancing pole, he had used words. Now, those words were in conflict with reality. It was as if the man on the rope suddenly lost his pole. He began to sway, wildly. With panic came innumerable dangerous and disturbing related stimuli of the thalamus. Swiftly, threshing violently, he fell.

Madness.

It was the madness that comes from unresolvable inner conflict. Through all the ages of human existence such conflicts have been set up in the minds of millions of men. Hostility to a father conflicting with the desire for the security of parental protection ; attachment to an over-possessive mother conflicting with the need to grow up and become independent ; dislike of an employer conflicting with the need to make a living. Always, the first step was unsanity, and then, if the balance became too hard to maintain, escape into the relative security of insanity.

Secoh's first attempt to escape his conflict was physical. His body blurred, and then, to the sound of a faint moan from the spectators, it grew shadowy.

The Follower stood before them.

For Gosseyn, still in control of the untrained nervous system of the 'god,' Secoh's transformation into his Follower shape was expected.

But it was the crisis.

Slowly, he started down the steps. Slowly, because the 'god's' muscles were too stiff to permit swift movement. The exercising they had received within the confined space of the sleeping chamber had opened up vital nerve channels, but only on a limited scale.

Without Gosseyn's knowledge of how it was done, the almost mindless human thing could scarcely have crawled, let alone walk.

Driving him was the ever more desperate realization that he only had minutes—minutes during which the Follower must be defeated.

Down the steps he faltered, and straight toward the wavery shape of blackness.

The strain of watching one's god walk towards one with hostile intent must be a mind-destroying experience. In a very frenzy of terror, the Follower protected himself by the only method at his disposal.

Energy poured from the shadowshape. In a flare of white flame, the god-body dissolved into nothingness. In that instant Secoh became a man who had destroyed his god. No human nervous system trained as his had been could accept so terrible a guilt.

So he forgot it.

He forgot that he had done it. And since that involved forgetting all the related incidents of his life, he forgot those also. His training from early childhood had been for the priesthood. All that had to go, so that the memory of his crime could be utterly banished.

Amnesia is easy for the human nervous system. Under hypnosis it can be induced with almost alarming simplicity. But hypnosis is not necessary. Meet an unpleasant individual, and soon you will not be able to recall his name. Have an unpleasant experience, and it will fade away, fade as a dream fades.

Amnesia is the best method of escaping from reality. But it had several forms, and one at least is devastating. You cannot forget the memory of a lifetime of experience, and remain adult.

There was so much that Secoh had to forget. Down he went, and down and down. To Gosseyn, who had returned to his own body instantly when the 'god' was killed, and who stood watching now from the doorway that led to the back office, what followed was anticipated.

The Follower's shadow-shape disappeared, and Secoh was revealed teetering on legs that supported him a few moments only.

He fell limply. Physically, he had only a few feet to go, but mentally his journey continued down. He lay on his side on the floor, and his knees drew up tightly against his chest, his feet pressed against his thighs, and his head flopped loosely. At first he sobbed a little, but quickly he grew silent. When they carried him out on a stretcher, he lay unaware of his surroundings, curled-up and silent and tearless.

A baby that has not yet been born does not cry.

READERSHIP SURVEY

The Editor of **Digit Books** asks for the co-operation of readers in conducting a brief survey by means of a questionnaire. In doing so, we wish to establish a closer relationship with our readers, and so ensure that they can rely on **Digit Books** for increasingly popular titles.

Would you kindly reply by letter or postcard to the following questions:

(1) What other books, or types of book, would you like to see published by **Digit** in a Paperback edition?

(2) Would you please name one title you particularly want to see in a Paperback edition. If possible, name the author.

(3) What is your favourite subject:

Fiction	Biography
Travel	Theatre
Sport	Films
Handicrafts	Adventure
Crime	Science Fiction
Ballet	Western

(4) If you are a student, or are attending an educational course are there any Textbooks you would like to see in a Paperback edition?

When writing, please state your name, age, occupation, and address.

Replies to this request should be addressed to:

The Editor, Messrs Brown, Watson Ltd.,
Digit House, Harlesden Road, Willesden Green,
London, N.W.10

THANK YOU!